No one is listening.

No one is listening.

A Novel

matthew sanchez

little
beast
feet

Published by Little Beast Feet, New York, New York.

Edited and Designed by Girl Friday Productions
www.girlfridayproductions.com

Editorial: Alexander Rigby, Clete Smith, Scott Calamar, Carrie Wicks
Interior Design: Rachel Marek
Cover Design: Jesse DeFlorio

ISBN (Paperback): 978-1-7326136-2-1
e-ISBN: 978-1-7326136-1-4

First Edition

Printed in the United States of America

For Michael

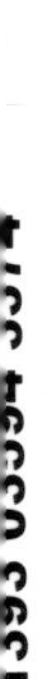

BROOKLYN

All across New York, people in black suits and black dresses were leaving their nine-to-fives hungover from the workday. I, on the other hand, was sitting on my couch, nursing a hangover from the night before, when the phone rang. It was Francis.

"Something's up with Mom."

He said this to me like it was breaking news.

"What's wrong with her?" I asked.

"I dunno, man, she's forgetting stuff. I think she's got, like, early Alzheimer's or Parkinson's, or some shit like that. She doesn't really know who I am, and she's, she's acting like she's afraid of everything."

"Afraid?"

"Well, she freaking called the cops on me for showing up and knocking on her door. She was yelling at me to go away like I was a robber or something."

I grinned. "Well, you *are* a thief."

"Yeah, but this time I just really wanted to see her and make sure she was okay. You know?"

I rolled my eyes. "France, you *never* go there unless you need something."

He let out a puff of what sounded like thick smoke. "Well, I was going to ask her for twenty bucks, but I was going to pay her back. You know I'm good for it."

Francis is a fuckup. He has tremendous heart, but he's lost and searching for something he'll never find. Mom had that whole post-partum depression thing with him and never got over it. When I came along, he saw how different she was with me. I was her favorite. Padre said France acted out his whole life just to get her attention. He still hasn't stopped.

I opened the door to my balcony and brushed the hair out of my face. I could see in the window's reflection that it was violently thrashing in a gust of wind and looked like an angry black flame. I breathed in the cold air and stared through the bright lights of Manhattan. After hearing Francis blow out another puff of smoke, I thought it sounded good, so I reached for a square and lit up.

"Well, did the cops come?"

"No, she called them back and told them never mind. I hope she doesn't do this on the reg . . . some sheep-who-cried-wolf thing or some shit."

I smiled. "*Boy* who cried wolf."

"What?"

"It's the *boy* who cried wolf."

"Oh."

I looked down past the black patchwork tattoos on my arms and at my cigarette, relishing the way the filter felt when I pinched it. "Hey, why the fuck do you call these things squares anyway?" I asked.

"What, cigarettes?"

"Yeah."

"Well, bro, it's a prison term. We had to hide them in our back pockets and when we sat down, they'd turn from circle to square. So that's what we'd call 'em."

I shook my head. "The things you learn in prison."

France grunted, "Yeah well, only thing I learned is I ain't ever going back."

"I thought you learned that accent in there too?" He sounded like a cholo.

"What accent?"

"Never mind. Hey, did you get that shirt I sent you?"

"Which one?"

"The one that has our logo on it?"

"Yeah, like two weeks ago. Shit, I'm wearing it right now."

"Fit alright?"

"It's fine, bro. I don't care how it fits . . . It was free."

I pictured him in the shirt and grinned. "Yeah, free's good. So, did Mom say anything to you?"

"Well, what do you mean?"

"I dunno, like, 'Get the fuck off my lawn, you idiot'; 'Get a job, you middle-aged weirdo'; 'Go to the dentist, you—'"

"Ha fucking ha, bro."

I laughed.

"See, that's what I'm saying. She did, but she looked all glazed over and shit. Like, I look her in the eyes and it's like she's not even there. She recognized me, but I don't think she knew exactly who I was. Know what I mean?"

"Well, what'd she say?"

"She said something about missing Grandpa, but the weird thing was, she asked if you were clean. I was like, who, *Bell*? Mom, are you asking me if Bela Mar, your immaculate, sent-from-the-gods angel son is clean? And then that's when it clicked, like a fuckin' lightbulb, bro."

I inhaled smoke deeply and let it go.

"She thinks you're me," he said. "She thinks you're me. Weird, right?"

"Yeah, weird . . . I ain't no angel, though."

"Bro, you were never into hard drugs; you weren't into anything crazy like that! I mean, sure, you smoke weed and other stuff sometimes, but something's wrong, man—I gotta get her out of there."

Get her out of there? Where would she go?

Francis sensed my nerves. "You alright, bro?"

"Yeah, I'm good. How's Padre?"

"Same. Can't stop talking about how proud of you he is. Still stubborn as all hell though, and hates me living with him."

I laughed. "Of course he hates you living with him—you're, like, thirty-one."

He sniggered. "Yeaah, true. I'm only here till I can get enough cash to snag me a car and an apartment, though. I'll make it happen; it's just a matter of time, little bro."

"I know, I know. Well hey, I gotta run. I gotta go paint my face. I'm meeting Em for a Halloween thing. We're going to some party or something, I dunno."

"Paint your face?" he asked.

"Yeah, you know, for Day of the Dead."

"Oh, Día de los Muertos."

"What?"

"Día de los Muertos, you know, Day of the Dead."

"Oh."

"C'mon, Bell, don't you know your fucking heritage?!"

I laughed. "Fuck off."

"Well, be safe and call me later. Don't do nothing *I* would do."

I laughed. "Tell Padre hi."

"Will do, little brother. Oh and hey!"

"What?"

"Don't forget where you came from."

"I won't. I think you remind me every time I talk to you."

—

I hung up and pictured France's face. I missed him. We were so different. He was six one to my five nine. He was thin like a thread, and I had love handles. His skin was light like cream paper, while mine was olive like toasted hay. We did share our brown, almost black eyes and our straight-razor triangle-shaped nose; those came from Mom, but his hair was short and thin, while mine was shoulder-length and thick. Francis was my favorite human, while I, for better or worse, was my least.

In the distance, I could hear the sirens from a Brooklyn ambulance. I took another drag and briefly wondered what tragedy had just happened—a car wreck? An overdose? I guess it didn't matter all that much, but I always wonder. Ambulances don't get dispatched for flesh wounds.

Down below, my neighbors were arguing about something. He was defensive, and she was pissed; either way I knew they were going to make up later by fucking so loudly I'd have to put on my headphones and listen to Broken Social Scene or something noisy like that. The man across the street was complaining about the amount of trash he had to take out, while next to him, the neighborhood cats were eagerly waiting for him to finish. What a show.

I flicked the square, watched the ember fade into the sidewalk, trudged to the bathroom, and grabbed the white face paint I'd bought earlier from the corner bodega. I looked in the mirror and wondered if I should shave off the peppered stubble, and decided against it. No one cares. I took out my phone, typed in "Day of the Dead," then erased it, typed in "Día de los Muertos," and looked at the images. When I found one I liked, I smeared the white face paint all over, then I grabbed the black: first my nose, then my eyes, then ridged teeth across my lips and cheeks. I made a few intricate curved lines that looked like a violin's f-holes on each temple, and finished with a few dots on my chin and forehead. When I was done, I looked in the mirror at a proper skeleton and mumbled, "Dead already." I grinned, then threw on a white button-up, black skinny jeans, a black trench coat, and a black fedora, and walked out the door.

ANGELS & KINGS

Walking in New York reminds me of playing football. The object, for me, is to stay away from everyone, and when someone is walking slow, to find an opening and dart through it as fast as possible. The truth is, I enjoy it. I'm not home often 'cause of how much I travel, so any time spent here is time I treasure, even if it's dodging slow assholes.

That night the streets were particularly crowded. The costumed drunk college idiots were annoyingly loud, the noncostumed pretentious hipsters were annoyingly quiet, and the half-costumed prep kids, well, they were just annoying. People were in disguise every which way: Beetlejuice here, a mummy there, something gross with face paint across the street, and a guy wearing an oversized cock, although I'm sure that was the most accurate representation of him. Fucking moron. There was also someone in drag walking next to me, but in New York City that could have just been a normal, everyday person. Across the street a beautiful brunette was dressed like Superwoman. Her shorts were small and her ass cheeks were hanging out. Her breasts were there, nothing special, just there. I couldn't help but stare. A memory that didn't exist flashed in my head: she and I undressing each other, not saying a word, just smiling. It disappeared as fast as it came.

I was making my way toward Angels & Kings, stepping over trash, dog shit, and avoiding the bums begging for change. One of my friends, Oscar, was there watching some band play. It was still too early to meet Em, and I didn't feel like being alone. I made my way down Avenue A, and when I got to Eleventh, immediately lit up a square. I saw Oscar outside, smoking. He didn't notice me.

"Oscar," I said unenthusiastically.

"Bell!" he yelled.

I cocked my head, stopped in front of him, and we bumped fists. I didn't want to touch him. He looked terrible. Pale complexion, greasy hair, and ten pounds lighter than when I'd seen him last. He'd always been thin, but this was different. Looked like a blade of dead grass.

"What's new, Oscar?"

"Not much, man." He blinked one of his eyes and half smiled. "Happy Haalloweeeen. What are you 'posed to be? Some kind of skeleton?" He was slurring his words and talking drunk. Actually, he always sounded like this.

"Yeah, well, Day of the Dead."

"Oh, Día de los Muertos."

"Smart-ass fucking Francis," I mumbled under my breath, then spoke up: "Same shit, I guess. Where's your costume?"

"I dunno, man, I kind of, well, I kind of forgot."

This kid's an idiot.

"How are the rest of the guys?"

"They're good, man, you know, just still riding this wave."

Oscar smiled, then nodded. It was fake, but I didn't give a shit. I could tell he was thinking about "the wave" and how he wished he were on it, or on any wave, for that matter. He started to drift, probably thinking about an actual wave in the ocean, and how blue and green it was. Then he blinked, noticed me still standing there, and asked something he already knew the answer to.

"Drew still with his girl?"

I shook my head. "Actually, no. I'm the only one left. Asher and Luke have been single for a while now."

He grinned, one eye closed, and said, "Oh, man, I don't blame them with everything that's happening with you guys."

"Ha ha ha." I bit my lip. *Fuck you,* I thought.

"Say, my friend's band is playing inside. They're pretty good—you wanna check 'em out?"

Oscar always liked something purely for the fact that no one else did. What a waste of a brain. He liked Good & Plenty, for fuck's sake. Worst fucking candy on the planet. I had some time to kill, so I shrugged and begrudgingly agreed.

"I'm down."

"Cool, man. Let's go."

—

The place looked the same as it always did, only this time there were more cobwebs on account of the holiday. The glass chandeliers were lit up with white electric candles that bounced to the beat and had fake wax melting down their sides. The red walls were cast in the shadows of horns, masks, fake swords, and Titan spears. The underage girls were dancing in the dark, hoping not to be bothered by the guys, and the guys were playing cool, drinking, and hoping that the underage girls wouldn't mind being bothered. I hated this place. It was the same carousel all the time. Back in the day, the up-and-coming industry fucks all hung out here and tried to get laid. They'd hit on the minors, get drunk, and make them promises they couldn't keep. Drew, Luke, Asher, and I would just watch, encouraging them and congratulating them on the pussy they'd never get but thought they had a chance with. Half the time it would end in a kicking and screaming match, and someone always left saying, "Fuck you, fuck this, fuck that," and crying. It was a never-ending cycle of bullshit. Everyone there was just sick in the head, but in our business, that's how you survived. That's how you still survive.

We didn't know it, but at the time, this horrible shithole was the mecca of the NYC scene. Anyone who's made it big out of New York in the last ten years started here. It's where we all used each other to get ahead. After we stopped coming here, the ones who didn't make it never left and were still trying to hustle—and to hustle us, for that matter. It was sad. Oscar was one of those guys.

The band onstage finished a song that sounded somewhere between forks scraping the plate and someone vomiting their mom's chili while blasting XuXu. Thankfully they announced they were taking a break and someone put a dollar in the jukebox. Simple Minds' "Don't You" came on and all was good. The faint smell of body odor crept toward my nose, and I glanced around to see whose it could be.

It smelled good. It was Batgirl's, and she was dancing up a storm. She smiled and it was almost as sweet as her stench.

"Hi," she said.

I glanced at her but kept walking toward the bar. Priorities. I needed a drink.

"Well, never mind, then," she said, and kept dancing.

I ordered a Boulevardier with a straw. The straw because of the face paint. The bartender looked at me weird, but I didn't care; I just kept staring at Batgirl.

Oscar began telling me some story about one of his friends from New Hampshire who got arrested for robbing a convenience store. Supposedly the guy was guilty by association 'cause it was actually his asshole friend who did the robbing and yada yada yada . . .

"Sounds like he got a raw deal, if you ask me," I said.

Oscar could tell I was bored. "Heyyy," he said, "you wanna get high?"

I thought about it. "Yes, yes I do." I smiled and sucked up the rest of my drink. I looked down at my empty glass; the black straw had white makeup on it. As we walked out the door, I looked at Batgirl and inhaled her again. She smiled, and I kept walking.

When we got outside, we went to the corner, and Oscar pulled out a spliff from his pocket. He lit up, took a hit, then handed it to me. "Here."

I took a deep pull, held it in, then exhaled and coughed.

"Some good shit, riiight?"

I nodded and coughed for another minute while Oscar laughed at me and then began telling another story about someone else getting arrested. Why was I here with this guy? I decided it'd be better if I left rather than stand here listening to him ramble on in his slow, dull way. Why does it feel like it takes him ten minutes to finish a fucking sentence? Besides, I could be a little early to meet Em. She wouldn't care; hell, she'd be happy.

I interrupted him in the middle of a sentence and told him I had to run. "Em's waiting and she'll be pissed if she has to wait too long."

Just then the doors flew open. Some redhead in a black crow's mask was being dragged out, kicking and screaming, by a big, mustached bouncer. Her heels dug into the sidewalk and her leggings looked freshly torn. Oscar and I both looked up with raised eyebrows, then at each other.

He nodded. "I know how it is, man. Go meet your girl and hit me up later if you wanna go out," he said, grinning. His pupils grew to the size of golf balls. "Be safe, man. It's a craaazy world out there."

I looked at him, confused. "I will be," I said.

We bumped fists again, and I left. I didn't want to be alone, but being with Oscar did nothing to remedy that.

—

My mind was racing faster than usual, and my legs couldn't seem to keep up. I started walking up Avenue A and turned onto St. Mark's, darting through holes of slow walkers with my head down. Thoughts of Em flickered in my mind. Her face, her smile. I thought about the phone call with Francis. He's such a fuckup; I hope Mom's not as messed up as he says. Then I began to think about Batgirl. I could still smell her.

I picked up my pace and could hear every sidewalker's footsteps. It sounded like rain. Everyone in front of me was turning into a frightening blur: masks, legs, laughing, echoes in my brain, Batgirl, chandeliers, my band playing for ten thousand people. I was racing toward an invisible finish line. I just didn't know it yet.

MARK BAR

I got to Mark Bar where Em worked and sat down. The place had a college feel to it. The bar was black and poorly painted, the floor had cracks where stools had been dropped, and the taps looked like they hadn't been cleaned in months. Em was pouring drinks and looked like a whisper in a loud room. Her hair the color of small hours, her eyes soft and beryl like the feather of a bluebird, and her frosted skin like fresh cream. My perfect woman. She noticed me and grinned. My brain slowed and focused on her.

"Hey, gorgeous."

"Hey." Her smile grew even bigger. "Nice skeleton face. Want a drink or something? I'm not off for another half hour, and I still have to put on my costume. Do we need to take anything to the party?"

"I dunno, I thought *you* were in charge of this whole thing."

"I'll call and see. I don't think we need to, but I can always just sneak a bottle from here if we do."

"Perfect," I said.

"Want a drink?"

"Okay. Give me a Tempranillo," I said in a low, rumbling voice.

She laughed, poured me a glass all the way to the top, dipped her fingertip in the red, and sucked on it.

"I love this wine," she said biting her finger.

"I can tell."

She stuck her tongue out at me, then went to the other side of the bar to tend to some pirates as I sat there patiently waiting. Usually in these circumstances I became an internal knot, full of tangled thoughts, but this time, I was just blank. I thought the drugs were kicking in. How did I even get here so fast? Someone put on Willie Nelson's "Are You Sure," and I began to lose myself in the lyrics.

I looked around and stared at a few of the customers. Most were in costume, eating burgers or drinking beer, none of them doing both at the same time. Then I looked at Em and smiled. This was exactly where I needed to be. Thanks, Willie.

Suddenly, I became dizzy and nauseated. I got up to go to the bathroom and stumbled. I pushed through a group of vampires, or superheroes, I don't know what the fuck they were, but they had capes.

"Get out of my way!"

I tried to open the bathroom door, but it was locked.

I looked around, feeling for the wall, knowing that something was about to happen. Right before I blacked out, I found a chair next to the bathroom door. I sank down into the green velvet just as I started seeing silver pops of tiny lights. In my head, the sound of a million gnats searching for a ripe blood orange and swarming furiously around me began to grow louder than my thoughts.

The dark sparked like a million tiny Christmas lights, only they were on lightning speed, firing off like sparklers on the Fourth of July. My brain was a TV screen with an unplugged cable wire, and the sound was loud and terrifying. My body was doing whatever it could to keep me from passing out; either that or it was melting. I blacked out, only I was conscious. I was blind, I was coherent, but I couldn't move.

As soon as the bathroom door opened, I came to. I looked without using my eyes, like my body was on autopilot. *Get to the bathroom, get somewhere safe,* I thought. I tripped inside fast, closed the door, locked it, felt around, and kneeled over the toilet to vomit, then passed out.

I woke up in a pool of cold sweat, arms and head on the rim of the porcelain seat, my makeup smeared everywhere and my shirt transparent from sweating. I looked in the toilet—no vomit. I looked in the mirror, and my skin was as white as my smeared makeup. I was a wreck. I heard Em knocking and yelling. When I opened the door, I had an audience. Apparently, they'd been trying to get into the bathroom for a solid seven minutes. Since I wasn't responding, someone almost called 911. I guess they thought I was dying.

I was in a dense cloud of toxic confusion. Em would talk to me, but then she'd have to repeat herself just to make sure I heard her. She asked what I was on, and my only response was "I dunno. Fucking Oscar."

We got into a mustard-yellow cab and headed home, skipping the party. The Iranian cab driver kept looking at me in the mirror. His eyes were dark and angry, like he knew something about me no one else did. It's as if he was looking at me and saying, "Fuck you."

—

We got to my apartment. Em undressed me, washed my face, and helped me into bed. She was pissed but it didn't stop her. She started kissing my neck, then my chest. She worked her way down and disappeared below the bedspread, while my mind wandered off to someplace else.

I was eight years old. Mom gave me a card when she dropped me off to live with Padre. The front had a detailed drawing of a brown teddy bear holding a big red heart; the back had nothing. I can't remember what she wrote inside, but I remember her handwriting and how beautiful it was. That day, the sky was blue and the leaves were burnt orange. The air was cold and quiet. She got out of the car and held me, then let me walk inside. She was silently holding back her tears to be strong for me, but her silence was louder than the sound of dry leaves crunching beneath my feet.

I woke up to a phone call from our tour manager, Hank. When he calls, there's always a brief moment of silence because he's thinking. When he thinks, it's slow and calculated, like his speech, and it kind of freaks me out.

"Hey, don't forget you're shooting a pilot for that TV show today at exactly twelve p.m. Please get up and shower, 'cause you need to look good."

Unfortunately, I was pretty sure that I looked exactly the way I felt.

"Fuck them. They know what we do, who we are, and what they're gonna get."

"I know, but shut up and get up. You take extra-long showers before noon, and we just don't have the time."

"Hey, Hank."

"What?"

"Am I your first wake-up call today?"

"Yes."

"What's the count?"

"Twenty-one minutes."

"Twenty-one?!"

"Well, Drew will answer right away, but he definitely forgot about it. So I'll have to allocate an extra three minutes to convince him that the pilot is happening today, not tomorrow and not the next day. I need an extra two minutes to argue with Luke about pickup times since he always seems to think noon means one thirty, and I need an extra ten to wake Asher up. I swear he could sleep through a hurricane."

I counted. "That's only fifteen minutes."

"Correct, but I figured this phone call would take four minutes, and I need an extra one to push the buttons on my phone."

I shook my head. "You're fucking weird, man."

"I know. See you in one hour."

"Hey, Hank, fuck you."

"See you in fifty-nine minutes."

BOWERY BALLROOM

I looked around the room, but Em was gone. I was burning up in sweat, so I rolled in the cool white sheets, hungover as all hell—my legs were the only part of my body that didn't hurt so bad. I rolled to the left and felt the fiery vomit rise. I rolled to the right and felt the same. My head was pounding violently, like a hammer hitting all of my nerves. With each little strike, a memory of last night flashed: masks, chandeliers, and that fuckhead Oscar and his stupid spliff. Each fraction of a second between throbs was the only time I could put my thoughts together. I reached inside my bedside drawer and pulled out a family-size bottle of Aleve. I popped three, and hoped I could keep them down.

I got up, walked to the bathroom, avoided the mirror, and got in the shower. I let the hot water run down my neck and began feeling bad about last night. I should make it right with Em. The band's leaving tomorrow, so if I'm going to make it up to her, it has to be tonight. I thought about her face, and what it felt like to kiss the patch of sun freckles on her right cheek. Then I thought about her ass, and how perfect it was. I wanted to bite it. Then, like a spider, Batgirl's BO slowly crawled into my mind and made me wonder what her other parts smelled like. I shook it off, turned the water as hot as it could go, and jerked off.

—

We shot the pilot at Bowery Ballroom on Delancey. This place was a shithole. Brown rooms, covered in dark, shiny shit-looking brown wood. It had multiple levels so it was great for different scenes, but the whole place smelled like the vomit that was finally settling in my stomach.

The biggest problem with these TV things is that they always require a lot of hurry up and wait. They get you dressed as if you're already twenty minutes late for your scene, shuffle you into a cold waiting area like you're cattle, say they'll come and get you in three minutes, then leave you there to freeze for hours on end. We found ourselves having to deal with the shit rooms and the vomit smell for what felt like eight hours. We were only in three scenes, and we barely had any lines, so you can see my issue. I had to tell some hot birdie, "All we want to do is sound check." I had to say it around what felt like a hundred fucking times.

Around number forty-six, the director started giving me direction: "Repeat the line, only this time try not to sound so mean," he said.

What a fuck. His kinky hair curled out from under his backward Yankees cap, and his tight navy shirt flowed over his loose-fit Levis. He was wearing white Chuck Taylors, the leather ones, and the most prominent thing I could see was his shit-eating grin.

I nodded. "Okay, I'll try not to sound so mean, sir."

He yelled, "Action!"

I repeated the line in a tone that resembled a squeaky fart.

He looked at me and his grin widened. He was uncomfortable.

"Okay, you know what? Just be you."

"Yeah." I nodded and mumbled, "No shit."

Drew's line was "I want to eat sushi." The only comment the director gave him was to say the line a little bit faster. He nailed it the second time, which to me sounded exactly like the first. And usually it would take him several tries to nail anything besides music or rolling a spliff, but sushi was his favorite food, so he said that line at least once a day anyway. Luke and his black porkpie hat weren't given a line, so he was just mumbling in between other people's dialogue, hoping someone would hear him. When no one did, he proceeded to tip the hat in between phrases, probably thinking he'd at least get noticed. I for one was thankful he didn't get a line. His deep southern accent made it impossible for most people to understand him. We probably would have had to be there another ten fucking hours. Asher had to hit on the birdie with cheesy lines like, “How often do you come here?” and “You look like an angel.” After hearing him say, “Man, these lines are great!” I retreated into myself for a moment, wondering how I became involved with such an idiot. Then I remembered that Ash was a robot. Yeah, he was the lead singer, and yeah he was nice to look at, but everything he said felt programmed. Lacked feeling. He was the human version of Applebee’s.

I looked down at the script and sighed. Who wrote this fucking thing?

All I wanted to do was get the fuck out of there. I was surrounded by people who would forget me as soon as they realized I was nothing special. I’m not special, I’m nothing, no one is, but I remind myself of that enough; I don’t need or want help from anyone else, whether they mean to or not.

—

Seven bullshit-filled hours later we finally finished. The producer was nice enough to set us up with a table at the Box. It was one of those exclusive clubs that offers a risqué variety show where celebrities go to escape. When you arrive, you have to check your phone, ’cause the club has a strict no-pictures rule. If you get caught, they take you out in the back and leave you with a broken phone and, if you give them attitude, a broken nose. The amount of famous people I’ve seen at this place fucking out in the open, blowing lines off their date’s freshly shaved twats, and getting jerked off by trannies is uncanny. It was everything I hated to love, but part of me couldn’t help it. It was fun, when our lives didn’t feel like it anymore. The Box was just another way for us to feel alive. I thought Em could be into it, so I called her up and told her to meet me there.

THE BOX

We walked in and were met by a skeleton-thin girl in a white Venetian mask asking us if we wanted to party. She was holding a few pills in the palm of her hand. I'm pretty sure they were Ecstasy, but either way they looked like Pez candy, only one had a picture of a bomb on it, and the other had a revolver.

"No, we're good. Where's the pisser?"

She closed her hand and looked at me. "I don't fucking work here."

After we checked our coats and I pissed, a bouncer led us up the stairs to our table. We passed the usual: people smoking; strangers fucking; a crying girl whose eyeliner was running; and two strong-looking tan men in white leather gloves, giving each other hand jobs. I grabbed Em's waist to comfort her just in case she was overwhelmed. She turned to look at me, stuck out her tongue, and giggled. She was fine.

Our table was front and center on the second balcony and had a clear view of the stage below. Being on the second floor guaranteed that we took no part in the show, which we were very happy about. The guys invited their friends to meet us, and naturally, more showed up than we wanted. Most of them we hadn't seen in over a year. Fucking leeches. They'd all arrived before we did, and had already taken all the seats.

I turned to Em. "Well, where do you want to sit?"

"I can stand."

"Nope." I shook my head and walked up to one of the bloodsuckers who was sitting front and center.

"Get up."

He looked at me, smiling.

"I'm not fucking joking." I didn't smile back. He stopped smiling, got up, and we sat down. A server dressed like a mermaid brought us drinks. Casa Noble and soda with lime.

Em pinched my arm. "You didn't have to be so mean to that guy."

"Oh, fuck that guy. He doesn't deserve to sit front row; you do." I laughed. "This is here for us, not them. They can all go to hell as far as I'm concerned."

She grinned and rolled her eyes. "You could have asked him nicely."

I looked around at the scummy drugged-out clientele and shrugged. "Yeah, I could have." Then I grabbed her hand. "I'm sorry, I just hate feeling used. Especially by someone I've never met."

She nodded. "I get that."

I thumbed my glass. "So, what do you think of this place?"

"It's pretty cool," she said, smiling.

"It's kind of weird, right? You only hear about these places existing; you never really get to experience them."

She took a sip of her drink. "Yeah, I was just thinking that. Do you?"

"Do I what?"

"Well, do you get to experience places like this, you know, often?"

My eyes moved to the left. "Occasionally," I said, lying.

"Hmm," she grunted. Suddenly she didn't look so happy—she saw right through me.

A muscled-out black guy wearing a teddy-bear mask was slowly dancing onstage. He was naked and his flaccid cock was the size of my arm.

"Do you find that to be attractive?" I asked.

"I find his body to be."

I looked and agreed with her. He was attractive. He could have had the ugliest face, but with a teddy-bear mask and his hard body, it didn't matter.

When I was younger, a childhood friend, Jon, asked me if I wanted to play touch. I wasn't sure what that was so I said yes. He reached down my pants into my underwear and played with my soft cock. He told me to do the same, so I did, only he was hard. I remember thinking I didn't want to do it, but I also didn't want to stop. I guess it was exciting and new; it was weird and different; it was wrong, but I didn't care. Padre told me Jon ended up marrying some redheaded girl he met at a Christian summer retreat years ago. Francis told me, last he heard, she left him, took their two kids, and he's back living with his parents. Neighborhood gossip runs rampant through San Antonio. Nothing better to do, I guess.

The show started with a gorgeous black seductress dressed in lingerie and a cat mask. She was singing some song that maybe a few people knew, but she was singing it with conviction, and her voice demanded attention. She would step left in her black heels, and people's heads would follow. She would lunge right and shove a man's face in her pussy, and everyone would look jealous, wishing it was them. In the middle of her song, she bit her lip on purpose and it began to bleed a little. A small red drop slowly descended down her chin, and I wanted to taste her. She turned around, exposing her tight ass and ended her introduction by putting the microphone all the way into her mouth. The crowd cheered and the lights faded to a purple and black-light wash onstage.

The crowd was like lightning, eagerly awaiting what came next. The cheering quieted down when a dark, sensuous song with a bass line you could feel in your gut started. A young, half-naked brunette birdie with bits of shiny leather began to do an acrobatic routine. She started on the floor, grabbed two chains that were hanging from the ceiling, and ascended up into them as though they were vines from a jungle canopy. Her body moved like a snake and contorted in every which way, while the cold metal pulled and tore at her skin. Every now and then the chains took bits out of her and she began to bleed. She sucked on each new wound like a vampire. First her arms, then her thighs, then she'd wipe the blood on her stomach and suck on her fingers. The clanking of the chains tightening every time she moved made everyone wince. But no one could take their eyes off her. The women in the crowd would shuffle and recross their legs, probably discovering that our chained vampire had made them wet. The men just stared with their mouths open, dicks as hard as the steel she was wrapped in. It was hot and bloody. What else could turn them on?

The lights faded to black and a spotlight switched on. There was a blonde, muscled tranny in an orange bikini and matching six-inch heels standing onstage. Her tits were faker than my enthusiasm for the pilot we shot earlier that day, and they were just as horribly done. Instead of looking like tits, they looked like two giant rocks that were smoothed into a dome with a nipple painted in the middle. Gross. When she walked, her thigh muscles would bulge and ripple like a horse. She'd bend over and expose her bare brown asshole, then she'd flex it so it looked like it was winking at you.

Immediately the dynamic in the room changed from turned-on to grossed out. The muscle sat down on the floor and pulled over a blue denim knapsack. On the front was a piece of white tape with the word "TREATS" written in all capital letters. She unzipped it, smiled at the crowd, and took out a small green veiny dildo. She started to suck on it, then she pulled back her orange bikini, displaying her fleshy, impotent dick, and started jerking herself off. She couldn't get herself hard, so a few seconds later, she shrugged her shoulders, took the dildo out of her mouth, spread open her ass, and began fucking herself with the veiny toy. Everyone shuddered in disbelief, but a few sick people, including me, were just staring, admiring the balls on this girl. Well, not literally, but you get it. When she was done, she put the toy back in her "TREATS" bag, and pulled out a bottle of Jack Daniels. She placed it on the ground and rode it like a cock. Up and down, up and down, her little prick bouncing every which way, grossing everyone out. When she was satisfied, she took the bottle out of her ass, took a sip, and spit the brown liquor on the front row. There was a moment of seven people all yelling, "Whoa!" in disbelief, unable to comprehend what just happened.

She stood up and walked to a red velvet throne, and the music started to quiet down. It was as though we were watching her backstage. She sat down, spread open her roided-out legs, and began jerking off again. When she couldn't get hard for the second time, she reached over to the table next to her, grabbed a handful of cocaine, snorted it, rubbed it all over her face, asshole, and dick, grabbed a large black dildo, and began fucking herself again. This time her veins were bulging and she was moaning. She finally got hard, and when she had enough of the black toy, she proceeded to wrap her dick in paper and light it on fire. She then turned around and somehow there was fake blood all over her body. I wasn't really sure what any of it meant, 'cause if it was supposed to be a metaphor for something, it was overshadowed by the pure shock value. What a horror show. Em was watching with one eye the whole time. I was watching with both. It was gross, and it was awesome.

The stage filled with fog, and a single red wash of light illuminated the floor. A small flame began to rise from the back of the stage, then another. A couple walked out holding two thin sticks with fire on the ends. The girl was a beautiful translucent-skinned redhead cloaked in white lace and wearing a black leather collar. She walked slowly with her back straight, pushing out her breasts, her pink nipples hard as diamonds. She would raise one leg, then the other, in a slow prance, and her heel would come down hard but wouldn't make a sound.

The man was dressed in a white shirt that exposed his bare chest and black leather pants. His skin was tan, and his beard was pencil-thin. He was wearing eyeliner, and his jet-black hair was in a ponytail to avoid the flames. He would lay his hands on her breasts, and she would lean back, deep-throating the flame. She would blow out a huge ball of fire, and when she slowly rose back to position, he would lick her nipples. At one point he took a swig of oil, then blew it onto the flame, causing an enormous roar from the crowd. Everyone's eyes flashed orange, looking like the devil had just set into their bones. I glanced over at Em, who was mesmerized by the naked fire breathers, and pinched her thigh. She snapped out of it, shifted on her chair, looked at me, and sighed. Then as the fire died down, she fingered her glass and grinned. The tequilas had us feeling pretty good.

I looked at her. "That was wild, wasn't it?"

"There were so many moments I wanted to look away but couldn't!"

I laughed. "I know what you mean."

"That Jack bottle routine, whoa."

"Tell me about it!"

We ordered two more Casa Noble and sodas and passed some time discussing the show. But something was off with her. I could see it in her eyes.

"What's with you?" I asked.

"What are you talking about?"

"I dunno, you just seem different, is all. Is something bothering you?"

She leaned in closer, then back farther. She sighed, almost as if she were in pain. "Well, actually, I need to talk to you but right now isn't the time."

The tone of her voice changed, so mine did too. "Why not?"

"It's just not, Bell. Not here."

I scratched my head and avoided her eyes. "I dunno why anywhere else would be better. Just tell me."

"No."

"C'mon."

"No, Bell, I'm not gonna do this here!"

"Do what?"

"Fucking shit! Fine!"

Her eyes moved left, then right. "I've been thinking about this for a while now. With your schedule, and with mine, I think that we, well . . . this is hard for me to say, but I think we should stop seeing each other."

My heart cracked. "Huh?"

"Listen, I never see you. And when I do, it's fun and all, but it's not enough anymore. What we have is great, but I need more, and you can't give it to me right now. You've got too much going on—hell, last time we had a night out, you got high and passed out at my work. You almost got me fired! I even took you home and tried to have sex with you and you wouldn't even fuck me! I just really feel like you're distant in every way. I just really feel like . . ."

She kept talking, but her voice disappeared and the music became louder in my head.

"Look, this isn't really optional—I just think we should enjoy our time together, and cut our losses."

She started to tear up.

I stood up. "Okay." I reached in my pocket and put a square in my mouth. "Okay, fine." I lit up. "I'm leaving."

"What else is new?"

"What the fuck does that mean!?" I shouted.

"You always do, and you already did, Bell!" As tears crowded her cheeks, I could tell they weren't out of pure sadness—there was a relief there too.

I started toward the stairs, and the guy who I made get up earlier smiled at me. I pushed him into the bar and yelled, "Fuck off!" Everyone stared at me as I left Em alone at the table. On the way out, I passed the smeared-makeup girl and she was still crying. The two strong men were now taking turns sucking each other off, and at the bottom of the stairs, the skeleton girl with the Venetian mask was planted like a gumball machine. I asked her if she still had any pills.

"Here you go, honey. Take this one, it'll make you forget everything," she said, smiling. "Everyone's got things they need to forget, at least for a while."

I looked down at the blue Pez with the bomb on it and thought, *Bombs away.* I popped it into my mouth and swallowed hard.

—

I walked outside, and the air hit me. It was cool, and the wind was strong and whistling. It felt like the first air from an opened freezer on a hot summer day. I closed my eyes, leaned my head back, and breathed deep. I began to walk aimlessly around New York. Tears rolled down my cheeks and my head began to spin. Life always had a way of reminding me that being on top and being on bottom were within arm's reach of each other. And right now it felt like I was holding on to both ends. I stumbled into a bar and sat down. The bartender looked at me and said, "You look like you need a drink." I half smiled and nodded.

"Give me two. Tomorrow's gonna be a long day."

JFK

I woke up in my bed, dehydrated as all hell with a pounding headache. Everything inside of me felt like thick sandpaper grinding away at my organs. First my brain, then my liver, and last my kidneys. I walked to the bathroom to piss, and out of me came a canary-yellow stream of radioactive urine that burned. It was the kind of hangover that makes you say, "I'm never drinking again . . . until tonight." I flushed away the radiation, flipped the seat, and sat down to take a shit. Evacuating your bowels after a night of coping with a bottle is one of the only things that feels liberating.

I sat with my elbows on my knees and tried to piece together the night. The last thing I remember is a black car—a Lincoln, no, a Cadillac—picking me up at some hole-in-the-wall, only I wasn't alone. Some blur of a person was with me the whole time. Who?

Parts of the night flooded my brain: a flat, tanned stomach; an echoing laugh; long, curly blonde hair; taking shots of something herby and dark green . . . but never a face. My pillow had the faint smell of vanilla, and there was a note on my bedside table. A number was scribbled on it. "Call me." It was signed "Mel" in blue ink and had a crudely drawn smiley face, which, for some reason, didn't look happy. Probably just in my head.

I got up and squeezed the carpet with my toes, grabbed Mel's note, and threw it in the trash. I breathed heavily, stretched my arms out, and burped loud. Then I walked to my fridge, pounded a soda water half-cut with blue Gatorade, and took two Aleve from the family pack.

I showered for a long time that morning. The water was hot and felt good on my gravel-tearing headache. My body was screaming at me for everything I had put it through the last few days, but my brain was saying one thing: *Em*. For a moment I let the hot water hit my face, and said aloud, "She cut me loose, and set herself free."

I opened my eyes and stared at my feet. I put them close together and noted how my two big toes bent outward more than anyone else's I'd ever seen. "Your feet are fucking ugly." Then I looked at my cock. It was hanging purple and limp. I tried to jerk off, but I couldn't get hard. So I stepped out, dried off, avoided looking at myself in the mirror, and got dressed.

—

My driver was an older gray-haired man who asked a lot of questions. He pulled up holding a sign that said "Beal Mar." I rolled my eyes and waved at him. He got out, grabbed my bags, threw them in the trunk, and opened the door for me. He had on one of those black driving caps that went with a cheap black suit and tie. His shoes looked a bit worn, and he had a yellow mustard stain on his left sleeve. It looked like he'd been doing this for a long time. I was staring at my phone, feeling like death, trying to distract myself from the fake "new car" smell that was lingering from one of those poorly scented hanging black trees. All around me was an ocean of stiff gray leather, and my sea legs weren't kicking in. The driver looked at me in the mirror and began talking in an endearing but creepy-uncle sort of way.

"Why do you look like you've just been through hell?" His rusty eyes were staring at me.

I just wanted to be left alone. I looked at the mirror, sighed, and answered. "Well, to be honest, last night my girlfriend left me, so I got drunk, took drugs from a stranger, and slept with some girl I don't even remember. Hell, I don't even know if it really was in fact a girl. I hope it was, but also right now I don't really have it in me to care."

He laughed. "Well, sorry to hear about losing your girl, but it's not *so* bad. At least you got some."

I wasn't sure if he actually heard me. Maybe he was fucking deaf.

"Yeah," I said.

I reached into the black leather seat pouch and felt for water. None.

"Do you have any water?"

At a stoplight, he reached over to the passenger seat and handed me a bottle. I ripped it open as though I had been stuck in the Mojave for a few weeks. My mouth was dry, my lips were chapped, and my body was hot.

"Say, aren't you in that band?"

I cracked my neck. "Yes."

"Big fan. Big fan." He was smiling bigger than a clown.

"Thanks, man."

"Say, would you mind signing something for my daughter? I swear she's your biggest fan, and she would flip out if I brought her something from you."

I looked down, touched my forehead, and massaged it. "Look, man, can we both just not talk? I'm not trying to be mean, but I had a long night and I don't want to talk or think; I don't even want to move. But at this point, I don't have much of a choice. Is that okay? Is that something we can both do?"

He looked at me again in the rearview, his eyes looking defeated, then after a few awkward seconds said, "You got it."

The rest of the drive was quiet. I keep forgetting that drivers are never alone. And when you're never alone, it's easy to feel like you always are.

—

I got to JFK, looked at the rusty-eyed man, and happily said goodbye. Before I opened the door, I took out a pair of drumsticks labeled "VIC FIRTH." They had my signature on them, and I tossed them on the front passenger seat.

"Here, for your daughter."

I apologized and blamed it on my hangover. He looked at me like I was still an asshole but grinned and told me thanks and he "understood." I didn't care what he thought, but his daughter shouldn't grow up thinking her favorite band was full of hungover, salty dickheads.

I grabbed my black duffel, stepped outside, and put on my sunglasses. My eyes were bloodshot. I walked through the airport swiftly, avoiding the slow walkers. It was like the streets of New York, only the airport idiots were slower than the walking dead. I had no patience for that. I could see their brains reminding them that it was "one foot in front of the other," and I swear a few of them were drooling. As they walked in their brightly colored tracksuits and H&M sweatpants with oversized Champion sweatshirts, my only thought was *There's no way any of these dead people are fast enough to be athletes.* As I neared the center of the airport, some of the dead were wearing cheap suits and were attached to their iPhones or Samsungs. They were sending emails and memos and setting up conference calls—you know, the real-life horror of nine-to-five job life. As far as I'm concerned, they aren't really living. They're all just traveling back to the graves they digitally maintain. Fuck this place. I walked into the Admirals Club and found Asher standing at the bar.

ROW TWO, SEAT A

When Asher expresses concern, it's about as believable as me running a marathon in thirty minutes, or shit, running one at all. I could never understand why he sounded so insincere, 'cause he *was* genuinely concerned, but he just wasn't convincing. It's not his fault—he's just a robot. His emotions were as deep as his skin, and as thin as his black painted-on jeans. That's how he was programmed.

"Dude, what happened last night?"

I shook my head. "I don't want to talk about it."

"Well, I mean, okay. But that shit was crazy, man." His tawny eyes grew.

"Em and I are done," I said.

His stare retreated to the ground, then back up at me, and suddenly he looked normal.

"Sorry to hear that, brother. I figured as much, but I thought I'd see if you were okay."

"I'm fine, thanks for asking."

"No problem."

He tried to change the subject. "Wasn't that show crazy last night?"

"Yeah. I kinda don't wanna talk about it."

He nodded. "Word, I get it."

"Where's everyone else?" I asked.

"Drew's in the corner staring at his phone, and Luke is over there playing a game on his."

"Where's Hank?"

"I dunno, man, was it my turn to watch him?"

I shook my head. "I'm gonna make a tea."

I sat down in front of a television alone and watched the news. Everything was shit. The state of the world was always worse as the days went on. A bombing here, a plane crash there, a child raped and murdered—it was just shit. Here I was feeling sorry for myself, 'cause somehow my insignificant problems were bigger than everyone else's. I finished my tea, grabbed my bag, and walked in silence to the plane.

My seat neighbor was an old man who stared at my tattoos. His gray pants, white shirt, and burgundy tie all screamed *big* business, but it couldn't be any bigger than his stomach, which looked like a low-hanging tire from a tree trunk. He didn't like it when I stared back at him. He'd look down and shake his head, and I would do the same. Why doesn't the pretty girl ever sit next to me? Shit, he was probably thinking the same thing. None of it mattered, though.

Behind me, Luke, his hat, and Asher were sitting together, arguing about something or other. You could hear the yelling and see their arms flying up above the seats. Idiots. Those two were always yammering about this and that—a dick-measuring contest, really. Hank was buried deep in his emails, calculating how much time he had to answer them before the plane took off, and Drew was buried deep in his eternal cloud of THC; he always gets high before flights.

I looked at the blonde flight attendant who was in a blue skirt and heels. She bent over to grab some waters, and I stared at her ass. She looked over her shoulder and caught me, then casually lowered her ass so she was kneeling. I smiled quick, looked up and to the left, then put my headphones on, turned on James Blake, and began to fall asleep.

Thoughts of Em couldn't find their way out of my head no matter how hard they tried. I already missed everything about her. Part of me couldn't blame her, 'cause it was a hard life she didn't know she signed up for. And the other part of me had to blame her, 'cause it was the only thing that helped me. So I sat there falling asleep, convincing myself that it was her and not me. And just like Mom, everyone leaves. Before I passed out, I grabbed a pillow and put it on my lap so I could hide the midsleep hard-on I get. I don't know why, but it always happened on planes.

—

I woke up as we landed. It startled me 'cause it felt like we were crashing. The plane jerks you in every which way and creates the hard-hitting sound of three hundred tons being dropped from thirty thousand feet, smashing into hard blacktop. When we came to a stop, I looked down and realized I had drooled all over the blue headrest. It was now blue with an added foamy white. *Great.* The blonde flight attendant was laughing at me. I smiled back and awkwardly tried to cover it up with the flight blanket.

I usually dream on planes, but this time it felt like I time traveled. A six-hour flight turned into a half hour, and it was glorious. We went to the Admirals Club to grab a coffee and I had to piss. I went into the tacky 1970s wood-paneled bathroom, whipped it out, relieved myself, and stared at my cock. I raised one eyebrow, listening to the sound of my piss hitting the toilet water, put it back in my jeans, then flushed. I washed my hands, then glanced at the full-length mirror. I lifted my black shirt, looked at my love handles, and said, "You're fat." I flexed my chest, made a popping sound with my mouth, and left humming the James Blake song from the flight.

Hank was waiting for me when I came out of the bathroom. He was in the same clothes as always—black jeans, black shirt, black baseball cap, and brown boots. It was his uniform. His red beard was thick but trimmed, and his tortoiseshell glasses were new Ray-Bans. On his left arm was a fresh colored tattoo of Mickey Mouse in skull form that had just started to peel. Bits of red, yellow, and black began to fall, looking like a snake shedding and coming into its new skin.

"What's up?" I asked.

He folded his arms and tapped on his side counting one, two, three.

"Nothing, just waiting for you."

I raised my eyebrow. "Well, let's go."

LONDON

Hank is a no-man-left-behind kind of guy, but that's because he has to be. He tells us when to eat, when to sleep, when to shit, when to wake up, and when to play a show. He tells us when not to smoke, what not to say, and most importantly, he tells us when to stop drinking. If we didn't have him, we'd probably all be dead. I felt bad for him most days. He'd jumped into this at the beginning of our career before this thing became huge. It was a jet taking off and he was a copilot with no training. You could tell by his wardrobe, his well-placed tattoos, and his slow, calculated speech that he was an overly intelligent man who didn't display much emotion. He showed it, but sometimes it didn't seem believable. He had all the makings of a sociopath, really: a perfect tour manager.

"Hank, you're a fucker, you know that?"

He took enough time to think of four reasons I could be saying this, and said, "Yes."

I laughed. "Well, I don't mean it, really."

"Yes, you do," he said.

A girl in a tight black skirt with four-inch Jimmy Choos walked by. I turned my head and clicked my teeth; Hank looked and did nothing.

"See, you got issues," I said, shaking my head.

"Well, we all do."

"See that brunette with the tight skirt and expensive shoes?" I pointed.

"Yep."

"Well, what do you think about her?"

"I think she's a great-looking woman," he replied.

"I honestly have no idea why I'm so bothered by your lack of passion. See, I would slowly take that dress off, fuck her, and put her heels in my mouth while she was moaning and asking for it harder."

He stared forward. "I'm sure you would," he said stoically.

I rolled my eyes, and the Jimmy Choos birdie smiled at me. I turned my head and ignored her. "I need a drink."

Hank said nothing and pulled out his phone to check his email. Before he opened the app, I could sense him counting in his head how many times I'd said that to him recently. Four, that day alone by my count, but I could be wrong. I imagine he counted just in case it was more than usual, and maybe today it was, but anomalies happen. It wouldn't be the first time, and it certainly wouldn't be the last.

He shook his head. "We're gonna be late to load in for this show."

I looked at him. "And you need three drinks."

Then he smiled and, without saying a word, held up two fingers.

—

Like Hank predicted, we were late to load in. But that part of the process didn't affect me or the band 'cause our jobs were just to play the damn music and look good onstage. When we arrived, Hank showed us to our greenroom and left us to our own devices. I sat alone in a corner and played with my phone. My mother's face quickly flashed in, then out of my head. *Bitch,* I thought. I shook it off, grabbed a bottle of Jameson, and took a swig.

"Yo, you alright, bro?" Drew saw me drinking earlier than usual.

"Huh? Oh yeah, I'm fine."

"You miss her, huh?"

I squinted. "Who, Mom?"

"No, maaan, Em."

I looked at the bottle in my hand. "Oh." Then I put it down. "Yeah."

—

The show was big, six thousand people or so. At one point some guy climbed the speaker towers and did a magnificent backflip into the crowd. He jumped and spread his arms and legs into a swan dive. He was an eagle among the swallows. The only problem was, no one caught him. He looked like a beautiful trapeze artist flying in the air, and then when he hit the ground, he looked like he'd just gotten the shit beat out of him. He left with a broken leg, a new appreciation for paramedics at concerts, and a great story.

Asher told the crowd not to be stupid, but no one was listening. They looked like a bunch of electric waves shimmering in the cobalt, red, and apricot lights, high on Ecstasy and drunk on endorphins. Screaming white girls were screaming white obscenities at us in their harsh British accents, which made me want to scream even more vulgar obscenities back at them. Bald, bearded, horrific-looking men were holding their ash-blond, room-temperature, disgusting cask ale high in the air with their overweight, crooked-toothed women on their shoulders, calling us wonderful cunts.

It's amazing how the word "cunt" is used in the UK. Personally I love it. Saying things like, "You magnificent cunt," or "He's a wild cunt," or even better, "Fuck that cunt," makes me smile, and it feels good. But like all vulgarities, it depends on the context. When the show ended, I immediately ran back to our greenroom to avoid the crowd. The stage had suddenly become a shadowbox of my good feeling, and my time up there was over—I did my part. I let my offstage life settle in, then to take the edge off, I poured myself an Espolòn and soda, sat down, and looked at my drink. The bubbles rose from the bottom to the top like colorless, gauzy hot-air balloons. Hank sauntered in and told us we had a meet and greet in exactly four minutes and forty-seven seconds. I grabbed a black towel, wiped my face, and told him, "I'm skipping this one." Luke and his hat looked at me and said they were too. He also didn't care for the spotlight. We both loved our fans, but if they knew everything we thought of them, they'd probably try to vote us out of the band like it was an episode of a bad reality show. I tried to keep my distance from them because I found our relationship to be the same as anyone from the old Angels & Kings days; they just wanted something from me—they were social beggars. I didn't blame them. It was a way for them to feel larger-than-life or to at least distract themselves from the everyday routine. The only problem was I had no interest in it. I was a wave-at-you kind of guy, you know, from far away. I didn't want to hug you; I didn't want to talk to you; hell, from where I sat onstage, you were just another blurry face to me.

When the meet and greet was over, Hank came back and stared at Luke and me.

"The other guys already left, but there's a car in the back, and it is ready to take both of you to the hotel. It's a fifteen-minute drive, so pee now."

Luke adjusted his hat as I drained my tequila, then he looked at me.

"You ready?"

THE HOXTON

It was dark, and the sidewalks looked orange and cream in the streetlight. A few cracks in the pavement had been poorly covered in tar and were choking out the green plants trying to escape the entrails of a cold concrete death. People were walking fast, dressed in black clothes and carrying black umbrellas, prepared for the random drizzles in London. Down the street, an artist in tattered jeans and a blue face mask was spray-painting the side of a building in a hurry, hoping not to be caught.

We were staying at the Hoxton, a hotel known for its expansive ceilings and hip bar where fresh daisies are set on each table every day. Some nights they have an open mic, where strange people get up to sing strange songs and read strange poetry. Those are the nights I hope to avoid. Luke and I walked in, talked to the beautiful dreadlocked brunette with catlike green eyes, and went to our rooms. The wooden floors were covered in black-and-white cowhide carpets, and the bed was lofted. The massive windows overlooked the London street, and the small desk held a few tan and yellow books.

I set my bag down, sprawled on my bed, and texted Francis.

B: you hear from mom?

F: no word bro.

It was getting late and the guys were tired, but Drew was in the mood for a drink. I got up, changed my shirt, avoided the mirror, and played with my hair a bit. "I'm having a terrible hair day," I said to no one, then I flipped open some pomade, rubbed it in my palm in a clockwise motion, and put it through my hair. "Ugh, fucking terrible looking."

I threw on my black leather Schott jacket, my black hat, and took the elevator downstairs to meet Drew at the hotel bar. He was dressed like he was on the hunt, in his black suede bomber and his tan Chukka Frye boots. I looked down at myself and felt insecure but shook it off and waved at him. As he approached, the faint smell of weed lingered, but it always did around him.

"What are you, going on a date?"

"Weeell, just with you, man." He laughed.

"I'm surprised you actually put on clothes today," I said, smiling.

"Yeah, ha ha. I gotta look good, maaan. I can't put myself out there looking like a homeless walrus."

I shook my head. "I don't even know what that means. Let's get a drink."

"Well, yeeaah, dude, what kind?"

I smiled. "Rye old-fashioneds, of course."

Two women were sitting in the big green velvet chairs by the front window. Two fawns completely aware of the hunt. They seemed deep in conversation: one not smiling and listening politely, the other rambling on about something that's more than likely as interesting as shit on the street. I tend to avoid those types of situations 'cause I find myself not knowing what to say half the time. I'm better when there's one girl; two intimidate me. Drew, however, is quite the opposite.

"I'm gonna go talk to those two babes."

I nodded. "Go for it. I'm gonna order another drink." I took a deep pull from the rocks glass and drained it.

I noticed that the brunette looked like my ex, Ames. Same haircut, same olive skin, and even the same shade of coral lipstick. Her eyes weren't as sunless, but she was damn near close. It intrigued me. I watched Drew make his move. I couldn't hear what he was saying, but his big dumb mouth was moving fast, and whatever he said made the girls laugh loudly, and then he pointed at me. They both looked over and I tried to ignore them. I took a big swig of my fresh old-fashioned, and then Drew waved me over. I sighed and reluctantly obliged.

"Hi, I'm Bell."

"They know who you are, maaan," Drew said. They started laughing.

"Yes, we know who you are," said my ex. The other one was blonde and had features I didn't care for. Drew liked her, though.

"I'm Julie," said the blonde.

"I'm Sarah," said my ex.

Sarah's accent was proper and ladylike; Blondie's was a little rougher.

"Nice to meet you." I shook hands with both of them. "So, how is your night going?"

"Well, we were fine until your frien' Drew over here walked over and started talkin' to us," Blondie said, winking. "He just kept sayin' that you two were famous and that it would be a waste if we didn' talk to ya."

"Well, crisis averted, I guess," I said, smiling. Sarah laughed and stared at me.

"So you two are soooo famous—who are ya?"

"We're musicians," Drew said.

I hated this routine. This always happens, and he's become so damn predictable.

"Oh. Well, which ones?" Sarah asked, unenthused.

"Well, we have a song on the radio," said Drew.

"Sing it," said the blonde.

"Oh no," I said.

Drew started to hum it; what a fuck. The girls instantly perked up.

"Holy shit, I know this song!" Blondie started to sing the words, and Sarah joined in. They laughed loudly.

"Shu' up, is that really you guys?"

"Yeeeeah," said Drew, drawing the word out even more than he usually does.

"I don't believe you; I'm going to search it." Sarah pulled out her phone.

"Go ahead." Drew was always more shameless than me when it came to this shit. I couldn't quite figure it out. He was always picked on 'cause he was a little shorter, and a little darker, and because of that he had to fight a little harder. Now that we were on top, it seemed like all he thought was, *Look at me now, fuckers.* He's got nothing to lose, I guess.

Once the birds were done with the search engine, they seemed to just enjoy hanging out with two people who seemed more important than they ever could be. I wished they knew how unimportant we were and how much bullshit idolizing anything is, for that matter. Sarah didn't talk much; she mostly just stared. Blondie seemed to enjoy talking and did enough for the both of them.

"Soooo, how do you two know each other?" Drew was making sure to keep them talking.

"Well, we sort of work together," replied Blondie.

"What do you do?" I asked.

"We're dancers."

Drew perked up. "What kiiind of dancers?" he asked. I could tell he was excited.

"Well," said Sarah, "we are dancers of the exotic type."

"Bullshit, I call bullshit," I said.

"No, really," said Blondie. "We strip, we take our clothes off, we get naked."

I could tell Drew was thinking we'd hit the jackpot. Not because they were exotic dancers, but because they were happy about it. They were proud about what they did, and they were happy with where they were in life. It didn't look like the status quo was important to them, but every book has a cover.

"Dancers here are different, though," said Sarah.

I raised my eyebrow. "How?"

Blondie sat up straight and recrossed her legs. "We strip from behin' a bar, and no one is allowed to touch us."

What's the point? I thought. "Good money?" I asked, knowing the answer.

"Well, these cocktails are twelve pounds each—you tell me," Sarah said proudly.

"Speaking of pounds, I'm hungry," Drew said. "Know of anything open this late?"

"Have you ever had *döner* 'n' chips?" asked Blondie.

"Nope," Drew said, licking his lips.

"Follow us—there's a spot right around here," Sarah said, standing up from her throne.

CHESTER ST.

A couple of hours had passed since we'd arrived at the Hoxton. Outside, the streetlights were spotty and dull. They seemed to hum to each other with electricity and glow in the cool, moist air. The brightest thing around us was a neon purple light that outlined the roof of an ugly two-story building. Blondie pointed to it and said, "That's where we work." Halfway to the food stand, the exterior of a dilapidated wall had a painting of Audrey Hepburn sprayed in every color imaginable. The outlines were on top of each other and made it seem as though you were looking through blurry plastic. Next to it, a lamp illuminated a black-and-white poster advertising the suicide hotline.

+44 (0) 8457 90 90 90
LIFE IS WORTH LIVING

We strolled slowly behind the girls down Main Street, staring at their pendulum asses. Back and forth, back and forth, hypnotizing us into deep wonder-lust. For a second I took comfort in listening to their heels clack on the cracked pavement. I lit up a square, gave one to Blondie and one to Drew. I offered one to Sarah, but she smiled and said, "Life is cancer enough." I thought about that sentence and tried to imagine what it would mean to me if I were a stripper.

—

As we arrived, Sarah looked back and grinned. "Döner meat and chips, it keeps us dancing girls healthy." Everyone laughed.

"Whaaat do we order?" asked Drew.

"We'll get it, yeah?" said Blondie.

As far as I could tell, döner was pork parts that were served on top of french fries. It was good, but that's because we slathered it in some sort of vinegary BBQ sauce. I asked if they had anything hot: the guy pointed at Sarah and Blondie and laughed, then handed me sriracha. I grabbed the bottle, ignoring his stupid laugh, and poured on the sauce. If I'm going to eat crap, I like it to be spicy. We walked past all the sad faces eating their meat and into the small dining room. It looked terribly old, with broken bits of off-white tile on the floor and shabby wooden tables with chairs that didn't match. The lighting was bright and fluorescent, and all it did was reveal the truth—at this point I was sure I looked like a wrecked car.

We sat down, joined the rest of the sad people, and ate our meal over tired, unimportant conversation. I mainly focused on Sarah playing with her hair, wrapping it around her finger like it was a string reminding her of something she might forget. She bit her lip and looked at me like she ached. I barely touched the food, but when everyone was finished, the girls wanted to go dancing. "The irony," I said to my plastic fork.

They took us to a club where they knew the bouncers. The giant men took one look at me and gave me shit for my hat, so I said, "Fuck it," threw it on the street, and walked in. I hate lines—I don't do them—so I was happy we got to skip it. Drew and I bought the drinks—two Herradura and sodas with lime, and two Grey Goose and sodas, no lime.

Drew was dancing with Blondie while Sarah danced with some little prep fuck in a popped collar. I don't like dancing, so I sat and watched. She was good, and you could tell she genuinely enjoyed it. Every move she made enhanced whatever part of her body she desired. Her curves bounced up, down, left, right and moved in ways only a trained dancer could. She was sexy, and she knew it. She came up to me, grabbed my hand, and tried to pull me onto the dance floor.

"No, no, I'm good. I don't like dancing. I'm just enjoying watching you."

"Don't be such a prude, you just gotta let go. Who cares what anyone thinks? Try to have a good time and give no fucks."

For a second, I thought this girl actually *was* my ex. What the fuck did she know about me anyway? She was reading me like I was one of her regulars at the club, and I couldn't say no.

"Well, at least let me finish my drink."

"Bottoms up," she said, smiling.

I gulped down the tequila and she pulled me fast. She stared into my eyes and started grinding me. She grabbed my hand and put it on her ass. I had a hard-on; she felt it too. Then she looked at me and said, "See? No fucks."

We danced a bit more, slurped drinks a bit more, and left before a bit more became too much.

Hank had put an SUV on call for us. When we walked out, I saw the driver and waved him over. Drew and Blondie jumped in the back, while Sarah and I hopped in the middle.

"Well, that was fun," said Blondie. "We need to make a stop."

"Where to?" I asked.

"She needs to pick up some coke," said Drew.

"What? Drew, just give her a spliff, I know you got one. Besides, Blondie, aren't you fucked up enough?" I asked, half joking.

"Look, it's no big deal, I just need to make a stop. Why's it matter?"

"'Cause I'm trying to have sex with your friend." The whole car giggled. "And I'm trying to do that sooner rather than later."

"Look, she's prolly going to; what you worried about? I'm prolly going to with him too." She was annoyed.

I looked in the rearview mirror. "Well, don't get too excited about it."

Sarah interjected, "We can stop, we can stop; it's no big deal."

"Pull over!" screamed Blondie. "Pulla fuck over!" She started hitting the seat with her fists.

I turned around. "What? What the fuck are you screaming about? Pull over? I was just joking around with you. If you need to get some coke, let's get you some coke. If you need us to stop and get you some H or pills, I guess we can do that too—I don't give a fuck what you do!"

"Shut th' fuck up, you judgmental cunt piece of shit! Pull th' fuck over; I'm walkin' the rest of the way. I'll find my own fuckin' ride. How dare you call me fucked up! I don' need no fuckin' pills! I don' need no fuckin' pills!"

"Fine, you fucking psycho!" I screamed.

We pulled over and let her out.

"Fuck you all!" she screamed.

I turned around and looked at Drew, then I looked at Sarah next to me. Drew looked pissed, and Sarah wasn't too far off.

"Guess your friend really needed that coke," I said dryly.

Sarah sighed. "It just makes her feel good; it makes her feel normal, I guess."

"Not feeling normal is normal to me," I said.

"I get it," she said, blinking hard. But Drew was pissed.

"Maaan, fuck you, Bell! You're such an asshole sometimes. Why do you have to ruin people's nights, man? So what, she wanted some coke! Who gives a fuck, duuude?"

Drew caught me off guard. "No, fuck you, Drew! Get your shit together. If she wanted coke, you should have taken it upon yourself to find it for her. Not wait till we're all in the car headed somewhere together. Who knows where we would have ended up? Who knows who we could have encountered! What the fuck is wrong with you? We're not in the position to just go out and get coke. If we get caught and we go to jail . . . well, fuck, Drew, we're in a big band. It affects our fucking lives!"

Drew turned red and looked at the floor. "Yeeeeah, I know, you asshole; I just wanted to get laid."

Sarah was sitting there quiet, then she looked up and smiled. "Well, you probably still could, want me to call her?"

Drew shook his head. "Nooo . . . Forget it. Just drop me off."

—

The rest of the ride was quiet. Sarah reached for my hand and held it the whole way. We dropped Drew at the Hoxton, then went to her flat. She asked me to come in and naturally I said yes. Her flatmates were all asleep, so we had to tiptoe on hard wood and be quiet. She went to the bathroom to change while I lay on her bed examining her lifestyle, which was spread all over her room. She lived clean, almost too clean.

The bed was made up with white sheets and blankets, the clothes were all color-coded and hanging, except for a pair of blue jeans crumpled up on the floor, and her vanity was decorated with perfume bottles and makeup brushes and jewelry. *Surely she shaves bare,* I thought. Bursts of Blondie circled my mind, screaming and getting out of the car. I felt bad; she seemed like she was a good person. I truly didn't care about her habit—I was just kidding around. But then again, she called me a piece of shit so fuck that cunt.

Sarah came back into the room, wearing black boy shorts and a light-pink bra. She sat on the bed, asked me something I didn't hear, and we started kissing. I undid her bra easily and her breasts fell out. She was breathing heavy and rapidly. I turned her over and made her put her ass in the air. I slowly took off her shorts, and I'd guessed perfectly: shaved bare. I started to go down on her. She ripped off my pants and stuck it in her mouth. When she came, she pulsated and whimpered like a dog. We lay in her bed under the covers, staring at the ceiling. My mind was blank. A cloud of guilt began to circle my brain—it was time to go.

I got up, put my clothes back on, called a car, kissed her, and said goodbye. She asked for my number so I gave it to her, knowing she would never call and knowing I didn't want her to.

I stood outside the apartment to smoke. I hated this fucking place. Somewhere along the line I'd lost my lighter, so I fumbled through my jacket pockets and found a book of matches from the Box. It was black and white, and had a drawing of a devil on one side. I turned it over in my hands a few times, staring at it, thinking about that night, thinking about Em, thinking I wasn't enough.

A black minicab pulled up and the driver rolled down his window.

"Bela?"

"Yeah. Hey, listen, I'm gonna stand here and smoke a cigarette, so just keep the tab going."

"All right, then."

—

In the car ride to the hotel, I saw a streetwalker who resembled Blondie. She was wearing a similar blouse and a leopard print coat, and she had the same black four-inch heels. She was leaning into a car's open window, chatting and laughing. For a second I could have sworn she looked over at the minicab and straight into my eyes. Was it her? No, it couldn't be.

We kept driving through the windy streets of empty London. This place was horrible; I could never live here. Even the car was annoying. A black throwback to the times when cars were classy, but London, no matter what it pretends to be, is just as classless as anywhere else. It's full of prostitutes, drugs, and violence. I don't have a problem with those things, I just hate when something pretends to be what it's not. Also, London just seems like a place . . . well, it seems like a place where it's enough to dream, and to just keep dreaming, and to never get anywhere. I already dreamt about the good life once, and now that I had it in my hands, there was no turning back. Fuck London, the land where dreams die. I was happy we were leaving.

I got to the Hoxton and walked into the lobby. There were a few couples sprawled out on the couches surrounding a solo pianist. He was playing pop music like Elton John and Billy Joel, which I didn't mind. I went to the bar, ordered a bottle of red wine, and went up to my room.

I was nine, and it was Sunday in the middle of a Texas August. We were at my great-aunt's house. The sky was blue and had patches of white and gray clouds all around that let the sun peek out every once in a while. Francis and I were on top of my dad's truck, staring and pointing at the sky, saying what the clouds looked like—a fat lady, a rabbit, an angel; and we laughed until our sides hurt. In front of her redbrick house and black steel window bars, my aunt grew roses in her garden. She was so proud of the big white and red flowers. She would tend to them religiously, pruning their branches, trimming their leaves, watering them, and fertilizing the dirt. How much she cared about them was incredible; they were her children. At the right time, when it was warm and the roses were in full bloom, she would cut one off for both France and me. She would smile with her bright-red lipstick, which she had also gotten on her teeth, laugh hysterically, and say, "Stop and smell the roses, kid." Mom and she never liked each other—actually, they hated each other. My aunt didn't like the way Mom handled the postpartum thing with France, and Mom didn't like the way my aunt looked at her. I understand being looked at and judged for my decisions. It's harder to look back and stare truth in the face. Mom never kept up with her garden.

I opened my door, walked into the foyer, and caught a faint smell of roses. It was quiet and I could hear my feet crunch into the cowhide carpets. The tinnitus in my right ear was softly humming, reminding me it was there. I opened the bottle and took a swig, then another and another until I couldn't anymore. I put the bottle down on the floor, plugged my phone in, fell on the bed, and passed out with all my clothes on.

—

"Wake up."

I opened my eyes. Hank was staring at me.

ROOM 328

My eyes widened, and I was confused for a minute. I looked to my left and there was a half-empty wine bottle. Apparently, I'd spilled most of it on the floor.

"What?" I asked, disoriented.

"Wake up, we gotta go."

"What time is it?"

"It's nine."

I sat up and looked to my right. My clothes were on the floor in a pile, and the TV was on. BBC news was covering someone who had just gotten shot or something.

"Okay, I need to shower."

Hank slowly shook his head. "No time for that. Here."

He handed me a cup of coffee and I sucked it down. Bitter and black, just like I like it.

"What the fuck did I do last night? My head is pounding."

"I dunno, but there's some Advil next to you."

I reached for the two little brown bits of heaven like a zombie discovering a pile of brains and stuck them in my mouth. Pills and coffee, all just distractions for my body so it doesn't realize to its full extent what an asshole I am. These days I have no regard for it.

I looked at Hank. He was staring at me with an expression that was somewhere between judgmental and apathetic. The guy's a fucking psycho.

"Okay, ETA?" I asked.

"Twenty minutes."

I jumped out of bed. "That's plenty of time to shower!"

He began to speak slowly. "You take fifteen minutes to shower and, on your fast days, ten minutes to get dressed. You are already packed, which if you weren't would take you around seven minutes, but either way, it'll take you an extra four minutes to get to the car, two to wait for the elevator, and two to walk to the car. So no, that's not plenty of time."

I looked at him with one eye closed, then grinned. "Well, you just got it all figured out, don't you? Get the fuck out of my room. I'm going to shower—I'll be five minutes late, you crazy ass!" I said, laughing.

He reached for his phone, opened an email. "Hurry up, see you downstairs," he said.

"Oh and Hank."

"What?"

"Can you send France some of the new merch? I don't care what, just something, anything."

He blinked rapidly, then began to nod slowly. "I'll add it to the schedule."

"Thanks."

He opened the door and walked out.

"This guy is insane," I said to the air. "Can you imagine living your life in minute form?"

It's what we pay him for, but he *timed* how long each one of my tasks takes? Next time I'll ask him how long it takes me to shit and to fuck. I'll bet he knows. I walked into the bathroom and stripped off my underwear. I turned on the shower and stared at my body in the mirror. I avoided my face. I turned to the left and looked at the one stretch mark I had on my waist. "Goddamn it, this thing is ugly." I squeezed it and prodded it for a second, and then I shook my head and jumped in the hot water.

Thirty minutes later, I hopped into the black SUV and we headed to Heathrow to catch a flight to Paris. The streets were wrecked with people, all in black, all going on with their lives like they had a purpose. But to me, they all looked the same: focused, lonely, and soulless. On the way we passed the dizzy Hepburn street art. It looked like Em.

Hank was quiet, ass deep in emails; Drew was already asleep, definitely high; and Asher had his headphones on, ignoring the world around him. Luke and his hat were facing forward, but when the car got too quiet, he saw that I was awake and started talking.

"What'd you get inta last night?"

He had that southern accent, not really a drawl, but some words flowed together differently and awkwardly.

"Went home with a stripper," I said, smiling.

He turned around quickly, like I had just told him I was secretly a transvestite.

"Wait a minute, ya did what now?" He was excited.

"Went home with a stripper."

"Y'all went to a strip club and didn' tell me?"

"No, they were in the lobby, drinking. Drew went up to them, did the whole 'I'm in a famous band, and this is my song, and lemme hum it to you' like a fucking idiot, which convinced them we were cool, and then we had a night. It was fun."

"So how'd y'all find out they were strippers?" His eyes were wide cause he was in disbelief.

"Well, they told us."

His bright-green eyes got wider and he shook his head. "That sounds fake. No way. Yer makin' it up."

I can't understand why he thinks I would lie about something like this. This shit happened to all of us, *especially* him. He's tall, white, blond—although you would never know it 'cause of the hats, wears expensive leather jackets all day long—shit, he gets laid just as much as, if not more than, anyone else.

"Okay, I'm making it up," I said.

"Well, if it ever happens for real, you need to call me. Even if I'm asleep, I'll wake up for that."

"Sure thing."

At this point I was in no mood to convince him of anything, so I thought it was best to shift the attention onto him.

"What'd *you* do last night?"

"Just went t' sleep. I's tired, I guess."

"Maybe I should try sleeping one day."

"It'd be good for ya."

I chuckled and popped open the window to smoke a square.

"Yeah, I guess so."

"Dang, I can't believe y'all hung out with strippers and didn' call me!"

"Meh, there was only two of them; it wouldn't have mattered."

"Well, if I was there it woulda been game over, that's f'sure."

I rolled my eyes and blew a puff of smoke in his direction. "Yup. Woulda been over."

—

We got to Heathrow. I passed through the usual zombie crowd, stared at a strawberry blonde in Louboutins, and got on the plane. I chugged water, put on my headphones, and didn't play any music. I just listened to the warm hum of the engines and began to fall asleep.

I was awakened by my parents yelling, arguing about something. They were both downstairs while France and I were in our room. I started to sob, screaming at the top of my lungs with tears rolling down my chunky face. Mom came in and picked me up to try and calm me down. She looked at France and walked out of the room. I saw him open one eye. She put me in my gray-and-blue car seat, revved up the 1988 blue Oldsmobile, and drove me around the neighborhood. It was pitch-black, and the moon was new and nowhere to be seen in the Texas sky. The Big Dipper was bright, and Orion was sparkling. I immediately stopped crying and started to watch the streetlights glow and leave light trails as we passed. The whole time my mother was saying something sweet to me so I would calm down, and I could see her dark-brown eyes in the mirror. As my eyelids got heavy, the light trails became longer and the hum of the car became warm.

PARIS

Paris rarely likes American pop bands. They like those "superstars" who are always in the tabloids, being larger-than-life. They get that we're nothing special, but they seem to be blind to the fact that neither is anyone else, especially those "superstars." Asher has trouble with things like this. His brain isn't programmed to think that anything else in life is as or more important than becoming a star. I can understand that, 'cause he's basically the most surface-level human being I've ever met. His computer brain makes sure he walks through life with blinders on, with only stardom as his primary objective. It's rare that he can break through his shell, but when he does, he's not so bad. The only difference between him and those "superstars" is effort. They don't try, but he has to.

"You know what our problem is?" he asked.

"Here we go again," I said, shaking my head.

"I just think our music needs to be more modern, more current, you know like those new young hip bands that are coming out right now."

"You mean the ones who've been trying to replicate *us?*"

He ignored my question. "All I'm saying is, they're the ones rising on the charts right now, and we're not."

"Dude, you're ridiculous. Why would anyone think that stripping away our identity as a band would be a good idea? I mean I hear you, but we have an established sound, we have an established vibe—we do our own thing. I'm not saying we can't take pieces of what we do and make it more modern, but I would rather die before I begin to chase trends."

Asher turned red. "You're not hearing me! I'm saying we can replicate what these guys do, and do it better."

I grinned at his frustration. "Or we could just do what we're doing and become bigger and better."

"Bro! Never mind." He turned and walked away from me to be alone with his mechanized vision.

Just then, Drew walked up and asked what had just happened. I rolled my eyes, knowing he was way too high and that I would have to repeat myself for him to understand. "Just Ash wanting to be something he's not again."

Drew shrugged his shoulders and began to speak, slow and quiet, "Ah, I see. The saaame old shit."

"Yeah. You know, it's bullshit. The only time I ever feel alive is when we're on that fucking stage playing our hearts out. Sometimes I think that idiot would be fine with getting rid of all that, as long as it sold more."

Drew nodded. "What?"

"Fuck. I said: he'd be fine with taking the heart out of our music as long as it sold more."

Drew nodded again. "Oh yeah, for sure. He's a robot, duuude."

After a sold-out crowd, we were all feeling pretty good. The promoter set us up with an after-show party at a club whose name I could never pronounce. On the way there, I could see the Eiffel Tower in the distance, flashing its lights, standing tall in all its glory. It reminded me of all the flashing lights I saw before I passed out at Em's bar. And it reminded me of how much I missed her. We passed the Bastille and made our way to Oberkampf, a trendy neighborhood known for its nightlife.

We pulled into one of our favorite restaurants, Chez Justine. The awning is proud, burgundy, and big. It covers light-colored wooden tables outside that all face the same way. Each one has an ashtray and two flimsy chairs. Usually these are the first seats to be occupied because Parisians like to drink and smoke in the fresh air. They've been doing that since the country was first conceived. Good style is just in their blood.

Chez Justine has some of the best steak frites you will ever have, and we were all famished from the show. We walked in, Hank told the manager who we were, and we were instantly seated. All around us were beautiful girls in black skintight jeans, loose-fitting cream tops, and dark jackets. Most of them were brunette, and the blonde ones were more dirty or strawberry blonde, since they seemed to dye their hair. Some were high fashion in Yves Saint Laurent and Givenchy; others weren't, but just fucking looked good. Some of them were accompanied by French men, with their long dark hair and their Johnny Depp beards; others were just with their girlfriends, hoping to get picked up by a man they deemed worthy.

We were seated in the middle of the restaurant, so everybody could see us. It wasn't our choice, but we didn't mind. Luke, Asher, Drew, and I all sat in the middle like it was a king's table. We ordered steaks, half-bloody, with pepper sauce, and well-done fries. A bottle of wine came, and we immediately ordered two more with a round of Fernet shots to get the night started. As we ate, Luke, his hat, and Asher argued about some brunette in a black cape they were both gunning for.

"Dude, I saw 'er first."

"Luke, man, you're crazy! Who cares who saw her first? You can't see someone and just claim them on the spot!"

"Fuckin' watch me."

"Ohhh, fuck it, bro, you can have her! This shit isn't worth it."

"Okay, 'kay, 'kay . . . let's flip for it."

Asher looked at Luke like one of his circuits had just shorted out.

"Huh?"

"Let's flip for it. Heads she's yers, tails—and well, that tail's mine." Luke was smiling with both of his hands on the table.

"Whoa there, don't get too excited, your hat's gonna fly off," I said dryly.

Everyone laughed, then Luke looked at me. "Oh shut up." I just smiled.

"C'mon, man, let's flip for it."

"You mean *her*," I said to no one.

Asher looked to the left and thought about it for a second, smiled, and said, "Fine."

Luke reached into his pocket, pulled out a quarter, said, "Call it in the air!" and flipped it.

"Heads!" Asher yelled. As the coin came down into Luke's hand, someone on the other side of the restaurant blew a loud party-favor horn, in celebration of a birthday. Luke looked down and half bit his lip in disappointment. Asher, feeling like the world was celebrating his victory, stood up and threw his hand in the air. "I won, man; that's it—she's mine!"

Luke's half smile changed to a full smile. "C'mon, best of three!"

Hank was staring at Asher and Luke, apparently confused. He looked at me blankly. "You'd think that grown men, especially of your status, would have a better way of doing things."

I nodded. "You'd think so."

Asher and Luke have the same taste, and at times even if they both have incredible-looking women on their arms, they try to purposefully steal the other one's girl. It's like a dysfunctional tag team that somehow actually works. At the beginning of the night, sometimes I ask them why they don't just switch, and Luke usually responds with, "It's more fun this way."

Drew and Hank started talking business, something about the cost of the bus we were getting. I just listened, ate, and stared blankly at my world. Halfway through the meal, champagne and Noah's Mill bourbon shots arrived. I shot the champagne and sipped on the bourbon.

Hank stood up slowly and raised his glass. You could tell he had been thinking about this for the past five minutes or so.

"Cheers to constantly growing in these foreign countries and cheers to this lavish life you've bestowed upon me."

We all looked at him silently, thinking, *Did he just say* bestowed*?*

Luke and his hat chimed in, "Oh, and cheers t' me winnin' the coin toss!"

I rolled my eyes. "Why don't we ever toast to the prospect of one day not having to tour anymore?" I asked.

Asher looked at me like I was trying to change his primary directive. "'Cause that's fucking sad, man!"

Everyone laughed. "Whoa, fucking Buzz Killington over here," clamored Drew.

I felt like an idiot. "I just mean, I don't want to tour when I'm fifty, you know?"

"Hell, I plan on bein' dead," laughed Luke.

Asher was shaking his head. "Geez, bros, this just got dark."

My heart started to race a bit, and I was annoyed at myself. "Okay, okay, okay, fuck this!" I said, fake smiling.

Hank, being the tour dad, began to speak slowly and forcefully and a little bit louder than usual. "Everyone shut up!"

We all stopped talking, still with our glasses in the air, and listened intently.

"Cheers to one day being so damn successful that you never have to do coin tosses 'cause the girls you want are everywhere. And cheers to you having so many hit songs that you don't ever have to do a reunion tour when you're old, and cheers to you guys for making so much money that you can finally give me a fucking raise and put the rest of the crew on retainer!"

We all started laughing and screaming, "Cheers! *Prost! Salud!*"

We finished our meal, Hank paid in cash, and we sucked on Jameson's neat. Luke charmed the coin-toss girl, picked her up, and we were all on our way to a Paris disco. She had friends meeting us there. We told her it was fine, but we had conditions.

"Dude, tell her absolutely no guys allowed," said Asher, grinning. "'Cause the truth is, we don't have any interest in making friends and none of us are going to sleep with the dudes."

Hank was speaking and staring at his phone, then he looked up and smiled. "Well, maybe you would sleep with the dudes, Drew." Then he pounded the Jamo.

Drew smiled and winked his eye. "Ayyyyyyyy, ha fucking ha."

I chimed in. "They're dead fucking weight. No guys allowed." Then I playfully punched Drew in the arm. "They're a waste of our time."

"Yer such a loser," said Luke, half smiling.

We all jumped into the SUV, Drew in the back left, Hank in the back right, me middle left, Luke and his hat next to me with coin-toss girl on his lap, and Asher in the front seat. The ride was short, loud, and obnoxious. Luke was sweet-talking the coin-toss next to me,

Asher was playing "Footloose" on the stereo and scream-talking to Drew, who was rolling a joint and scream-talking back. Hank was as usual staring at his phone.

I loved and hated these moments. Sometimes it feels like the driver is going to get distracted and ram us into a telephone pole, sending us all to our early, albeit deserved, deaths. I've pictured this exact moment several times. Luke would be the least hurt because he always wears his seat belt. At most, he would hit his head on the seat in front of him and get a concussion. He'd be so upset that his porkpie was ruined that he would try to straighten it out before even looking back to see if anyone was okay. Then he would make sure that everyone knows how he knew this would happen one day and that he was better for it. Asher would fly through the front window, cutting his face and arms, and more than likely cracking his skull open. This would reveal above all else that he is in fact a robot sent here from a different world and that's why he's devoid of any emotion. Drew would slam face-first into the seat, forcing the joint he's rolling into his mouth. He would get most of his front teeth knocked out and break his nose, but twenty minutes later he would be so high that he wouldn't care. I would somehow get ejected out the side window, but I would fly, hit the ground and roll, and be fine. Then to complete my expectations, I would be hit by an oncoming car, a Toyota Camry, breaking both of my legs literally in half—bones sticking out and everything. My face would be flattened into the hood, but I would still be alive, if not to witness the disbanding of my career, then to be reassured that the wreck did not in fact do anything to improve my already ugly soft body. The sharp window glass wouldn't cut off my love handles as I went flying through it, and the Toyota Camry wouldn't somehow increase my cheekbone-to-face ratio as my head smashed into it. I would sit there, stare at the SUV, curse the driver, lay back, and light up a square. At this point I'd be in shock, but nothing would keep that smoke from entering my lungs. I would lay back, stare at the clouds, and just feel like dying.

We came to a stop and waited our turn getting out of the SUV. The line to the disco was wrapped around the block, and it was full of young Frenchies all dressed in black, all smoking cigarettes. They were gathered here knowing they would be seen as if it were cool to just stand in line. Fucking idiots. They reminded me of hungry town pigeons all black, gray, and white, circling around yellow seed on the ground. We got out of the SUV and walked straight in, skipping the smoking birds. They all looked at us like we were offending their air. How could this group of Americans with one French coin-toss girl be better than them? Impossible. They stood there blowing smoke out the sides of their mouths, quietly cursing us under their breath. We smiled at them and just kept walking.

LA FIDÉLITÉ

The building was dark, and you couldn't really make out where the ceiling started or ended. There were candles everywhere, lighting the walls, illuminating posters promoting various amateur DJs that are a complete waste of space. The music was loud and pumping, and the crowd sweaty in passion. It smelled like sex and felt humid enough to steam your voice. Hank ordered us a bottle of Woodford with sodas and ice. The coin-toss girls arrived and asked for gin, so a bottle of Tanqueray with tonic was also ordered. They brought coupe glasses because that's how they do it, all fancy and shit. I lit up a square and sipped on my whiskey while mostly keeping to myself. One of the coin-toss girls' started eyeing me. Playing eyes had always been a specialty of mine. She would look, I would keep looking; she would smile, I wouldn't. She would whisper something to her friend, I would sip my drink; she would look at me again, I would puff on my square.

At one point her friend pushed her toward me.

"Sorry," she said, smiling. "My friend's a . . . umm . . . an idiot?"

Her accent was hot. Her English was fine, but when she finished saying something she was unsure of, it sounded like a question.

I laughed. "I get it," I said. "All of my friends are idiots."

"Do you want to, ehhh, dence?"

"What?" The music was loud. I hate clubs and discos for this reason alone.

"Ehhh . . . Do you want to dence?"

"Dense? I'm not dense, Oh, *dance*! Um, no. I'd rather finish my drink. Can I get you another one?"

Her large lips were pouting and rouged. Her face was one of those that said what was going on behind it. Her half-closed dark-brown eyes looked like she was saying to herself, "This is how it starts," and her furrowed brow made it seem like she couldn't say no.

"Emm . . . okay, sure."

"Gin or whiskey?" I held up both bottles.

"Whiskey," she said. The caramel color of the liquid matched her hair, and her olive skin complemented it when she held the coupe.

"So, what do you do, umm . . . in ze band?"

"I play drums mostly," I said.

"Oh, ze *batterie*!" she exclaimed. "I wish I could play ze *batterie* . . . ze drums."

Everyone says this to me in every single country. It makes you think, every now and then. I, with extreme certainty, don't wish I could be an accountant, or drill people's teeth. Maybe they don't either.

"Oh, you could definitely do it; it's not that hard. Just like everything else, it takes time."

She smiled. "My friend, he hez a drum set and he showed me once . . . eh, how to play?"

"Well, how'd you do?"

She started laughing. "I was real badly."

I laughed and sipped on my whiskey, then poured myself another. Drew was in the corner, dancing with some brunette, Asher and Luke were off with their girls, and Hank was answering emails. I wondered for a second if he was going to get laid.

"What's your name?" I asked.

"Sophie," she replied.

I looked over and her friend was sitting alone, sipping a gin.

"What's with your friend?"

"Her English . . . emm, it's not good. She's, um, embarrassed?"

Her friend saw us talking about her, looked down at her drink, then back at us, and half smiled.

"Call her over here; she shouldn't drink alone."

Sophie winked, said something to her friend in French, and she walked over. She was beautiful too, a tall brunette in jeans and a halter top. Her hair was up, but pieces of it fell onto her pale shoulders. She had a black tattoo of a coffee cup on the inside of her forearm, which made me think she had been a barista at some point.

"What's your name?"

Sophie translated.

"Abby . . . emm . . . Abigail."

"Abby Abigail, nice to meet you," I said, and we all laughed.

—

We downed our whiskey and were feeling it. Most of the conversation was surface level, but that's okay because deep conversation was left for people you cared about, or the barflies you might never see again. Sophie and I would talk, and then she would translate for Abigail. The two brunettes speaking in French had me feeling like velvet. They could curse my family into the depths of hell with the foulest expressions; they could tie me up and cut me limb from limb, blood everywhere. They could take giant sticks, shove them in my ass and out my mouth to spit-roast me, and I would still beg for more. I could listen all day.

Eventually, after enough liquor, we got up and headed to the dance floor. Sophie was sexy, Abigail was shy, but then they started dancing with each other, and that's when Abigail came out of her shell. Maybe she was a lesbian, but then again in France, they like it all.

I couldn't take it anymore. The fantasies were playing out in my head. I was half-hard with excitement and possibility. I needed to leave.

"Let's get out of here," I said.

Sophie smiled. "I can't leave my friend."

I thought about it for a second. "Bring her with us."

She smiled, said something in French, and Abigail nodded.

"I'm going to the toilet. I'll be right back."

I walked toward the back of the room, thinking that I didn't want to be here anymore. I stepped on someone's foot. "Sorry," I said, but they didn't even feel it, and if they did, they were too Mollied out to care.

I walked into the bathroom. Black tile lined the walls, and the stalls were red. There was a drain in the center of the floor that reminded me of a murder scene from a bad Hollywood B movie. The pissers were all occupied, so I stepped into a stall. I could hear the guy next to me snorting coke and singing at the top of his lungs.

He would cough in between lines, and snort loudly. What a stereotype. Where's Blondie? Right in front of the toilet were words scribbled in what looked like a fit of enlightenment: "Life isn't about finding yourself, it's about creating yourself." Do people have these cliché realizations while they're sitting here? Do they think they're doing other people some sort of disservice if they don't write this dumb shit on walls? I guess the world *does* stop when you have to take a shit, but I can't imagine carrying around a pocketful of markers with the intention of writing my unoriginal thoughts on bathroom stall doors for all to see. Under the Sharpied words was a crude drawing of a hairy limp dick with a face on it, frowning and looking sad. I reached in my jeans for a Sharpie that didn't exist and then pulled out my middle finger and flicked off the entire stall and the guy next to me. Then I said aloud, "No one is listening."

—

I finished pissing, and on the way out of the bathroom yelled, "Fuck you," to the cokehead crooner in the stall. I passed the Molly idiot and spotted our table. Abigail was smiling at me. I smiled back. "Are you ready?" We grabbed our jackets. Sophie led the way out. She was holding my hand and I was holding Abigail's behind me. We were dodging the sweaty dancers who were moving with the beat, foreshadowing the night ahead. The music grew quieter as we got closer to the door. When we stepped out into the street, the line of gray, black, and white pigeons was still wrapped around the block. Our driver pulled up. "Bela?"

I nodded. "Yeah that's me."

Sophie jumped in, and then I pushed Abigail's butt up into the black Escalade and climbed in myself.

The driver turned around and looked at me. "And where are we headed?"

"The Saint James."

SAINT JAMES

I didn't know what they were discussing, and I didn't care. The whole ride Sophie and Abigail were speaking French to each other while I stared out the window—it sounded like heaven. Paris is beautiful; it's beautiful all the time. Raining, cold, hot, crowded, empty—it doesn't matter. Tonight it was bare and the streets were silent. It was as though the roads had a lot to think about. The street lamps were dancing, and the orange leaves of the trees were illuminated in their flickering. Fall was smiling and I was smiling back.

We got to the hotel and walked up to my room.

"Raid the minibar, if you'd like." I grabbed the Patrón and poured myself a glass. Sophie popped open the champagne and poured one for her and Abigail.

"I'll be right back."

As I walked to the bathroom, a wave of sadness hit me. I went in, closed the door, and stared at myself in the mirror. I looked angry. I hated looking at myself. I kept staring, then my face became blurry. Was that Blondie leaning into the car, looking for coke? Was that her or some other tramp who's lost in life? When Em was staring at that teddy-bear guy's dick, did she decide I wasn't enough? An image of a bloody steak bleeding onto a white lily entered my mind. Finding and creating myself? Does she even remember me? My face became clear again, and I shook my head and started talking.

"You piece of shit. You're a piece of shit. You're fat and ugly and your music sucks. People only like you 'cause of what you are, not who you are. Your own mother doesn't even like you. You failure piece of shit." I stared at the mirror for two more minutes, knowing what was about to go down. Then I laughed, stuck my tongue out, and walked into the room. No one is listening.

The girls were half-naked, laughing on the bed. The champagne was gone. I undid my belt, took it off, and slapped Sophie on the ass with it. They both laughed and moaned and told me to do it again. I did, and then Abigail got up and undid my jeans. I was there, but my mind wandered off to a different place. Abigail grabbed me and stared hard into my eyes, then kissed Sophie. Out of muscle memory, I unclasped Abigail's bra as Sophie took her own off. I rubbed Abigail's breasts while kissing Sophie, then Abigail went down on me. As she was sucking, I was still soft; Sophie took off her thong and grabbed my belt. She handed it to me, bent over, and told me to spank her again. I grabbed the belt, and it came down hard and fast, sounding like a whip. She flinched, turned around, looking concerned, and took the belt away from me.

"I'm sorry," I said, "that was too hard."

She shook her head. "No, I liked it."

Abigail chimed in, "You did too."

I looked down and my cock was hard.

After we finished, we all lay on the king-size bed under the cream sheets. We were drunk, hot, and breathing heavy. Abigail grabbed a square, lit up, and smoked in bed. I just stared at the ceiling in silence, listening to them both breathe. Before I passed out, I looked at Sophie; she had the same nose as Mom.

—

I dreamt about *Breakfast at Tiffany's.* Behind it was a soundtrack of a symphony I had never heard before. I remember it being beautiful and lush in strings and brass. Bursts of color emanated from the sound—reds, blues, violets, oranges, and yellows shot out, painting the world. A sun rose over the horizon, shadowed by the moon. Birds flew, dipped, and carried the timbre of violas on their wings. The cellos hit their open C and everything went into slow motion. A chord of ecstasy that would make Mahler proud.

My eyes opened and I stared at the eggshell ceiling for fifteen minutes, getting lost in a hallucination. A boat crossed the water to search for an island that mysteriously disappeared and reappeared from time to time. The island contained treasure revealing all of life's greatest mysteries. Alas, when a sea monster with seven arms destroyed the boat and all life was lost, I counted to ten and got out of bed.

Abigail and Sophie were still asleep, naked, Abby on her side curled up with her breasts in her arms halfway under the comforter, one leg out. Her mouth was open and she was snoring softly. Sophie was on her back under the covers up to her chest. Her breasts were falling to the side a bit, and her hair was surrounding her head, looking like brown flames engulfing a beautiful sun. They were both stunning in their sleep. Even more so than when they were awake.

I walked into the bathroom, avoided looking in the mirror 'cause I felt like hell, turned on the shower, and got in. I was washing my hair, standing under the hot water when the door opened. It was Sophie.

"Hiii."

She still sounded sweeter than jam. "Umm, hi."

She sat down on the toilet and began to pee. The stream of piss hitting the water echoed throughout the bathroom. I pulled back the curtain enough to look at her; she was still naked, head in her hand, hair falling every which way, and holding a piece of toilet paper. Her fingernails were slightly chipped but red, and her skin looked magnificent sitting on top of the white porcelain. I looked down and had a hard-on. I stepped out of the shower, and she looked at me, then my cock. She smiled at me, finished peeing, and started rubbing me. Then without moving from the toilet, she began sucking me off. At some point, she let out a small fart. Exactly five seconds later I came hard in her mouth. She swallowed, squeezed my balls, kissed me, and walked out. I stepped back into the shower to finish washing my ugly body.

When I got out, both of the girls were gone. I threw on my jeans and a T-shirt, packed my bag, grabbed my black trench, and walked to the lobby. Asher was sitting cross-legged in a chair, silently waiting for everyone to come down.

"What's up, dude?"

"Nothing. Just ready to leave this place."

"Why the rush, man?"

I looked at his black shirt, which had a cum stain on the lower right side.

"Not in a rush, I'm just ready to get on with it." I pointed to his cum badge. "Looks like you had a good night."

He looked down, then at me, then down again, then back at me. One of his eyes blinked, and I swear I saw it flicker. Then he started laughing. "FUCK! I didn't even notice that, bro!" I started smiling . . . idiot.

"Man, thanks for telling me. I woulda walked all through the airport with a cum stain on my shirt, shit."

"Well, at least you got laid," I said.

"Bro, you don't even know. This chick was slamming, let me tell you. She had the biggest fakies . . ."

He kept going on and on, but I didn't care. I just stared at him, pretending to listen. This is what he was programmed to say. It was the same routine. Girl's hot, guy comes. I doubt any of these fuckers of mine had a chick give them a blow job on the toilet. Whatever.

"What about you?"

I blinked. "What about me?"

"Well, how was your night? I saw you leave with those two tenderonis from the club—how'd it go?"

I shook my head. "It was fine."

"Did you smash both of them?"

I looked to my left, annoyed. "No."

"Damn, man! Well, next time."

Just then the bus pulled up. It was the color of tar and reflected sunlight in a similar manner. "Yeah, man, maybe next time."

BUNK ALLEY

I walked in, ignored the driver, glanced at the front lounge, and went straight to my bunk. Every bus has twelve coffin-like sleep tubes, each with a small window. They're not glamorous in any way, but they serve their purpose. My bunk is the place I go to escape the weight of other people, it's the place I go to masturbate, and it's the place where I used to call Em. Sleep is my bunk's least important function. Consistency is important to me, so I get the same bunk no matter which bus we end up in. Driver's-side back, middle bunk. Asher walked in behind me, but he stopped and talked to the driver for a minute. All I could hear was his voice sounding like an actor rehearsing lines. When he finished his hello, he glided to bunk alley and put his stuff in the passenger's-side back, middle bunk. Drew and Luke and his hat came out of the hotel, laughing about who the hell knows what, and Hank followed slowly behind them in his black uniform. Luke and Drew both got the front middle bunks; and Hank got the one on top of me. The bus began to move. It felt like wading in a high tide. My body followed each movement of the tires but somehow stayed centered. We made our way through a few city streets and merged onto the autobahn, passing gold and marble statues. I could see the Eiffel Tower in the distance, laughing at me. I wondered how many sad, faceless people at this exact moment were looking at it and dreaming of everything it emptily promised. As it began to disappear, I quietly said, "Fuck you," and shut my window. Then I drifted off to sleep.

—

I woke up in a haze, everything blurry. I tried to remember what I did the previous night, but I recalled something that happened three nights ago in a completely different part of the world. Bars and restaurants and clubs and stores have all started to blend together in a way that makes this world feel so tiny. Boots, food, signs, dentists, monsters—it's all the same wherever I go. Most nights the driver pushes through six hours while we all sit around watching bullshit movies, drinking, writing, sleeping, or getting high; mostly I just drink, bored. Normally I'd go smoke a square in the front seat with the driver, but today I can't stomach it. He's horrible. He just sits there listening to conservative talk radio criticizing the left, saying, "Damn wetbacks taking our jobs," under his breath. When he stops to get food, he comes back with grease-filled cheeseburgers the size of his fat fists; and when he eats them, his mouth and eyes widen like a shark devouring its prey. I'm not even sure he chews. Today he smells fine, but most days he doesn't. And no one knows what it is. I have a theory that he pays prostitutes to take a shit on his chest, but it's just a theory. It's either that or there's a dead mouse stuck in his boot or something. I just can't stand to be around this smelly, racist sludge meat on wasted bones. Not today.

—

Hours passed and nothing happened. We pulled over to a truck stop, and I went outside to make a phone call. Interestingly enough, I found a pay phone, which I had assumed didn't exist anymore, and came up with the idea that she might answer if she saw a random phone number. I bit my lip and dialed. It rang three times, and she picked up the phone.

"Uh . . . uh, hello?"

She sounded the same as I always remembered. But I couldn't muster the strength to say anything.

"Hello?" she said again.

I stayed quiet, then she hung up the phone.

I could see her sitting on the couch, thinking to herself that it must have been the wrong number. But if Mom knew it was me, would she think the same thing?

—

I walked back inside, blank and heavy. I went to the cabinet, pulled out the Fernet, and took a shot. Then I began to think about Francis and Padre. Where did we go wrong?

Years ago Padre called to tell me Francis was getting out of prison. I went back home 'cause it had been a few years since I'd seen his face. It was a warm day in Texas, and the car ride to the prison was quiet. Usually Padre has on some sort of talk radio, but I could tell he was so nervous that he either forgot, or just wanted to be quiet with his thoughts. The highways were bare, and the sun was shining. All around us were fields of golden wheat and stems of green corn spanning miles and miles. When we parked, Padre turned to me and said how proud he was that I was trying to live out my dream. I smiled, thinking about my first drum set he'd purchased and told him I couldn't do it without him. When France came out, he was wearing the blue jeans and white polo shirt we sent him. He looked good, healthy, and happy. He got in the front seat, and I sat in the back. The car ride was just as quiet, only this time it was awkward, and no one knew what to say. Out of nowhere France broke the silence and began telling us a joke. "You know, I saw the funniest thing written on the wall the other day. It said, "For a good time, hire a hooker; for a lot of time, hire my attorney." For the first five seconds Padre and I were quiet, not knowing if we should laugh. France began to laugh, and we saw that childlike smile and began laughing uncontrollably. We stopped to buy him a burger, and I remember looking at him eating it like a hungry, happy child, feeling closer to him than I ever had before.

The next morning we all rolled out of our bunks, hungover or still drunk; I, of course, in my unflattering fashion was last. I could hear them all take turns brushing their teeth, scraping away the sex and alcohol buildup from the last few years, and talking about how they were looking forward to what lay ahead tonight. They sounded like flies talking about shit.

Luke and Asher were ambitious and went for a run, competing against each other's mile times or something like that, fucking pricks. I just lay in my coffin, staring into the dark abyss above me. Most mornings I emerged from my cold, dark cocoon, not looking like a butterfly, but more like an angry wasp that's been marinated in piss and vinegar. Today was no different. I opened my sandpaper eyes, angry at myself, and pulled back the Arizona-patterned curtain to see if everyone else was gone already. My muscles and tendons ached when I moved, and I grunted when I stretched, hoping for a quick fix of endorphins. I looked at the ground, then all around me.

"Fuck!"

BADEN-BADEN

I rolled out, put both feet on the ground, and felt the shit-brown carpet between my toes. It felt sticky and hard like it had been jizzed on repeatedly. I lurched to the bathroom, brushed my teeth bones—even they hurt—and moved to the front lounge. The brown leather banquettes on both sides were empty, and the TV above the left one was on. A movie called *The Descent* was playing. It's about a bunch of cave dwellers who get lost and have to escape weird-looking, gross, hairless, and blind cave monsters. Like us in the mornings chasing coffee, there's no escape. One seat behind the left-side banquette was acting as Hank's desk, and he was sitting there working. The Keurig machine was blinking, and it felt like a siren calling my name. I trudged over, rubbed my eyes, and made myself a cup of coffee, black and strong.

"Hank, what's the count?"

He looked up slowly from behind the screen.

"The event's oversold, so don't worry about it. Nine thousand isn't gonna look that much different from ninety-five hundred."

I took a sip, annoyed, and winced as it burned my lip. "I know that, I'm just curious. How'd we do on merch last night?"

He peered down and began punching keys, then looked up at me.

"Four bucks and twenty cents a head, give or take. I haven't accounted for comps yet."

I raised my eyebrows. "Not bad. What's the most popular item?"

He looked back down and began stabbing keys. "Umm . . . lemme see." He hit those letters and numbers faster than anyone I'd ever seen before. It sounded like tiny machine guns in a war against Hank's own personality. His speech was slow and calculated, but his fingers were fast and accurate, like his brain.

"The black-and-white tour shirt," he said.

"With our faces or the logo?"

"Faces."

"Makes sense."

I took another sip, then saw a pack of squares next to the microwave. I grabbed one and tapped it on the counter like I had a tic.

"What's up with our driver? What's his name?"

Hank was staring at my square, probably counting my taps. "Hugh." He kept staring. "What do you mean?" he asked.

"I mean, every morning we roll out of our bunks, that motherfucker is sleeping on the seats. He's snoring too, and it's loud. I swear to whatever god you believe in, you can see his mustache move up and down every time he fucking breathes."

Hank smiled, then began to chuckle. "Yeah, I dunno. He's a weird guy; I'll talk to him."

I gave him a "no shit" look.

"I get it—he's tired, he's gotta drive long hours, but c'mon, man, where the fuck are we supposed to sit in the mornings? Why doesn't he just go to his hotel when he stops driving?"

"I don't know. I leave all the info on the steering wheel and he just tells me he doesn't know what to do. I'll talk to him."

I shook my head. "What an asshole. Also, what's with the racist shit?"

I started tapping my square again, this time on purpose.

Hank looked at the square. "What do you mean?"

"Well, yesterday we pulled over into a rest area so Luke could take a shit. As we were leaving, a few black dudes were walking in front of the bus. I could hear him saying shit like, "Fucking porch monkeys," and "They should all go back to Africa," some shit like that. That waste of clean air is a straight-up racist."

Tap, tap, tap. Hank started to blink one eye. "Weird man," he said.

Tap, tap, tap.

"Weird? More like fucking crazy. Pretty sure he said something about not liking faggots too."

Tap, tap, tap.

"I'll talk to him," he said as one eye twitched.

Tap, tap, tap, and then the square broke in half. I looked at it, then at Hank, and narrowed my eyes.

"Yeah, fucking talk to him before I do."

He didn't say anything, just looked at me. I could tell he was thinking, *Number twelve,* in his head. I reached into the cabinet, pulled out the Advil, popped two, then I grabbed another square.

"Fuck you, Hank." I smiled, sipped my coffee, and walked out the door, leaving my tobacco bits all over the counter.

—

In my darkest of times it's hard for me to tell the difference between right and wrong or good and bad. Well, it's not hard. I just don't care. I introvert more than usual and sometimes lash out. I break things, and chain-smoke, but mostly I'm just mean. And I'm mean to the people around me. They get it, though, because they deal with me on a regular basis. They'll leave me alone, thinking to themselves, *He needs some time by himself.* Really, though, they just don't want to be around me, and I don't blame them.

The one constant I have in my life is an unexplainable sadness. I fantasize about the things in life that matter to most people, and I wish they mattered more to me. We're here for an insignificant stretch of time, then we're gone and forgotten like the season's first snow. I think about love, and how I'm scared of it because all I've seen it do is fail, and ruin people. I think of my parents, my brother, my aunt who never had it, and I think of Em. I want a family one day, but there's a wrench turning knots in my stomach, making me feel like it will crumble in front of me. I'd rather go on without it. I can live with ruining my own life, but I can't live with ruining the lives of people I love.

I dream about a future as an old man in a cabin somewhere with a collection of tattoos, platinum records, an orange cat, and a wife with kids and grandkids. The reachable dream made not so by the frailty of my own personal guilt. I'm not sure what there is to feel guilty about, but usually guilt isn't fake. I want the life my parents never had. I want a healthy garden full of white, red, and even pink roses. I want it to live on longer than I ever will.

—

It was cold outside, but I was warm. I closed my eyes, took the square out of my mouth, and moved my neck toward the sun. It felt good on my face. "These shows are all the same," I grunted. I still loved playing, but the overwhelming feeling of excitement diminished a long time ago. It's like the first snort of coke. The first is always the best. Then it just becomes an obsession to try to replicate the rush of the first line.

—

Almost ten thousand people stared at us with their hands in the air, singing our songs and chanting. White-knuckled fists moved back and forth, resembling a rally, all to the beat of my kick drum. Every time my wrists flicked the sticks and stroked the toms, or when my left foot kept time on the hi-hat, I felt my blood smiling inside of me. When I hit the crash cymbals, white noise sang in my ears, and when I hit that beautiful deep-sounding snare drum, I could hear parts of my soul applaud and beg for more. These were the moments I lived for and so often took for granted. Today, I blocked it all out and thought about the dirty blonde in the front row. She was staring at me, grinning and fucking me with her eyes. Her breasts were bouncing every time she moved, and at one point she bent over the railing on purpose to show me more. She knew I was staring. As soon as she waved at me, I looked away and moved on to another girl. She ruined the mystery.

—

After the show, Drew and I decided to explore the city. We kept hearing about Baden-Baden having the best red-light district, so we decided it was worth a look. Drew enjoyed that sort of thing, and it intrigued me. I never liked the idea of paying for sex, but we all pay, one way or another. We took a car, passing beautiful buildings and statues. Purple and red flowers lined the streets, and bees were buzzing, looking for nectar. We got to a corner, got out of the car, and Drew stopped in his tracks. He couldn't stop staring.

RED-LIGHT DISTRICT

"Drew, what're you doing?"

"Maaan, I think I'm going to go in there."

He was smiling bigger than I'd ever seen, like a child spotting giant swirly lollipops for the first time. I fumbled in my pockets for a square, looked at him, and chuckled. "So do it."

He kept his eyes on the building and, without blinking, reached out of his haze to grab my shoulder. "Well, come with me."

I lit up and inhaled big. "Eh, I dunno, I'm not into that kind of shit."

Without moving his eyes, he nudged me on the arm. "C'mon, don't leave me by myself."

I looked at him with a fuck-you face, then laughed. "Fucking shit, okay, fine." I took another puff. "Let's go."

The houses were all three stories and had whores hanging out the redwood-paneled windows. Some were old, a lot were young, and most were middle-aged. A few waved at passersby, hoping to grab their attention; others read a book, not giving a shit; and the rest were talking on the phone to their husbands, boyfriends, or mothers and pretending not to care. One thing they all had in common was their skimpy lingerie; another was how they acted, as if fucking you, no matter who or what you were, was a walk in the park. It was just business.

The very front of the house was prime real estate. There were huge windows that had two great-looking whores occupying the space. Drew had his eye on one particular place. The brunette was young and looked anorexic. She was dressed in black lace, wore glasses, and sat on a chair filing her nails, not giving a fuck. The redhead was in her forties, pale and topless with red pasties. She was dancing, putting on a show, really working for it. The young one could mop the floor with the middle-aged one without even trying. The difference was incredible and sad. We rolled through the house and walked up the stairs. The girls were standing in their doorways, looking at us like we were walking dollar signs, and we were eyeing them like they were rib eye steaks. On the second floor, a thin, pale fox was sitting and reading a book, ignoring us. Her lips were skinny and her hair was straight and jet-black.

"Hi," I said.

Drew kept walking and she looked up from her page, annoyed. Her eyes looked like the abyss and she didn't smile. She looked familiar.

Without even a smirk, she snarked, "Hi."

I smiled and shuffled my feet. "Aren't you gonna invite me in?"

"I wasn't planning on it." She had an accent but spoke perfect English.

I laughed. "Well, ask me anyway."

She dog-eared the page she was on, rolled her eyes, and said with a sigh, "Would you like to come in?"

I stopped smiling. "No." I turned to walk away.

"Well, I'm not gonna suck your little cock right here."

I turned around and smiled. "How much?"

"Come inside and let's talk about it."

I couldn't put my finger on it, but I felt like I knew her. I walked into her room. It was small and had a bed made up with purple sheets and bloodred pillows. She had incense burning to cover up the countless body odors that lingered, and her black curtains were drawn so no one could see in. Next to a wooden chair was a pile of folded sheets, and next to that was a hamper full of used ones. Every day she could tell how much she'd been used by how much laundry she had to do. I was glad she only had two sheets in the hamper.

I didn't want to fuck her, so I asked for a blow job. She smiled, took down my pants, got on her knees, and slipped a purple condom on with her mouth. Halfway before I came, I realized that she looked like Jon's sister. I had a vague memory of Jon jerking me off and his sister walking in and watching and not stopping us. She was a few years older than us, but I remember her being hot.

I looked down at her, sucking and gripping my balls. "I'm going to call you Chloe."

She stopped and looked up at me. "You can call me whatever you want, Daddy." When I came, my brain flooded with memories of a childhood birthday. I came hard and mumbled, "Happy birthday."

"Chloe" looked up at me, confused, probably making a mental note to add this to her weirdest stories list. I pulled up my pants and stayed quiet. She walked to the bathroom and brushed her teeth; I could hear her humming something that vaguely sounded like the "Happy Birthday" song.

"Leave the cash in the book on the dresser, fifty euros."

"Okay."

I took out a wad of cash and began counting it. When I got to fifty, I stopped and took in the room again. I picked up the book *Brave New World* and quickly stuffed all the cash I had in it and ran out in silence.

When I got outside, Drew was waiting on the stoop, rolling a spliff. We began walking and drifting toward the bus. I felt guilty and he felt hungry so we stopped to get a currywurst. Chloe circled my mind like a carousel.

"Life's strange."

Drew was eating and smacking his lips. He spoke without looking up. "Yeeeah, man, it is. I wouldn't trade it for the world, though."

I exhaled smoke. "Well, no shit, we live *incredible lives.*"

"I know you're joking but we really do, maaan. I don't know, though, maybe we're just in our own bubble. I guess everyone lives an incredible life one way or another. Know what I mean?"

His lips smacked faster and harder, and ketchup was going everywhere. I thought about killing him. "Are you high?"

He stopped, and looked up. "Well, yeah . . . But not just on green, also on endorphins—oh, and the memories I just made with Anna."

"Who the fuck is Anna?" I asked.

"The slag."

"Oh." I thought about Chloe and wondered if anyone loved her.

"What's she look like?"

He stopped eating. "Duuude, she had the fattest ass and the biggest fakies I've ever seen. She was hot, and I think she said she was from Russia."

I laughed, and Drew started smacking again. I shook my head and tried to ignore it.

"So you came to Germany to fuck a Russian?"

He nodded and laughed. "Nothing wrong with exported goods, brah, and that shit was goood, if you know what I mean."

I narrowed my eyes. "Shut the fuck up, Drew."

He laughed. "Dude, you know what I mean. What about you?"

"Well, mine was German, skinny, hot, perfect tits, not too big, not too small. The weird thing is, she looked like an old friend's sister."

He bobbed his head. "Dude, that's hot."

I scratched my ear. "Meh."

"Did you fuck or just get head?"

"BJ, but in the middle of it, I started calling her Chloe, my friend's sister's name."

He looked up from his food and stopped chewing. He was confused. "Word." He looked down, then at me again, shrugged it off, and began to chew his food. "That's weird, bro, but whatever floats your boat. I mean, you paid for it, so you can call her whatever you want, right?"

I looked at the cloudy sky and began nodding. "That's exactly what she said. So what about you—what did you do?"

He smiled. "I fucked."

"How was it?"

"Fast. Duuude, I came so fast. She was so hot, and I was literally in and out."

I laughed. "You're fucking hilarious, dude. Finish your food so we can get the hell out of here."

—

On the way back to the bus, I stopped in a bar. Drew didn't come with me 'cause he was tired and wanted to go smoke more, so he caught a car. I needed a drink. A wooden sign was hanging from a piece of metal above the door: “Die Kneipe.” I looked at the heavy door with black steel bars on it. “This looks good for me,” I said to no one.

I walked into the dark, damp candlelit hole, sat in a chair, and ordered the “bartender’s choice.” A few men were seated around the bar, all looking tired and lonely. The bartender brought me something slightly sweet, made with mezcal and a berry foam on top.

“This is nice,” I said.

He looked at me apathetically, said, “It’s my favorite,” then walked away.

An older gentleman dressed in faded jeans and a torn brown leather jacket sat down a few seats away from me. He was alone, just like the rest of us. He ordered a beer. He seemed to be bothering the people sitting next to him. He saw me looking over and started speaking to me in German. I didn’t respond. I just stared. He kept speaking to me; I kept taking sips of my mescal. Then he turned his head, took a big gulp of beer, and broke out in song.

He sang the same line to me repeatedly, smiled, and then just stared. He said something to me and then a blond guy turned around and translated just so the old drunk would shut up.

“He wants to know if you know who sang that.”

I took a sip. “The Doors.”

He laughed and nodded. “Maybe he’s had a long day.”

“Most likely,” I said and fake smiled.

The old guy kept looking at me. I ignored him, then he pointed at me and said, “Rock star.” He smiled, winked, drank his beer, put his head down, and fell asleep. His white stubbly face was etched with wrinkles that stayed after his smile had faded. They looked like cracks on a vase that wasn’t yet broken, but soon would be. His blue eyes were turning gray from being an old and tortured soul. He was alone, and the world was whizzing by without him. People drank, laughed, and dreamt he was just there, tired, asleep on the bar, and gone. The bartender looked at me. “Maybe he’s had a long day.”

I lit up a square and stared at my drink. Then my phone buzzed.

PADRE

P: Francis is in jail.

B: What did he do?

P: He says nothing, but you know him.

B: Well what did the cops tell you?

P: They told me they caught him
trying to break into a house.

B: You think he did it?

P: Bell, you know your brother.

B: So, he did.

P: I think he had another
one of his Xanax fits.

B: What do you mean?

P: He takes a bunch, then
claims he blacks out.

B: How can he steal if
he's blacked out?

P: I don't know, but he blacks out, breaks
into houses, cars, mailboxes. takes
anything he can get his hands on.

B: How does he get it?

P: He has a prescription.

B: Well fucking call the doctor
and tell him to stop prescribing.

P: He won't take my calls.

B: Give me the number
I'll find a way.

P: Don't worry about it bell. You have
more important things to do.

B: This is my brother. What's
more important than that?

P: I'm just afraid if he stops the
Xanax he'll go back to heroin.

B: One replaced the other padre.

P: He can't go back to heroin. I
can't live like that again.

B: I know Padre. I'm on my
way to Norway, I'll shoot you
a text when I get there. Are
you gonna bail him out?

P: What else am I supposed to
do? Be safe, and I love you.

B: Love you too.

BODØ

Norway is gorgeous. The sun's different here, and the moon's worshipped because of its constant presence. The mountains are green and capped with white powder. They triumphantly tower over the land, daring anyone to try and conquer them. The roads wind every which way and look like snakes trying to find prey in a grassy paradise. I'm sitting in the front lounge of the bus, drinking coffee, thinking those midwestern fucks know nothing. God's country isn't the US. Fuck that. If there is a God, *this* is his country.

—

Being trapped in a bus makes the air stick to your skin, so when we arrived at the venue, we grabbed our bags and took showers. It reset our brains. The club was small, no more than six hundred people, but it got a lot of international acts, so the amenities were better than most. Catering was home-cooked food consisting of pickled herring, roasted meat, potatoes, bread, butter, and a fresh green salad. Ferociously, I smeared the meat onto the bread slathered in butter and inhaled the greens. Then I repeated the process two more times.

The people hosting us were nice except for one security guard who yelled at me for smoking in a nondesignated area. He was short, stumpy, had glasses, and was wearing a yellow security vest.

"You can't smoke here," he said, hands in his pockets and a smug look on his face.

"What?"

"You can't smoke here." His face changed as if he just smelled dog shit on the bottom of his shoe.

"Here, like, in your country?" I'm an asshole.

"That's not what I mean." He took his hands out of his pockets and began waving them around like he was trying to signal me in sign language. "This isn't a designated smoking area. You Americans think you can just do *what* you want, *when* you want!"

This asshole. Why do they always have to bring up the American thing? As if having the luxury to hate authority, and stupid rules that inconvenience me, has anything to do with where I was born.

"Well, I'm not sure what smoking a cigarette has to do with me being American, but now that you mention it, we are back-to-back world champs."

He put his hands down at his sides and looked puzzled. "What?"

I smiled sarcastically. "Nothing. Where's the *designated* area?"

He pointed to a spot ten feet to my left like he was a parent punishing a child, and said, "Over there."

I looked at him like he was batshit. "Don't you have anything better to do? Shouldn't you be stopping someone from stealing our gear, or making sure no one brings in a gun and kills us all? Or hell, shouldn't you just, I dunno, do something else besides bother me? I'm not hurting anyone."

He put his hands back in his pockets and shrugged. "I'm just doing my job, sir."

I puffed a cloud of smoke toward him, smiled, and walked eight feet to my left. "Far enough?"

He shook his head. "A little farther."

I walked twenty more feet, cussing him out under my breath, stopped, and turned around.

"How about now, you fucking prick?" The last part was unfortunately drowned out by a jackhammer.

He looked at me and tried to yell over the pounding metal. *"What!?"*

I shook my head and pointed down at my feet, then put my hands up in a "What about now?" manner.

"That's too far," he yelled.

"What?!" I yelled back, grinning, even though I heard him.

He cupped his hands over his face, and just as a truck blared past me, yelled something that was drowned out by the loud sounds. It started with an *F*, and I'm pretty sure it ended with a "you."

I gave him a thumbs-up, and when he turned his back to me, flicked him off, then finished my square.

—

The show went well, nothing special. When I walked offstage, my shadow, after taking a break to let me enjoy my existence, reattached itself and snapped me back into reality. I pounded a shot of Espolòn and walked upstairs to a bar that was exclusively for employees and VIPs. It was small and could only hold around fifty people. On the back wall there was giant mural of a Pepto-Bismol-pink elephant. And like all the pink elephants I've ever seen, it was smiling and flying. All around me were Viking men and Viking women, who were built differently than us: strong, tall, muscular, and thick. I entertained the idea of fucking one, but I couldn't wrap my head around it. I honestly wouldn't know where to start.

I sat down at the four-seater bar, saw Drew walk in, and immediately ordered four shots of Fernet-Branca—one for Drew, one for the bartender, and two for me. Hank crept up slowly, like a shadow in a stairwell, and ordered a shot for himself. He looked around and took it all in, processing the room number by number. "This place is nice," he uttered.

"Not bad, not bad," I replied, sipping on the second shot.

Hank counted the stools, the lights, and the people. There were twenty-three bodies total, four stools at the bar plus two more hidden in the back, and sixty-seven lights, with sixty of them working at full capacity. Then he looked at us and began to speak. "So, the girl who's been taking care of us says she wants to take us to another bar. She's got a hookup and she's bringing friends."

Drew's ears perked up. "Sweeet! Are they hot?"

Hank sighed and stared at the bar. "How am I supposed to know?"

I slapped him on the back and his beard moved. "Hank, you're the TM; you're supposed to know these things." I grinned.

"That's not what you pay me for. I already have to deal with taking care of you pricks. I'm not a dating service."

"Haaaank!" said Drew. "You're telling me you're not, like, a walking Tinder?"

Hank smiled, slightly annoyed, and said, "Look, they're fucking Norwegian; there's no way they're not hot. Even if they aren't, hooking up with a random four out of ten is still just that, hooking up."

I leaned back, smiled, and pulled out a square. "Define 'hooking up,'" I said, then lit up.

Hank sighed heavily. "I dunno, a blowsie, or a make-out session, or a heavy petting."

I laughed. "First of all, I'm assuming a 'blowsie' is a blow job. Where did you even learn that word? Secondly, I don't wanna make out with someone I'm not gonna fuck. And lastly, heavy petting is meant for preteens, or cats or dogs, not grown-ass men with grown-ass appetites; I mean, come on!"

Drew looked at Hank and began laugh-talking: "Oooh shiiit, he got you there, man! He got you there!"

I laughed. "Alright, alright, alright. But you're saying that a blow job from a random pretty girl is the same as a blow job from a random beautiful girl because either way it's just a blow job?"

Hank nodded. "Yes."

I took a puff from my square. "I guess you got a point there."

"Yeah, I fucking do. Besides, it only takes Drew two minutes to come, it takes Luke five, and it takes Ash ten. I'm not sure how long it takes you, Bell, 'cause I don't know what it is that you do differently, but any way you look at it, that's less than twenty minutes."

I looked at him and put down my drink. "What does that have to do with anything?"

He shrugged his shoulders. "Nothing. I dunno, I just think all of you are gross. And unfortunately, my brain knows more about all of you than even you know about yourselves."

I blinked rapidly for a few seconds, then looked at him. "You're a fucking psycho, and you need to get laid."

Drew laughed and shrugged his shoulders. "Welll, I'm down, bro."

I turned to him and said, "You're always down."

"Comes with the territory—I'm crazy, duuudes!"

We all laughed. I took another pull from the square and asked, "What are Luke and Ash getting into?"

"They're coming, meeting us there."

Hank was leaning into the bar, and I looked around and noticed that he seemed to fit in here.

"Okay, I'm in too. When are we leaving?"

Hank pulled out his phone to look at a message.

"Right now, let's go."

I pulled out my wallet, slammed down five hundred kroner, grabbed my jacket, and followed the guys out.

"What kind of bar is it? It's not a club, right?" I asked.

Hank slowly shook his head. "No, no club. I know you guys hate those."

"Well, I seriously can't hear people talking to me in those things, let alone hear my own thoughts."

"True," said Hank.

I turned to see a tall, thick brunette smiling at me.

"Is it far from here?" I asked.

"I don't think so."

I thought about taking her from behind, but where would I start?

—

We walked in, and the smell of vomit hit my nostrils. Thankfully the farther we got into the place, the fresher the air became. The bar was dark, lit only by the lamps that accompanied every table. The mirror behind the bar had gold lettering that listed the beers on draft. Everything was made out of beautiful dark wood that looked recently stained. It was crowded, but our table was ready. We sat down and ordered three whiskey smashes made with Old Overholt and waited for the rest of the crew.

Luke, his hat, and Asher showed up five minutes later with tall, beautiful blue-eyed blondes on their arms, and our brunette friend was behind them, smiling. She had chocolate hair, teal eyes, and breasts the size of watermelons. Her smile looked like it was once widened by a knife 'cause it seemed to cover half of her face. None of us were interested, but you could tell everyone at least thought about fucking her. After introductions, I sucked on the lemon that came with my drink and listened to the same dull conversation we always had in those situations. It bored me, but I didn't want to be alone. I looked around the room and spotted a beautiful girl sitting at the bar.

I got up from the table and turned to look at everyone. "Excuse me, I'm going to go talk to that girl."

Asher looked at me with his wide animatronic eyes. "Whoa, man, that's not like you."

I bit my lip and agreed. "Yeah, well, you and twiddle-dick here are hogging up the rest of them, so I figured I'd take my chances."

He laughed and on cue so did the mindless blonde birds.

"Dude, go for it. What're you gonna say, what's your move, bro?"

"My move is the hell away from this desolate playing field and you idiots. I think I'm just gonna say hello."

Just when I thought they couldn't get any bigger, Asher's eyes widened and he looked as if his programming had just been attacked by a virus. "That's it?"

The mindless blonde bird on his left said, "I think that's perfect." She smiled. I looked at her, nodded, and thought to myself, *That's right, but who the fuck asked you?*

Asher's eyes returned to the normal amount of wide, and he smiled and held up his glass like he was giving a farewell speech. "Well, good luck, bro."

I smiled, flicked them off, and walked toward the bar. I set my drink down, hoping to get her attention, and leaned on the bar next to her. She had platinum-blonde hair. It looked natural and not fake. She had the body of a ballerina, thin but fit, and she was dressed in black skinny jeans and an oversized black sweater. Hell, she was the woman I dreamt of without even knowing it. She was perfect.

I looked back at the table, and Asher was robotically fist-pumping the air with one hand, cheering me on, while the others were winking, pointing, and laughing at me. I turned red, then looked back at the platinum-haired girl at the bar.

"Hi," I said.

She looked over, said, "Hi," then smiled. Her big green eyes had a tint of amber with a streak of honeysuckle, and her smile could make nations fall. She smelled like fresh linen. "How's your night going?"

"It's good," she said, shifting her weight and staring into her drink. She was not very talkative, so everything felt up to me.

I watched as a piece of her hair fell in front of her face, like a feather in the snow. "What did you do tonight?"

She brushed the hair back and blushed. "I went to a concert."

Bingo. There aren't too many concerts happening in this town on the same night. According to promoters, that would be a disaster. This is one of those places where, when there's an event, the whole town goes.

I smiled. "Which concert?"

She looked up from her drink and grinned. "Some band."

She was playing hard to get. "What band?"

"I don't remember. They have this one song that I like, though, maybe you know it." She turned toward me and started humming.

It reminded me of "weed-boy" Drew over there whenever he's trying to impress some rando' he's into. But when she did it, she sounded like fine red wine. "I know that song."

She laughed and took a sip of her beer. "Who doesn't?"

I looked down at my drink and stared at a black speck on the lemon rind, trying to think of what to say next. "Was the concert good?"

"Oh, it was very good. I don't know much of their music, and some of it I don't like, but they have so much energy onstage. I wish I remembered their name."

Her English was perfect, with slightly accented vowels. Sometimes she'd say the silent letters in words, but she didn't know any better.

"Ah, don't worry about it. Did you go alone?"

She began shaking her head. "Well, I went with some friends, but they all had to wake up early tomorrow, and I guess I just wanted a drink. What about you?"

I bit the inside of my cheek. "What about me?"

She began moving her leg back and forth nervously. "Well, what are you doing here?"

"Oh, I'm here with friends," I said, pointing to our table. "Those guys over there."

Luke and Ash were laughing with the blonde dodo birds. When they noticed us looking, they began waving, whistling, and winking at us. Drew was talking to our knife-mouthed friend, telling her why everyone was laughing at me, and Hank as usual was looking at his phone, writing an email.

The girl laughed. "Well, why aren't you with them?"

For some reason I felt embarrassed. "Oh, I see them all the time. Besides, you looked interesting and I wanted to talk to you."

She laughed and her lipstick glimmered in the light. "Am I interesting?"

A tingle went through my body. "Well, I'm still here, aren't I?"

She smiled, took another sip of her beer, blinked, and thought with her eyes. "Do you have a cigarette?"

I fumbled in my pocket and pulled them out. "Yes, I do."

She got up. "Let's go outside."

We walked out the back door, and I could hear Luke whistling a catcall in our direction while the others laughed. The door was red and led directly to a gravel path beyond the dumpsters. I grabbed a matchbook on the way out and pulled out two squares. I stuck them both in my mouth, pulled out a match, and lit both cigarettes at the same time, inhaling the sulfur dioxide and tobacco smoke. I waited for the ends to turn bright orange before handing her one.

She took the square and put it between her lips on the side of her mouth, being careful not to get it wet. "Thanks. So, where are you from?"

I blew out a puff of smoke, ignoring the question.

"By the way, my name's Bell."

I held out my hand; she took it. She hadn't heard that name before.

"Bell? What kind of a name is that?"

"Well, Bela. My parents are weird. They named me after a famous composer they liked."

"Oh, that's interesting. Bela—I like that."

She exhaled a puff of smoke and I breathed it in.

"Yeah, I guess so. That's kind of how they named my brother and, well, my dog, my cat, my fish—all after famous people they liked; it's pretty weird when you think about it."

She laughed. "Well, I think it's cool."

Smoke was swirling like waves all around us, behaving like misted pheromones.

"What's *your* name?" I asked.

"Jane," she replied. Her feet moved and crunched on the gravel.

I blinked rapidly. "Nice to meet you . . . You asked where I was from?"

"Yeah."

"New York." I exhaled more smoke.

"Oh, I love New York."

"You've been?"

"Several times. I travel there for work."

The smoke was intertwining and wrapping in on itself. It looked like two clouds combining into one. I started to become anxious, and a horrible word vomit was forming. Before I could stop myself, the sentences escaped my mouth like air through a crack in the wall.

"Jane, I'm going to be honest with you. That band you saw tonight, that was me. That was us, over there at that table. Now, eventually you were going to find that out, and it was going to be an awkward moment, and well, I just wanted to avoid that. Yes, I do know that song because, well, because I wrote it. But truthfully, I end up talking about that, and people often become somewhat starstruck. But I'm just gonna say, I'm not important. I'm not anything special. And there's absolutely no reason why anyone should find me more interesting than anyone else. I think *you're* beautiful and I want to get to know *you.* I don't want whatever this short-lived meeting is to be based on the fact that you think I'm something I'm not. Frankly, I'd rather not talk about what I do—it's exhausting. You just seem like someone I could have a great conversation with, and you seem like someone who could maybe want the same thing."

After that word vomit, I was sure she would put that square out and go back to her spot at the bar alone, but she didn't. Her eyes lit up for a second, then she looked at me adoringly, like I was a new puppy or something, and smiled.

"Oh, really?" she said. Then she closed one eye and turned her head. "It's not like a lot of people who are all dressed in black, wearing leather jackets, and who just so happen to be from New York, come through here often."

I looked around. "Wait, you knew the whole time?"

She smiled and exhaled more smoke.

"Well, I didn't really know, but I had an idea."

I don't know what it was, the alcohol or the air or her acceptance of my vulnerability, but I immediately became intoxicated by her mere presence and began feeling the world wrap around me in a warm blanket. It was like heroin.

"I think I'm in love."

She laughed. "Don't be stupid."

We finished our squares and went back into the bar. I introduced her to the guys, Luke's hat, and their girls, and we continued to drink and talk about life. We talked about the stars, and how we were all made of stardust, and that's why we were all connected in deeper ways than anyone let on. I don't know how I truly feel about any of that nonsense, but she was passionate about it, so I was too. We talked about how lucky we were to have been born in our countries, and that most people take that for granted. We could have been born to disease, lived in a shack or even worse, had swollen stomachs because we had no food to eat. We talked about the ocean and how it's mind-boggling that we still have no idea what's in its deepest parts. Then eventually we *did* talk about the band and Jane's art director job and about how it's all we thought about, and all we did. We were both constantly hungry for more when it came to our life's work, never satisfied. We were both addicts to our own cause.

"We're falling stars," she said.

"What do you mean?"

"Well, we are set on a path, a course, in life, just like a falling star. We're fueled by our desires and our passions, and the closer we get to our destiny, we start to burn. As soon as we reach it, we return to the universe, forgotten and cold. But if you think about it, we made our mark on the way. Someone looked up and saw it, someone looked up and made a wish, someone smiled. We improved the life of an individual even if it was for a mere half second. And if you ask me, that's pretty good for just being stardust."

I had no intention of thinking that far ahead in my life. I never cared about the end, 'cause I always focused on the now. But I couldn't argue with her, 'cause somewhere in the most ignored parts of my heart, I knew she was right. Then my soul skipped, and for a minute I felt euphoric.

I smiled. "I'm in love."

She laughed. "It's amazing how quick we are to use that term."

I nodded. "Do you find it wrong?"

"Well, no, it's a real feeling. I feel it too; I don't know if I feel it for you. I don't know if I ever will feel it, but let me put it this way: I know I'll never forget you."

I liked hearing that, and I felt like cashmere.

The rest of the night was about Jane and me, me and Jane. We grabbed more drinks—Van Winkle's, neat—and talked until the bar closed. The guys peeled off one by one with their girls, and eventually it was just me and Jane, Jane and me. At one point we played shuffleboard. In between turns, we would kiss furiously and I would grab the small of her back. We would joke around and playfully fight, I would pretend to let her kick my ass, and she would laugh as I rolled on the floor holding my stomach and screaming, "Help, I've been kicked by a crazy lady who keeps calling me a falling star." At one point in the night another man came and hit on her, and I pretended to be gay and started to hit on him. He left, uncomfortable, and we left laughing. We caught a car to my hotel.

I looked at her face glowing in the dark. "Come up with me."

She shook her head. "No, I shouldn't."

I knew she shouldn't, but I had to ask, "Why?"

"'Cause I don't want this to just be a one-night thing. I don't want this to just be another forgotten moment; I don't want to just be some girl you fucked."

I stopped smiling. "I don't either, trust me, but you live in Norway, I live in New York, we don't have to have sex, but what else could this possibly be besides *one night?*"

She bit her lip. "I'm leaving for Bali next week. Come with me."

Not an ounce of me wanted to say no. Jane knew I would never go, and I knew she didn't really want me to. The fact that we had one night together of feeling in love, and respecting that, made a bigger impact on me than most other things in my life. It made me remember for a second that it was all possible. If you can feel that way for a night, then maybe you can feel that way for a lifetime. Maybe this is what my grandparents had. Maybe my parents only had the idea of long-lasting love. Maybe they were still searching for that first snort of coke.

—

We kissed and held each other outside the hotel. We didn't say a word. We just let our energy, like the smoke, do the talking. Everything my body said was everything hers said. People were walking past us in both directions, but we didn't notice them. I called a car for her and put her in it, staring at her and thinking about the night. She rolled down the window and without a word kissed me and reached for my hand. It was warm and a little damp. She held it and stared into my eyes, looking like everything that mattered was right in front of her. The cab drove off and I watched her glowing face disappear into the dark, then the car became one with the city lights.

—

What a good night this was.

—

It didn't occur to me until later that evening: Jane might not be single. I never even asked her. I can imagine her getting in the cab and opening her phone, which she'd been ignoring. I can see her sending the message: *I'm on my way home.* And I can see her walking up to her door and being greeted by a tall blond man with glasses and a beard. I went up to my room and began to sink into the floor. I began to imagine her hugging him and thinking about *our* night. She would kiss him and think about *our* night. She would make love to him and think about *our* night. Of course this would happen, all the good ones in my life are taken. Either that or they leave me.

—

I lay in my bed for hours and wallowed in silence. Feeling sorry for myself was a specialty of mine. As I began to fall asleep, I thought about Mom. I wished I could ask her for guidance. I'm not sure what triggered what happened next, but that night I had the most terrifying dream I've ever had.

THE DREAM

Twenty thousand people were screaming our songs back at us. Their faces were lit up by the different shades of reds and purples emanating from the stage. The fake fog was thick—it swirled like waves on a sandbar and smelled like vanilla chemicals. The strobe lights flashed like lightning in a plasma globe. The sky was pitch-black, and the dead stars winked from light-years away while the moon peered down and begged for us to look up. In the middle of the set, I let go of my drumsticks and began to float toward the Milky Way–peppered sky. The music shrank and became quieter and quieter as I slowly drifted farther away until everything became a faint and muffled hum. It sounded like it was coming from behind a wall. I glanced below me, and everything looked tiny like specks of dust. Eventually the hum of the music disappeared, and I could hear the earth breathing. Suddenly the universe became a radiant white light, and I was thrown into a different location. I didn't recognize it, but it felt familiar. I was standing in an open field, looking at a small house. The grass was amber and green, and the front of the house was brown and speckled with cream and crimson splotches. The tall mountains in the distance looked like they were cut out of a magazine or a painting. And they looked glued to the construction-paper sky. The oak trees in the front sat still and didn't move even when the wind blew. On the wooden porch, I could see Em and France sitting at a farm table, laughing and drinking with Padre. I walked up, and everyone looked happy to see me—smiling and laughing like I had just told them a good joke. I looked inside the house and saw Mom, holding a child in her arms. I didn't know whose it was, but she held it like it was her own. Her dark-brown hair was glistening from the sunlight, and her earrings dangled like they did when I was a baby reaching out to play with them. She looked at the child, happy and laughing, then she looked at me. I reached my hand out to touch the infant, and Mom stopped smiling. She just stared at me blankly. A ringing in my ear started to grow loud, and the rest of the room faded into silence. As the ringing grew, my mother's face twisted into a sneer, and her stare became violent. "What're you gonna do, Bell? What are you gonna do, huh? What are you gonna do, Bell?" She screamed. I grabbed the child from her and frantically ran outside. Tears began to fall off my face, and the world began to echo. When I reached the front porch, everyone was staring at me vacantly. I began yelling, trying to tell them what had just happened, but they couldn't hear me, and when I looked down at the child in my arms, nothing was there—it was just cloth. I dropped everything and reached for Em's arm. She turned to me and started to scream. The sound of footsteps grew louder. Em pointed behind me, and I turned around. Mother was standing there in her blue dress, but her face was now contorted. Her mouth was literally ear to ear, her eyes had disappeared, and her nose was replaced by one large black hole. I turned back around to Em, Francis, and Padre, and their faces began to melt like wax in a hot oven.

"What are you gonna do, Bell? What are you gonna do, huh? What are you gonna do?"

BUSHWICK

I woke up in a panic and reached for my phone.

"Hello?"

"Hank, I need to go home."

He was quiet for a second, but I could hear clicking from keys on a computer. "You're going back to New York tomorrow at eleven thirty-five a.m. You fly for eleven hours and forty-five minutes and land at five twenty p.m."

"Right, but I mean *Texas*. I need to go back to *Texas*."

"Is everything okay?"

"Yeah, everything's fine. I just, well, I don't really want to, but I have to go see my mom and deal with something."

He sounded flustered. "So you want me to reroute you to Texas?"

Even to me it sounded ridiculous. She's not dead, at least not in real life. "No, I guess not. But when do we have time off?"

"We have the next few weeks off. Want me to book you a flight?"

I closed my eyes and pinched the top of my nose. "I don't know." The image of her twisted face entered my mind like a worm. "Ummm, no. Don't worry about it; I'll figure it out."

"Are you okay?" Hank asked.

I snorted. "Hank, am I ever okay? I mean, I'm always fine, but, well, you know what I mean."

"Well, get some sleep. You need to be at the airport by eight a.m."

—

The flight was long and uninteresting. The only thing notable was Drew's large Hispanic neighbor constantly reaching over Drew's seat and opening the window shade he kept closed. At one point, Drew looked at her and said, "Heeey, lady, can we chill? Trust me, there's nothing out there except large oceans and weird clouds. Sooo, can we just keep this closed so the light doesn't keep us all awake?" She looked at him and frowned, then opened a bag of potato chips and whispered, *"Dios mío,"* under her breath. I laughed and closed my eyes.

When we landed, I said bye to the guys, grabbed my bag, and got in a car. The drive home was always something I looked forward to. We'd start west on North Conduit Avenue past Ozone Park, where the immensity and beauty of Manhattan looked like a gray mountain range. Then we'd get on Liberty and sit in the creeping traffic until it reminded you that it was like city tax—just part of what you do to live in the greatest city in the world. Then we'd turn onto Bushwick Avenue, and drive slowly past the Evergreens Cemetery. It was gorgeous. Dark- and light-gray tombstones stuck out of the ground like teeth surrounded by luscious green grass. Crosses and statues of saints praying for the dead speckled the grounds, adding weight to the feeling of impermanence in this world. It was oddly calming. We all end up the same when we're finished. When I got out of the car, I sniffed the air. It smelled like bad Chinese food.

"I'm home," I said to no one.

—

For the next few days I mostly sat around writing music and drinking red wine, trying to ignore the mounting problem in Texas. I'd force myself to keep writing, even on days I came up with nothing just so I could have a distraction. At night, I went to cocktail bars alone and chatted with the bartenders. They were always nice to me and poured shots freely. One even gave me his metal flask that was fashioned to look like a fish. I took a pull and coughed; it tasted good and strong. It was rye—Michter's. I took another pull and felt warm all over, then smiled. I have a habit of telling myself that being out in the nightlife is "part of my job" and it's "important," fully knowing that it isn't. Yeah, drinking copious amounts of alcohol *is* part of the job, but really it's the best way I know to deal with my problems. Most nights when I'm finally good and drunk, I'll catch the train home and try not to stare at the bums who make the plastic seats their beds. I sit on the train, stare at the ground, and hum songs in my head. When I get home, I shower, crawl into bed, and stare at my ceiling. Sometimes I swear I can hear Em's voice, but it's not her. It's probably just my neighbor downstairs singing to herself. I've listened to her fuck; I wonder how it is. I guess I don't care that much.

—

Drew texted me the next morning and said he wanted to meet up later that day and go to dinner. It sounded like a fine idea to me, so I told him to meet me at Mominette that evening. It was a beautiful day, so I figured I could meet up with Ash beforehand and walk the city. I texted him and told him where to meet me. He responded in his programmed fashion: Word, dude. I got out of bed, pounded the Gatorade cut with soda water, popped the pills, drank some black coffee, threw on black jeans, grabbed my jacket, and walked out the door.

UNION SQUARE

Maybe it's the bums walking up and down in ragged, shit-stained clothes, begging for change, or maybe it's the naturalist who doesn't believe in wearing deodorant, but either way, getting on the train reminds you that New York City is the land where your senses are going to be insulted and your space is going to be invaded. That's just how it goes. I haven't been home in a while, so I don't mind it that much.

I was sitting in a corner blue seat, keeping to myself and people watching. Across from me sat a couple: two gay men, holding hands, smiling proudly 'cause to them their love was a statement of sorts. One was tanned and had smooth-combed hair with perfectly shaved lines; he was wearing some sort of black designer sweatpants. The other was a blond, messy-haired, jeaned-up white guy, who obviously made it a point to avoid the sun. Down a ways sat a spiky overgelled Hispanic man in a red-and-white-striped polo; he seemed on his way to work. His cheap oversprayed cologne always told the same story: he probably worked some food-industry job in the kitchen, maybe cooking, maybe cleaning. Either way, he made his honest keep doing something most Americans wouldn't do, and they still complained about him.

I was running ten minutes late and counting the stops I had left to Union Square, when in walked a tall, white, jock-looking college fuck. His dumb-ass blond hair said more about him than he ever could. He took one look at the gay couple, then looked around him and said,

"Faggots," out loud. The couple didn't hear him, but I stood up and looked him in the eye. "What's the matter? You think they might make you question your sexuality? You find yourself thinking about sucking cock often?" He looked at me but didn't say anything. At the next stop, he flicked me off and walked out. I just shook my head and smiled.

Every time we stopped, the train doors would open and close, sounding like wooden shutters on an old farmhouse. The automated lady would announce, "The doors are closing," and it always made me think about all the mishaps in my life: the doors left open on Em, Mom, Francis, you name it. Hearing "The doors are closing" fifteen times a day can have an impact on your morale. I'm just glad there's some left in my dumb head.

I got off the train, darted through holes of unimportant people, noticed a redhead in a Burberry coat, and then walked up the yellow concrete stairs to the street. When I reached the ground, I inhaled deeply and felt relieved to be surrounded by the gray city and semifresh air. Asher was standing on the corner with his legs crossed, looking at his phone. He was tall and slender, body like a ski with broad shoulders, and his skinny jeans made him look like a heron. His skin looked like it was programmed to always be the right amount of tan, and his hair was long and dark like waves of cocoa that perfectly framed his face. He was clean-shaven today, which was strange because usually at all times of the day he has a perfect five-o'clock shadow. Maybe there's a glitch in his system.

"What up?"

He kept staring at his phone and replied, "What up, man?"

"Well, just figured it was a nice day to walk the city and catch up."

He looked up with his wide eyes and brushed his hair behind his ear. "Hell yeah, dude. Where you wanna go?"

Asher has this weird accent thing. He grew up an only child between the Valley in Los Angeles and a lake in Michigan to a divorced flower-power mother and a dad who doubled as a musician and a magician. His mother did most of the upbringing because his dad passed away at a young age. I often wonder how different Ash would be if his father were still around. His extended family was rich in Jewish roots, all doctors and lawyers, but his immediate family was rebellious and full of gypsies, homosexuals, and artists. A modern American family at its finest. When Ash was drunk, the Midwest accent would come out, and his *o*'s would sound like *a*'s, and his *t*'s always sounded like they had a *ch* attached to them. When he was sober, he sounded like an intelligent surfer who couldn't get enough of the words "dude" and "man." An oxymoron really. More *moronic* if you ask me.

"I figured we'd do the usual. Hit up Washington Square Park, make our way to the West Village, then the water. Let's also stop by Blue Bottle—I wanna get a cold brew," I said.

"Sounds good, dude."

We started down Fourteenth Street and began to talk about business. It was our icebreaker—we liked to get the stress out of the way, and move on. The day is much more enjoyable when issues aren't gnawing at the back of your brain like bacteria on cheese. Although for Ash, it's different. He's not programmed to deal with stress. If anything, he puts it in a file in the back of his mind and lets it sit there until one day it pops open and breaks a circuit. It hasn't happened yet, but it will, and I don't wanna be around to see it, 'cause when it does happen, he'll probably kill someone.

I sighed. "We need to get the production figured out for this fucking tour."

He nodded. "Oh yeah, man, I agree. We gotta do something to keep it interesting. Maybe there's a way to change some of the songs around, like a remix or something. Maybe there's even a few songs we could do acoustic."

Maybe there's a way you could sing with feeling, I said to myself.

I shrugged. "For sure, man. There's a few songs that would really work acoustic. No more guitar solos, though."

He laughed, eyes looking wider than the Grand Canyon. "Dude, I agree. It wouldn't be so bad, but Luke doesn't spend any time on it. He's not a Frank Zappa who can just wail, you know? He's gotta, like, work it out."

"Yeah. I wish he'd spend more time practicing. He used to, but I dunno what happened." I pictured Luke and his hat bouncing up and down, playing a bluesy solo, thinking he didn't know what else to play, and I squinted my eyes. "Know what else? Luke is an asshole sometimes."

Asher nodded. "I agree, but what do you mean?"

"He can just be so condescending. He talks to you like you're a fucking idiot, and he's completely unapologetic about it. It's like, dude, we get it: something about you needs to be better than the rest of us, but you can keep it to yourself; we don't need to hear it all the fucking time."

"Dude, I know exactly what you mean," Ash said. "I was asking him about a song I liked and he was talking to me like I was stupid. Saying, 'I can't believe you like that song. That song is so wack.' Then he asked about how many copies it sold and started saying that a good song is only measured by how much it sells. I mean, I see the logic but that's craaazy to me."

I nodded. "Yeah, he's definitely one of those guys who gets his opinions mixed up with facts. Ya know what I mean?"

"Yeah, exactly," he said.

Asher licked his teeth. "Ya know, it's so interesting, though."

I turned my head and stared at a girl across the street. "What is?"

"Man, I dunno, I never really take that stuff personally."

I pulled out a square and lit up. "Dude, you don't take *anything* personally."

He shrugged his shoulders. "Yeah, I guess so, but what's the point; know what I mean?"

I shook my head. "No, I don't know what you mean."

"Well, people are people—they're not gonna change. So we can accept it or move on."

I nodded. "Yeah, well, sometimes I'd rather move on."

—

We made it to the park. There were old people sitting on benches, watching squirrels eat whatever shit people gave them, street musicians in tacky fedoras and ugly denim jackets busking for change, and even one of those weird Goth kids in all black with greasy hair, twirling red-and-black devil sticks. Parks are so stereotypical. We found an empty bench and sat down, avoiding the white bird shit, to listen to a jazz trio. It was a drummer, a trumpet player, and an upright bass player. They were talented musicians, but they all had bad style. The Asian trumpeter would bounce melodies like rubber off the tall

German-looking bass player. He in turn would shake his head to the rhythm of the ride cymbal that the French-looking drummer in big-framed glasses and a beret was finessing. We were both uncomfortable with the fact that they would always be better musicians than us, so Ash and I had to find a flaw. We sat there in silence, listening to the music, and quietly judging their lack of fashion. Bad style, man. I looked up at the oak trees—all the blackbirds were singing along. If there was one thing that bonded Ash, me, and the birds together, it was our love for good music.

"Dude, these guys are soooo good," Asher said.

"Hell yeah. Except for that shirt."

Asher giggled, and I laughed. "It's the loudest thing out here," I said.

Asher was hysterical. "Man, can you imagine!?"

I stared at the drummer's hands, admiring his technique while we calmed down. "What?"

"Well, not to discredit these guys 'cause they're incredible, but I'm glad our lives aren't like this."

"What do you mean?"

"I mean, I'm glad that we hustled our way to the top. We were always talented, but you know that's not important anymore."

"Whoa there, Ash, you're starting to sound like *me*."

He grinned. "Well, it's true. One thing we always had over everyone else was our work ethic. And I'm glad we can do what we love and not have to worry about when our next meal is going to be."

I sighed. "Me too. I'm so glad we became something. What *would* you do if you didn't do this?"

He thought about it for a minute. "Man, I think I'd try my luck at being a magician like my dad."

I laughed. "The only thing you're good at keeping secret is your emotions, my friend."

His wide eyes narrowed a bit. "I hate when you say that stuff."

"Well, I hate that you don't say that stuff. But why a magician?"

"I just think I'd like it."

"Yeah?"

"Well, when I was young, I would go with my dad to all the rad parties he would be hired to do magic at. Man, they were always full of little kids that were so amazed at his tricks. He'd pull quarters out of nowhere, separate those silver ring things, and even do cool stuff with those little red foam balls. He'd put two in his hand and somehow end up with four. It was sick."

I imagined his dad doing the ring trick and a bunch of kids laughing and clapping. "Did he ever do card tricks?"

He squinted. "Yeah, man, but not too many."

Then I imagined a man with a face I didn't know spit a whole deck of cards out of his mouth. "So was he your hero?"

"Who, my dad?"

I looked at him. "Yeah."

"I dunno, man," he said and pulled out his phone and shrugged his shoulders. "I guess so."

"That's as deep as it gets," I said under my breath.

The trio finished their last song. I got up and threw a dollar in the trumpet case. The blackbirds started squawking again, telling the band not to stop while I quietly told the birds to shut up. We kept walking through the park, staring at the idiots and talking. We passed a group in cosplay who were swinging fake swords at each other and fake fighting. One of the girls had bright-green hair and a lower-lip piercing. Her skin was milk white, and she had on fake brown furry cat ears. She was hot.

We passed a few travelers who had tribal tattoos on their faces, and who were all trying to hide the needle marks on their arms. A few of them were sitting with their eyes closed, fading into the ground slowly, the world not paying attention. A flock of gray-and-white pigeons landed on a man who was feeding them. He was fat, with wiry gray hair poking out of an old blue Vietnam War cap, and his jacket and jeans were spotted in bird shit. He was talking to the pigeons, who were listening with intent, but only because the food kept coming.

Asher turned to me. "Dude, I need to go on another bungee trip soon."

I rolled my eyes. "Where would you go?"

"Costa Rica, I guess."

"Costa Rica?"

"Yeah, I could even get in some hang gliding or something."

"Ugh."

"They have like the second-tallest bungee jump in the world, or at least I remember hearing that somewhere. Heck, I might even try to go shark-cage diving."

I shook my head. "Ash, you're fucking crazy."

Asher was into anything extreme. Luke and his hat were too, but for different reasons. Whether it was snowboarding, surfing, swimming with sharks, base jumping, cave diving, mountain climbing—hell, you name it, those two idiots were into it all. For Luke, it was his way of letting go of control. It was the only time he took off his hat. For Asher, it was something else. He coasted through life, going through the motions of the everyday mundane, suppressing his emotions, and not knowing why. He got girlfriends and lost them: he wasn't good at giving affirmation or attention. He ate food, but only for sustenance. If it were up to him, he'd just take a pill. He drank bad beer, because good beer wasn't worth it and did the same thing as bad beer. So did cocaine, but he didn't buy cheap powder.

"For the life of me I can't understand how or why you do those things," I lied. I knew that deep down in his robotic brain, he *did* feel things. Sometimes it just took jumping off tall buildings with a parachute to make it all come to the surface.

His eyes expanded to the size of ships. "Dude, you should come with me one day. It's such a rush."

"Nope. No fucking way. The only rush I need is the one I'm about to get from that cold brew."

He laughed. "Yeah, right, bro. Jump out of an airplane and tell me how it feels."

I shook my head again. "Aren't you ever afraid you're gonna die?"

"Are you kidding?" He looked at me like I was supposed to be in the psych ward. "Of course I am! All the time, but it doesn't matter. I mean, if you really think about it, man, it would be a hell of a way to go."

I nodded. "Yeah. That's for sure. I can see the headline now: 'Semi-famous singer jumps out of airplane to feel something. Feels hard ground and dies.'" I laughed.

"Dude, as long as you put out the good vibes, there's no worries—all will be good."

"What-fucking-ever, man: remember that when you plummet five hundred feet to your death. It's not like good vibes are gonna make that ground any softer."

—

We got to the West Village and began passing up the bums and tourists. You always knew the tourists 'cause they'd walk slower than the slow walkers, and they always looked up at the buildings. Usually they wore bright yellow or red sweaters with a camera or an iPad around their stupid necks. And usually they stuck out like a black eye. Even the bums looked more at home. In the distance I could hear a few seagulls yelling about something and the sound of a jackhammer. Asher and I made our way to the water, where it was calm and quiet. A cargo ship was moving, and the water looked blue and cold. We leaned up on a guardrail, and I lit up a square.

"You know, I've been thinking about it," I said.

"About what, man?"

"I dunno. It's just, we've had so many serious conversations, and I can't recall a single one of them where I feel like you being real wasn't provoked."

He stared at the water. "What do you mean?" I let out a puff of smoke, and he turned and looked at me. "What do you mean?"

I shrugged. "I dunno. I mean, yeah I do, it's just . . . well, we always talk about the same shit. Yes, we share our love of walking the city, our caffeinated drinks, and our love of women, right? But you know that's all surface-level shit, don't you? Tell me something *real, something I don't know*! How about that? Tell me something more than just these same skin-deep nothings we always talk about."

He put his hands in his pockets. "I dunno, man."

I looked at him, annoyed. "Is it that hard to do?"

"Well, I dunno." He started to look at the ground, 'cause he did know.

One drunken night, I overheard him spilling to some stranger that his father had always told him to "Man up and be tough, 'cause *you* are all *you* got." I'm not sure why he said it, but he seemed pretty down. Ash could be a sad drunk. I sat there drinking my tequila, pretending to be in my own world when I heard him say, "Up until his last day, my dad was the toughest motherfucker I'd ever known. One time when I was seven, I cried because another kid pushed me and I scraped my knee on the gravel. My dad told me to stop crying and wiped away my tears. He said not to let other people see how they affected me, 'cause if they see, they win." I looked over at him as he cheers'd the stranger, and I felt empty for him. I imagine that when his father passed, he let a few tears go, but then he wiped them away, took a deep breath, and spoke to his tears: "Man up, be a man."

"Okay, how about this?" I said. "Guilt."

"What about it?" he asked.

"Well, let's talk about it. The deepest, weirdest, most serious things that shape us as human beings are guilt and love. Tell me something you feel guilty about."

"I dunno, man."

"Okay, I'll start."

It was clear that a thousand-pound weight was lifted off his shoulders. He was always a better listener anyway.

"I feel guilty about leaving home. I feel guilty about leaving my brother there. I feel guilty about the idea of him being abandoned again. I feel guilty about the lack of energy I put into making sure he's okay. I feel guilty about not being a better person to those who love me."

"That's it," he said calmly, pointing his finger at me.

"That's what?"

"I feel the same way."

"What do you mean?"

"Well, not about my brother, but remember when I was still together with Coco?"

"Yeah, I remember."

"Well, she was always good to me, and I guess *I* just wasn't to her. I wish I could have been better. I wish I could have been a better person to her. I wish I didn't cheat on her with all those other girls, man. I see now how none of them meant anything."

He looked down, with his hands in his pockets. His face was a bit sullen and he had a vacant stare.

"I dunno, man. I wish people didn't always see me as this unemotional person. I feel things—I just don't like to talk about them. It never got me anywhere as a kid, and now it just seems like it's all anybody ever wants me to do. Talk, talk, talk."

I nodded. "Yeah, well, talking got you here."

"I guess so."

"You ever wish you weren't an asshole?"

He laughed. "Do you?"

"Well, yeah, but not enough to do anything about it." I smiled.

"Of course not."

We both laughed.

We walked into Blue Bottle and ordered our caffeinated drinks. The barista wasn't wearing a bra, and you could see her right nipple was pierced by the three bumps on her white shirt. I ordered a cold brew and Asher an iced green tea.

I sighed. "You know, it's a constant struggle. Hell, sometimes it's unachievable. It's as if, to be a better human, we have to ignore some of those very things that make us each unique."

Ash nodded. "I completely agree, man, but you know, if we can all just try, maybe the world would be a better place."

There's the robot . . . one step forward and two steps back. I just shook my head and finished my drink.

"I gotta go. I'm meeting Drew for dinner. Wanna come?"

"Nah, I'm good; I gotta go for a run."

"Okay, call me later."

—

Ash turned around and headed toward the train. I watched him walk away, thinking he'd never change, and that none of us would. "Hey!" I tapped my chest with my hand in the shape of a fist and yelled, "You know, man, you gotta dig deep! You just gotta dig deep!"

He turned around. "What're you talking about?"

—

I picture Ash getting home, stripping off his clothes, throwing on his black Nike running shorts, his matching Frees, tying up his hair, and starting his run. For the first half mile, he'll make a playlist on his phone. For the next mile, he'll try not to think about our conversation, but he'll picture his dad's face, 'cause he misses him. At mile four, he'll probably close his eyes and think about Coco and the one-night strangers that he let take her away from him. Then he'll run faster, trying to leave everything behind so that nothing matters anymore. He'll run so fast just to make himself numb again.

MOMINETTE

I got out of the car, thanked the driver, and walked into Mominette. The bell when the door opened caught the bartender's attention. He looked at me, nodded, and waited for me to sit. "What can I get you?"

"Lemme get a gin and tonic."

He sneered at me like I was an amateur. "Any particular gin?" His brow was raised nearly to the start of his ugly slicked-back widow's peak.

I looked around at the bottles. "Miller's." *You prick.*

The bell rang, and in walked Drew; he wasn't his champagne self today. His long, straight black hair was frazzled, and his dark-auburn skin was ashy. You could tell he had been scratching his tattoos 'cause they were raised on his arms. His expensive clothes looked ratty and torn, and he smelled like he needed a shower. He looked thin, like he hadn't been eating, and his guitar pick–shaped head had become thinner, making his soft jawline look hard and jagged.

"What's up, man?" I asked.

"Nothing reeeally, just wanted to hang with my homie, you know?" He gave a half smile.

"Yeah, I feel ya. Miss me?" I laughed.

"Well, yeeeah, man. I was feeling lonely, to tell you the truth. I figured my dude lived around the corner, so why not call him up and try to just be a friend?"

Even Drew was feeling the other side of this life. The offstage part. It gets to you after a while.

The bartender motioned to the server, and he promptly came and directed us to a table. We sat near the back, passing a few couples eating their food, laughing, arguing, crying—all the shit that couples do. Two birdies in the corner were gazing into each other's eyes, being in love; a few men were trying really hard to get their first dates drunk enough to sleep with; and a few barflies were just that—drunk and idle.

"Well, what have you been up to?" I asked.

"Duuude, I've been trying to write, but I'm finding it hard." He began to play with his napkin, tearing off little pieces of "loves me, loves me not." I looked down at my knife, which was slightly dirty.

"Why?" I asked.

"I'm feeling uninspired, man. We've been doing this for a while, ya know? And now, welll . . . now things are just . . . different."

I nodded my head and took a sip of the Miller's. "Yeah, man. We've been growing, but it seems like mostly apart. Not from each other or anything, more like apart from regular everyday people. It's hard to relate to anyone anymore."

I began picking at the knife, wondering what leftover crap was on it, then called the waiter over and ordered a bottle of Bordeaux and butter green pesto snails.

"Well, duuude, this life's not what I thought it would be. I mean it is, I guess; I just didn't know exactly what we were getting into. I dunno."

I shrugged. "Well, how could we know? They always say you don't know until, well, until you do." Drew nodded. "I mean what would you do if you *weren't* doing this?"

Drew laughed. "Oh, duuude, I couldn't do anything else! I guess I'd just be a burnt-out weirdo wandering around the city. One thing's for sure—if I wasn't homeless, I sure as hell would look like I was . . . I mean, even more than I do now."

We were both laughing as the snails arrived. We grabbed the perfectly toasted bread and began spooning them on and taking big bites, trying to speak in between the chewing.

"Hung out with Ash today."

"Oh yeah? How's he?"

"The exact same."

Drew smirked. "Yeah, maaan, that guy's not changing."

"Nope. Never will." I shrugged. "I just feel like whoever that guy ends up with is going to have to do all the heavy lifting. I mean, emotionally *and* physically."

Drew nodded and smacked on a snail. "Yeah, maaan. It's that only-child thing."

We ordered *moules frites* and relished the thought of soaking up the sauce with the leftover bread. Drew began talking about girls he was hooking up with or fucking, and I pretended to listen. I mostly just sat there eating, thinking about other things. By the end of the meal, we were feeling like kings, so we ordered a couple of Milagro and sodas to top it off. When we finished those, we decided to keep drinking and headed next door to Three Diamond Door, a bar named after the three diamond-shaped windows that appear on the front door.

I stood outside, watching the girls walk by in their leathers and jeans, puffing at a square like it was a fetish. I began thinking of Francis and how much he would enjoy this exact moment. Then I began imagining Mom and got angry. I pulled hard on my square, inhaling the smoke like I was getting back at her by ruining my lungs, then I began to calm down, remembering Em. I started to disappear into myself the way I always do, when Drew came outside, hit me on the shoulder, and snapped me out of it.

"Heeey, bro, let me be the emo one today. Come have a drink," he said.

I smiled and threw my square on the ground, then watched a tight brunette clack her heels and walk into the bar.

Drew and I were regulars at this place because it was so close, and both of us were too lazy to find anything else. Besides, we liked the name. It was a dive, but it had everything you wanted, and it was cheap. The only downside was the other regulars: the failed artists, writers, or other service-industry slags with shit tattoos, flannels, and Doc Martens who slumped over the bar like a bad yoga move and smelled like vomit and cheap fabric softener. They're a constant reminder of what we almost were. If you could get past all that, this place was for you.

They always had specials, and tonight it was draft champagne and batch Manhattans. We were in a whiskey mood, so we ordered two West Ends and skipped the specials. Fuck 'em. I cheers'd Drew and congratulated him on being one of the few people I could stand to be around.

He laughed and said, "Duuude, that's what it's all about—family." I rolled my eyes and fumbled onto a stool.

I ignored the image of Mom that flashed in my head. "Speaking of family, how is the fam?" I asked.

He shrugged his shoulders like it was the last thing he wanted to talk about. "Mostly good, I guess. But I will say, maaan, it seems like ever since all of this, everyone wants something from me; everyone has their hand out, know what I mean?"

I thought about my second cousin calling me out of the blue and asking me for three hundred dollars, and nodded. "Yeah, I get that."

"I dunno what they think, maaan. I mean it's not like we're sitting on top of millions upon millions of dollars here. I feel like they think we are sooo rich, and that we can just afford to do whatever we want."

I laughed. "Well, we can afford to do the things we find important, like order another two of these."

I shook the glass, and it sounded like the bell from Mominette. The bartender came over like a butler. "Also, when you *really* think about it, we *do* live in New York fucking City and have these extraordinary lives. It's not normal—what do you expect people to think?"

"I dunno, maaan." He sounded defeated and tired. "I guess I just thought people would understand the hard work we put into what we do. Everybody just wants a handout."

I pursed my lips. "No one will ever understand this life like you, me, Ash, and Luke. No one will ever understand what we put into it. Fuck 'em."

"Yeeeah. You're right, shit; my parents still want me to go back to college."

I laughed. "Well, that's not a shocker."

"Yeah, but I don't need college. I'm more successful than half of my family, maaan."

I took a sip of my whiskey. "I think it's different for them, though."

One time when Drew was high on a hybrid strain of green, he spilled his life story to me. It must have had him feeling pretty good 'cause once he started, he couldn't stop. He told me his mother had her cervix removed at a young age and couldn't bear children. She was tall, thin, blonde, well educated at Columbia, and in all considerations was a "knockout find." His father was tall, skinny to the point of looking like a cord, and was educated at Yale. Before their first date, he found out he was sterile due to an unfortunate incident with a baseball. Drew claimed that this alone was the reason they both knew it was meant to be.

They adopted five children, all of whom wanted to be doctors, lawyers, social workers, even a veterinarian, except for Drew. Here he was, a rock star, the black sheep. Even after the band made it, his parents still hounded him to finish school, though at this point he was making more money than anyone in his family. The pressure was nothing new. He grew up troubled and was sent to a reform school where he still didn't care to do well in his subjects. From an early age he knew what he was supposed to do, and he was doing it.

Drew stared at his glass. "Well, Max tried to kill himself."

I gulped, half choking on a piece of ice.

"What?" I coughed. "What? When?"

He had that same blank stare on his face that I had become so well acquainted with over the years. "The other day." He began shaking his head. "Says he's lonely, maaan. I dunno, I guess he's just, I dunno."

I looked up at the ceiling and noticed a black fly rubbing its front feet together and sighed. Drew began tapping his fingers on the bar and said, "I guess the weird part is, Max, my own brother, my own flesh, my own fucking blood, well, he feels I guess . . . what? Lonely and lost, right? I mean, man, I can relate, you can relate! So can the other guys! I don't think that ever goes away! Duuude, no matter how successful we become, it's there like a shadow. A *big* fucking shadow."

I nodded and looked up. The fly was gone. "That is the truth, my friend."

"Yeeeah, the only difference is, none of us would kill ourselves because of it." His eyes began to well up like water rising from a small hole in the earth. "All of this, maaan, we have all of this. And it's not important." He shook his head.

I sat there and stared into my drink. "What's important and what's not is a matter of perspective. Just make sure he knows that *you* think he's important."

He nodded and wiped his face. "Speaking of important, I'm gonna go. I gotta go work on these two songs I've been writing."

"Forget them for now," I said. "Let's do a shot, c'mon."

PEARL'S SOCIAL & BILLY CLUB

The bartender was close by, so I gave him a "fuck you" look and he came over. Two shots later, Drew and I were falling all over ourselves, trying to avoid our shadows. I asked him if he wanted two more, and he shook his head and then left 'cause he didn't want to wake up miserable, but I said, "Fuck it." I wasn't quite ready to call it a night. I went outside, put a square in my mouth, and reached for the fire in my pocket. I pulled out the box of matches and looked at them. They were the ones I got from the night with Jane. I held them next to my ear and shook the box. The two sticks made a marvelous wooden sound. I took one out, lit up, inhaled the square, and started spinning. I was envisioning all of the world's light surrounding her blonde hair. When I exhaled, I could see her cab driving away and disappearing into the smoke. I shook my head and mumbled to no one, "Everyone always leaves." As I walked toward the next bar, I made sure not to look anyone in the eye. I didn't have it in me. I didn't want to see them making fun of how fucked up I was.

Pearl's has always been the last stop on my way home. I knew the bartenders most nights, and they all knew me. They called me "Rosé" because that was all I drank there. The weird thing is I don't remember ordering it the first time. It's as if the highball glass just appeared in front of me. There was something simple about that, and I liked it. It was cold, it was easy, it was pink, it was in my hand, it was fine. I sat down and thought about Drew and his brother. I looked to my left, and there was a girl dressed in tight black denim and a circle scarf. She was fingering her glass and staring blankly at the bar like she had just gotten some bad news. I glanced to my right, and there was a whole line of sad men looking like they had just gotten laid off from some terrible job. It's as if this was the only place they wanted to be right now. I wondered if I looked any different. After about two more pink glasses, I threw my money on the table and walked out the door. I stood outside, lit up a square, and some guy asked me for one. He offered to trade for X. I told him not to worry about it and handed him two.

"Are you sure? You don't have to do that."

He looked like a Persian cat, very feminine and soft. He was tall, had dark skin, perfectly plucked eyebrows, and his lips were full. I was sure he was gay, but sometimes even when it seems that way, people aren't. He was wearing black leathers and had on a high-fashion black cape.

I shook my head. "Yeah, don't worry about it. I have plenty."

He smiled and stepped back next to me. "Thanks, thanks so much! So are you from around here? I only ask because you're so nice and not just anyone would help out a stranger. Not in New York City anyway."

I rolled my eyes, knowing he couldn't see it. I wasn't in the mood to chat—*just take the cigarette and be on your way.*

I nodded and looked at him sidelong. "Yeah, I live down the street."

He smiled and put his hand on my back. "Oh my God! Me too, whereabouts?"

His body language was saying more than his mouth was. He just smiled and looked into my eyes. Sometimes when a man looks at you in the eyes, you can read his soul. Right now his soul was saying, *Jerk me off.*

I looked at him and squinted. "Over on Central by Archie's."

His arm was doing that bend thing, holding the square. "That's so close to me! I'm on my way back that direction, you wanna get outta here? I have wine back at my place."

I was drunk off my ass, and I was seeing double, but if I concentrated hard enough, things merged together imperfectly.

I looked back at him and closed my eyes. "Sure, okay. One more, why not?"

We walked back to his place, smoking and talking about the greatness of the city or something or other, I can't recall. We walked into his apartment. It was small with white walls and bare wood floors. One side had exposed red brick with a wreath hanging on it, and a "Merry Christmas" sign in blue lettering. I walked to his gray couch and sat down on the big oversized cushions.

"Make yourself at home," he said, pouring me a glass of something red. I took one sip and the next thing I knew, I was waking up halfway through the night to him stroking my cock. I was hard but it still shocked me. I kept saying no but I didn't fight it. He just looked at me from in between my knees like he was a servant to Caesar. When he put it in his mouth, I closed my eyes, leaned my head back, exhaled, and came. He swallowed, then tried to kiss me.

I slapped him in the face and told him, "No! Don't you even think about it."

He cupped his hand on his face and said, "Oh, I see how it is." Then he smiled devilishly. "Well, we both got what we wanted anyway, now get the fuck out."

I stood, pulled up my jeans, and started to walk out of his apartment like I was running away. I started thinking of Jon, then Chloe, then that teddy bear big-dicked black guy.

He stood at the door and looked at me. "See you around, homo." He smirked.

I turned around, angry, and looked at him in the eyes.

"You better hope not. And if you do, ignore me or I'll fucking deck you."

His expression didn't change, and I didn't care. He was right—I got off and he was probably going to think about it later and get off too. We both did our part.

A brown rat ran across the sidewalk into a giant trash heap and made a squeaking sound. The yellow moon seemed larger than on most nights, but that could have just been my alcohol eyes. I stumbled home, hoping I could make it before I puked. I could hear the sounds of the city from far away, cars honking, tires moving, a few fireworks popping, and people yelling. A white dump truck with green lettering rolled past me, smelling strongly of death and rot. I gagged and threw up in a patch of grass. "I just ruined the only patch of grass for miles," I said aloud to nobody. Then I fell on the ground and started laughing hysterically.

My world was spinning in starlight and stomach acid. I had just gotten a blow job from a Persian cat guy, I had dinner with one of my best friends, I had a fresh pack of squares—my mother's nectar, and I had never felt emptier. Everything was the same. Everything was where it was supposed to be. My shadow was large tonight.

I got home and threw up again. I took off my shirt and stared into the mess in the toilet as if it were tea leaves telling me a story. It was red and mean, and reminded me of being sick when I was younger. My mother always took care of me and brought me popsicles. Of course, I would sometimes throw them up. I wiped my mouth with toilet paper, gargled mouthwash, and ignored myself in the mirror. I didn't want to see what my face was thinking or hear what it was saying. I flipped off the light, sighed, and crawled into bed. My downstairs neighbor was awake, listening to music. I could hear the faint sound of Joni Mitchell's "A Case of You." It reminded me of the night with Jane and how special it was. And it reminded me of the better times with Em. At least the girl downstairs has good taste.

I fell asleep half humming, half listening to the words, half dreaming of my mother, half wondering what place Joni got to when she wrote this song.

—

The next morning, Drew sent me a text asking me what time our flight was. I responded: I'm not your tour manager. Then I called Hank to ask him what time our flight was.

"Seven p.m. from JFK; we land at seven fifteen a.m. Did you ever get to Texas?"

I sighed. "No. I had too much on my plate."

"Hmm. Writing or what?"

I thought about it for a second—I didn't do a fucking thing. "Yeah, writing. Hey, I gotta pack. I'll see you in a bit."

"Copy."

I hung up the phone and lay in bed. I tossed and turned, but nothing made me feel content.

"You should have gone home, Bell," I said to no one.

—

A couple of hours went by as I lay in bed, nursing my hangover. I eventually got up, popped two pills, and drank my Gatorade and soda-water combo. I showered, packed, threw on clothes, and made my way to JFK. When I arrived, I avoided the dead people walking to their gates, threw on my headphones, and walked onto the plane. This was about to be a nineteen-hour flight, so Hank made sure we had seats that went all the way down, so we could sleep. As I sat, the flight attendant began her in-flight safety instructions. I've heard these things a million fucking times, so I always embellish to myself what I think they should say.

JFK

"Hello, everyone! Welcome aboard and thank you for your attention! It's time to get you ready for takeoff! We know you have lots of choices, so thanks for choosing us . . ."

And realizing that while we suck dick, we're not the worst! We definitely don't care about you, but we'll pretend to be happy to be your airline as long as you are seated in first class or the first three rows of the main cabin. The rest of you second-class fucks didn't pay nearly enough and will be lucky if your luggage makes it to your final destination . . .

"Now if you'll just follow along, we'll be on our way. Before we depart, there are some important safety instructions. First things first, let's buckle those seat belts. Insert the metal end into the buckle and pull the strap to tighten . . ."

Some of you fat shits—I'm talking to you, seat 7B—will need two belts. Fear not, we have plenty. We are a McDonald's nation after all! Yum, yum, yum! Enjoy your fried lard, you life-shortening fuck . . .

"To open, simply lift on the top of the buckle. Remember, seat belts should be fastened whenever you're seated just in case of unexpected turbulence . . ."

We don't want any of you fucktards getting in the way of the bar cart, now do we . . . ?

"To get us on our way, make sure your seat is upright, all electronic devices are put away, and your tray table is stowed. If you have a carry-on, push it all the way under the seat in front of you. If it won't fit, place it in the overhead bin . . ."

And know that at some point, some asshole will move it to another location just because they feel their luggage is way more important than yours . . .

"If you have a handheld device, please switch it to airplane mode now. You'll find our full electronic device policy in the back of our magazine . . ."

You know, that shitty plane magazine, with shitty interviews and shitty writing. The first page always has a positive "message" from our CEO; well, his hot secretary who he's fucking wrote it . . . not him, and there's a little section in the back with all of our electronic policies, but who cares? We flight attendants don't follow the rules, so why should you . . . ?

"US law prohibits smoking, including electronic cigarettes at any time. Tampering with, disabling, or destroying smoke detectors in the lavatories may result in a fine. US law requires all to comply with posted signs and crew member instructions. Now let's review the safety card. All exits on this airplane are clearly marked . . ."

If you can't see the giant doors, you're either fucking stupid or you're blind. You probably deserve to die . . .

"Take a moment to locate the nearest one, and keep in mind it may be behind you . . ."

If we do crash, however, the only way you're getting out of this metal death trap is in a body bag, and it won't matter where the exits are . . .

"All exits do have evacuation slides to use in case of an emergency. When directed to exit . . ."

Hope that I haven't lied to you about there actually being a slide, and jump onto it. It's fun, it's bouncy, and if the plane is on fire, you might feel euphoric and forget about it for a moment . . .

"Some slides may also be used as a raft . . ."

But if we go down in water, we will break apart piece by piece and, well, we're all fucked . . .

"This aircraft is designed with escape lighting on the floor. A sign will indicate you have reached your exit. In the event of an evacuation, escape path lighting will appear . . ."

Make sure to freak out, punch your neighbor in the face, and trample all of the slow idiots until you've reached your exit. Leave all carry-ons, including babies, behind and proceed to the closest exit . . .

"Now, if the airplane loses pressure . . ."

We're all fucked! But to seem like there's a shred of hope, "oxygen" masks will deploy automatically . . .

"Pull down on the mask to extend the tubing. The yellow cup goes over your nose and mouth, then slip the band over your head to secure the mask to your face. Normal breathing will start the flow . . ."

Of nitrous oxide, excuse me, "oxygen," but since we will all more than likely be yelling, screaming, praying, or whatever, erratic breathing will work too. Remember to always put your own mask on first before helping others. I mean, you always do your own drugs first, right . . . ?

"Life vests are located either under or next to your seat . . ."

Once again, if we land in water, none of this will matter 'cause we'll all be dead, but to remove the vest, pull the fucking box open, and yell loudly out of instinct. Place the vest over your head, pull the red tab, and hope that it chokes you and finishes the job. Eating your neighbor Sandy doesn't sound appetizing now, but wait till you're stuck in the middle of the ocean without any food for two weeks. If you're unlucky enough to survive, and you're indeed floating in the water, a little blinking light will activate so that all of the nearby sharks can see you clearly and hopefully put you out of your misery . . .

"Your seat cushion may be used as a flotation device . . ."

Except for, yes you guessed it, seat 7B. Sorry, sir or ma'am or whatever your fat ass is, you're just way too big and will sink like the boulder you embody . . .

"The crew will now be coming around . . ."

To quietly say fuck you, judge your grooming habits, and make sure you know that we're the assholes in charge. You're all in our house now, and since we all have a Napoleon complex, you had better fucking listen to us. Johnny's wouldn't be the first glass of water we've all pissed into. Anyway, we'll be back after takeoff, assuming we haven't blown up, with more information . . .

"If you need anything, don't hesitate to ask . . ."

We will be happy to listen to your request and either ignore or take our sweet-ass time to fulfill whatever stupid fucking thing you may want. As always, we're here to make your flight whatever the fuck we feel like at the time . . .

"Once again, thanks for flying with us . . ."

Now go fuck yourselves.

CAPE TOWN, SOUTH AFRICA

"This is horrible," I said.

"Yup. I always thought this's just somethin' Hollywood made up. I didn' realize people actually lived like this."

Luke and his hat were people watching as we sped by.

Our tour guide was driving us through the outskirts of Cape Town, where the townships were located. We were speeding the whole time, avoiding red lights, and most importantly, sketchy-looking trucks with piles of different-colored people in the back. Like a rabbit being chased by a dog, we never stopped moving. When we asked why, he said 'cause we'd get robbed and, worse, might not make it back.

The townships were divided by race—dark skin, light skin, and the poorest and most dangerous were a combination of the two. People lived in homemade shacks. The walls, if there were any, were made of cardboard and plastic plywood if they were lucky. Sometimes people acquired an old train car or a used shipping container, which they fashioned into a living space. No one knew or cared to ask exactly how they were acquired. One thing was always for sure: it wasn't legal.

I had to hand it to them—they did what they could to try to make life bearable and even somewhat normal. They made fruit stands and barbershops and even liquor stores out of these shanties, but everything still looked and smelled like a living hell. It was a speck of dust that everyone wanted to sweep under the rug.

The first township had a famous barbecue spot that we were headed to. Apparently, if you didn't go, it was bad luck. The town itself was so poor that it attracted tourists, because tourists don't live like this. Their *normal* was shocking to everyone else. Whoever ran the place made it well known that no visitors were to be harmed or robbed or even bothered. If any were, and they found out that you were the poor, unfortunate soul who disturbed the balance, they'd kill you, plain and simple. Fucking dead. For them, tourists meant money, so goodbye, you economy-ruining piece of shit. What a life.

We got to the BBQ joint and stood in line. There were about five people ahead of us. I hate lines, but I wasn't going to make a fuss about this one. A tall black man wearing a torn white T-shirt walked in the front door, carrying a goat carcass on a hook. You could see its tendons, sinews, and fat all out in the open, bleeding and everything. The meat itself had good marbling, but it was still a horrid sight to see. Halfway through, he yelled something in his language and dropped the bloody body on the ground, then continued dragging it to the back.

I watched as the plasma left a trail on the floor that led you to where the cooking magic happened.

"Well, that looks fresh," Luke said, raising his eyebrows.

I nodded and widened my eyes. "Sure does."

Asher began rubbing his head uncomfortably, like it didn't compute. "Man, where do you think they got it?"

A short black lady wearing a bloody apron came out from the back with a mop and started cleaning the red plasma that in some parts had started to bubble a bit.

"I'm sure there's a farm or something near here, I dunno," I said.

Drew looked around and rubbed his arm. "Preeetty crazy the way they just brought it in the front, right?"

I nodded and shrugged. "I mean, it is what it is. That dead, gross-looking thing, with all its bloody guts, *is* what we eat."

Asher made a gagging sound. "Yeah, man, it's just better out of sight, out of mind; know what I mean?"

I laughed. "You *would* say that."

"Think they'll clean it b'fore they throw it on th' grill?" Luke reached for his hand sanitizer, blinking rapidly.

"I don't know. Look around—the cleanest thing is that guy's gun."

I pointed over at two men wearing muscle shirts, shades, sweatpants, and big black boots. They sat there proudly displaying their real guns and fake Rolexes. They were placed there as a makeshift police force and looked scary as all hell. This was a way of guaranteeing no one would try to pull some shit. It definitely made you feel safe, and also not. On the off chance that something did go south, there was sure to be hellfire raining down on this entire fucking place. So I planned an escape route in my head, but came to the conclusion I'd have a better chance of surviving if I just hit the ground, lit up a square, and hoped for the best.

Our guide knew the owner from back when he was a kid and wanted to show us where all the cooking and preparation went down. He said, "In order to best appreciate the delicate flavors that are about to grace your mouths, you must hear from the pit master himself as to how, where, and most importantly why the traditional BBQ, or *braai* as we call it, started."

He called us to the back of the restaurant after we ordered and told us to bring our meat. A door opened to the outside and all you could see was the fire and smoke. Five or six wood-burning grills fashioned out of some sort of brown brick and black rebar all had meat on top of them. Pork chops, bacon, sausage, chicken—you name it; it was cooking. They would slather some type of dark-red sauce on it that was good and spicy, then flip it over and do the same again. They repeated the process until the meat was tender and nicely cooked.

Everywhere around us were gentle, dangerous men holding giant knives and red-hot metal pokers. Their toothless grins highlighted the fact that at any moment they could kill you if you crossed them. Hell, they probably *had* killed, but they all had time and honesty in their eyes. They seemed to care more about keeping their traditions and identity alive than anything else. I doubt they got paid enough to keep more than a pint in their stomachs, but this to them was an identity. Fire spoke to them like a god, and they couldn't help but listen, even if they didn't want to.

After introductions, a history lesson, and pictures, we took our perfectly cooked meat outside to the giant family-style tables covered in checkered red-and-white tablecloths. We sat down and started away at the feast. As we talked and ate, we battled black flies that were aggressive and uninvited. We laughed, drank glass-bottled Cokes, and smoked squares. Asher was sitting back in his seat, looking puzzled and stale.

I puffed my square. "What's going on?"

"Nothing," he said.

"Bullshit. *What's going on?*"

"Well, it's nothing, really, man. I just think it's crazy that we're sitting here doing all of this." He began making circles with his hands like he was trying to smooth over baker's dough. "And when you look around us, it doesn't make any sense." His hands fell to the table with a thud. "It's a big mystery to me, to be honest. How do people live like this?"

Luke stopped chewing, looked at Asher, and adjusted his hat. The expression on his face reminded me of Padre. "Well, Ash, they don't have a choice. They didn' choose this, but they're choosin' to make the best of it, really."

Asher sighed. "Yeah, I get it. It's just pretty depressing."

I looked at Asher, the emotions file tucked away in the back of his hard drive had suddenly started to open after being taped shut all these years, then I looked around the table. Everyone that I cared about outside of Padre and my brother were around me. Drew to my left, Ash to my right, Luke and his hat in front of me, and Hank to the right of him. We were in South Africa, and for the first time in a long time, I felt at home.

Across the street, a mother was holding her child's hand and walking with another one wrapped in her arms. She was thin, body like a dandelion, wearing ratted jeans, and her hair was wildly tied up. The boy was in blue denim shorts with a torn gray shirt, smiling and laughing. The expression on her face said she was happy, but her lightly etched wrinkles said she was tired.

I began to zone out and think of my mother—*she was tired*—then my vision corrected itself, and the boy and his mother were still there. When they had nothing, they had each other, and to them that seemed enough. Why wasn't that the case for my mother? Padre seemed overjoyed and said he cried at the very sight of his newborns. He was a man who got it, but she didn't. And Francis—most people will never know what it's like to have been born to his postpartum situation. Hell, I couldn't imagine it. When I saw how my Padre looked at Francis with adoration no matter how much he fucked up, I understood the undeniable love that parents were supposed to have. Maybe he overcompensated, but it's his blood, and it's his most important thing in life.

Francis had been dealt a bad hand. We're all dealt cards, but the game is rigged, if you ask me. When he was young and in and out of juvie all the time, he got sent to boot camp. He came back even worse. He made bad choices and got mixed up with the wrong people. He joined gangs, worked his way up in a gang, became a leader in a gang, had guns, pointed guns at me, shot guns, probably shot people, sold drugs, did drugs, made drugs, and probably worse. The thought of my own brother killing someone made me sick, but it was also a reality I thought about from time to time. It all happened and it all fell on deaf ears.

We were driving fast, like we were mad, down I-10 in Texas, speeding and laughing, heading toward the East Side. The whole time we swerved in and out of traffic like we were avoiding the cops on a high-speed chase. The red, yellow, and white cars blurred past us and became oil paintings framed by our windows. I didn't fear for my life; instead, I looked at him smiling and embraced it. France hadn't told me where we were going, and I remember thinking it didn't matter. When we got to the shit part of town, we pulled over and picked up some middle-aged man in baggy blue jeans and a bright red cap. France rolled down the window and told him to get in. He jumped in the back and started asking France how he was, and what he was up to. I remember looking at the man in the rearview mirror. He had a few teeth missing, and the wrinkles on his face looked like roads in the sand. He smelled like cheap liquor and thick tobacco, and his caterpillar mustache crawled on his face.

I remember feeling uncomfortable because he started talking to me and I couldn't take my eyes off his toothless mouth moving up and down. Francis assured me this guy was legit, but I didn't like how the man knew who I was, when I didn't know a thing about him. He asked how the band was, and how New York was. He asked what it was like to be famous. At one point, he told me my brother was proud of me, and I remember thinking, Who the fuck are you, and how would you know that? *I also remember thinking how different France and I were. We pulled over into some empty parking lot, and both of them got out of the car. Francis said they had business to take care of. I guess it had something to do with gang politics; he never told me. He left the keys and said to keep the car running. When they left, they did so in a hurry, and I remember thinking the whole time that either they were going to kill someone or France was going to score more heroin.*

I hated my brother at that moment. I turned the radio up and tried to tune out my thoughts. I could only think the worst. I felt fear for my life. When France got back in the car, he was alone. He had a vacant look on his face that I couldn't read. I yelled at him for having put me in that situation, and he apologized. Most of the way home we drove in silence, left to our own thoughts. At some point I looked at him and saw the child I remembered. I flicked the radio on, lit up a square, and started to tell him a story from when we were younger. We laughed like nothing had happened.

We finished our meals and got in the van. On the way back to the hotel, the car was silent. Everybody was full, but I could tell no one felt great about it. Somehow this place was a reminder of how much we take for granted. I rubbed my head to try to get some endorphins flowing. "I'm going to find a bar. Who's in?"

Asher didn't turn around, but he spoke. "Nah, I'm all good, brother. Been a long day."

Drew turned. "Yo, so I'd go, but I kinda just wanna chill in my room and get high. That shit was craaazy."

"Okay, what about you, Hank?" I asked. Without saying a word, he just shook his head and stared at his phone.

Luke and his hat turned around and looked past me, then he looked at me. "So you ask everybody else first, but not me?"

I rolled my eyes. "Just 'cause you're last doesn't mean I wasn't gonna ask you." I raised my eyebrow and looked at him. "Do you wanna go to a bar with me?"

He shook his head. "No, I'm good. We got an early flight. I'll go with ya tomorrow, though."

I looked at him and thought about stabbing him in the neck, blood going everywhere. "Okay. Tomorrow we go one for one, no excuses."

Luke grinned. "Challenge accepted."

SYDNEY, AUSTRALIA

The streets in front of the hotel were silent, and the white lines were flickering from the streetlights. People were smoking out of their second-story windows, and music was softly thumping in the background. Luke, his hat, and I were walking, looking for a bar. We found one on a lonely street. Outside, above a set of stairs, there was a wooden sign that had a bright yellow couch painted on it. It felt inviting, so we walked downstairs into the red-lit bar and sat at a small table.

"One Monkey Shoulder, one Michter's," I said.

Luke tipped his hat. "Here's t' you."

We drink.

I looked around. "What do you think about Australia?"

He took another sip, staring at me the whole time, then adjusted his hat and let out a big breath. "It's cool. I mean, it's th' same."

I noticed a short-haired beauty in the far right corner. "What do you mean?" I asked.

"Reminds me of bein' in California. Weather's always nice, sun's out, boobs out, ya know?"

I laughed. "Yeah! Only this is waay more pleasant than California."

He looked at me. "How?"

I watched the short-haired girl walk to the bar and order a drink, then turned to Luke. "Well, everyone here is so nice. No one seems fake, and the industry is smaller. It's just more pleasant. Less bullshit."

"I get ya. My only problem is, everyone here's *too* damn nice, and real fit."

I laughed, almost spitting out my drink. "Yeah, the struggle's real."

He started smiling and switched his crossed legs. "How can ya be that fit an' have bodies like that, when yer own country basically has the best breakfast? The bacon here is amazing!"

I smiled. "Yeah, man, I don't know. I gotta say, though, everyone here *is* nice, but we've only met a few people. And the few we *have* met have basically all been radio people and label people, you know—the ones who are *supposed* to be nice to us."

I fingered the rim of my glass and watched him think for a second. "Well, it's like that wherever we go," he said.

"True. So it begs my point. Australia isn't any nicer than anywhere else we've been. I mean, people are all the same. There's good, evil, good-looking, ugly—you know, the opposites. Australia is great compared to California, but that's because we know California, and frankly, we're tired of it. We don't know Australia. It's new."

He nodded. "I get yer point, but screw it. I'm enjoyin' my time; I don't care if it's the same as anywhere else. I'm enjoyin' the sun, the women. Hell, you could say I'm enjoyin' bein' in this wonderful *fit* of denial." Then he grinned at the pun he just made. I stared at him with fake disgust, then he shrugged and put a square in his mouth. "Well, I'd *think* it; I wouldn't *say* it."

I smiled. "Yeah, that was bad." He laughed and hit the table. "You know what I would say?" I asked. "I'd say, take it all in and enjoy it as much as possible. After all, we're on a giant island that took us twenty hours to get to on a plane. Get drunk, get fucked, and remember it for the entirety of your insignificant lifetime. As far as we know, we only get one."

He blew smoke in my direction and shook his head. "Ya sure do have a way a makin' things sound like impending doom."

I nodded. "What else is new?"

I called the waitress over. "Two more shots, and two beers."

Luke held up his glass. "Here's t' life."

We drink.

—

"What about it anyway?" I asked.

"What about what?"

I lit up another square and inhaled, staring straight into Luke's eyes, looking through him. "Life. Why'd you say cheers to life?"

"'Cause it's *awesome.* I know ya joke about it bein' overrated and all, but what else is there? How can it be overrated when there ain't nothin' else to rate it against?"

My eyebrows moved like two earthworms spasming in salt. "Yeah, I know what you mean. Life's not overrated, but sometimes you wonder if you'd rather be somewhere else, and if it would be any better."

His fingers started to tap on the table, as if he was searching for the words to say under the keys of a typewriter. "Hmm. Well, where'd ya rather be?" He lit up a square until the cherry was a bright ember illuminating his face. A beautiful brunette waitress walked by in short denim, and our eyes darted in her direction like we were hunters spotting a rabbit.

"Right now? Nowhere. I'm enjoying my time with you in this shithole bar. I like smoking, drinking, laughing sometimes, and having good conversation. And currently I'm enjoying looking at her."

He nodded, acknowledging his mutual satisfaction of the situation. "Me too, man. Ya know, life's purty fucked, but there's still beauty in all of it."

My esophagus started to burn from the smoke and chemicals, and I cleared my throat. "What do you mean?"

His right leg started to bounce up and down like it was an excited dog wagging its tail. He had a point to prove.

"Well, all the bad shit in the world; how'd ya hear about it?"

I shrugged. "News, internet, word of mouth, the usual."

"*Exactly.* They're real issues that people are talkin' about. There's people in the world tryin' to fix all the fucked-up things we done to it. The atmosphere has a ginormous hole in it, ice caps are meltin', and scientists are finally convincin' world leaders to do somethin' about it. Global warmin' has become a *hot* topic." He winked at me as he said it. "'Cause people are speakin' out against it. See, Bell, there's beauty in humanity. An' I truly believe there's good in all of us, but just like ya fight internally with what seems like . . . well, everythin'."

I smiled, then laughed. He was like a grandfather trying to teach me a lesson.

"We as a human race have to fight in our world for the greater good."

I rubbed my mouth. "Yeah, I hear you. I just feel that while we have to fight for the greater good, we've developed a mentality of fixing rather than preventing. Shit, we're in a 'it's too late to fix society' mindset, or at least it *feels* that way. I'm not saying we're fucked, but we aren't helping ourselves."

He nodded and took a sip of his beer. "Yeah, but we all got bad habits. Humans collectively got bad habits."

The waitress passed us, and I called to her, staring at her long giraffe legs. I could watch her walk all day as long as I was watching from behind.

Luke winked. "Two more whiskeys."

I held up my glass. "Here's to never having to work a shitty job ever again."

We drink.

—

The whiskey went down like a missile straight to my gut, warming my insides like my stomach was a hearth.

"Okay, okay, shitty jobs. I fucking hated 'em."

I leaned back in my chair and looked around, smiling. "Yeah, no shit. Remember when I had to do this?"

Luke adjusted his hat. "What, drink?"

"No, bartend."

His eyes moved to the bartender. "Yeah. Outta all the soul-suckin' jobs out there, this's one of 'em."

I took a sip of my beer and let out a breath as if the warm whiskey fire had just been smothered. "*Ha,* just one?"

"Well, you 'member when I was flippin' random electronics on th' internet? I mean, that wasn't even a real job, but I did it to scrape by."

"Yeah, that seemed like it was the worst."

"It was! I 'member one time, this guy made me meet him at the sketchiest McDonald's in the city. I mean, at least it was a public place. But I was just glad I didn't end up bein' scrapped fer parts myself."

I laughed, thinking about the horrendous idea of humans luring people to a place and killing them for their organs, or just for straight pleasure. "True."

"Remember when I was a butcher?" I asked.

"How in the hell could I forget that?"

I shook my head. "The worst part about it was, I was vegetarian at the time. Can you imagine having to slice various parts of various animals and wanting to throw up half the time? Tendons, plasma, just going every which way."

He winced. "Ugh, that's fuckin' gross, man."

"Tell me about it. Shit, that was the wildest job I ever had. It paid minimum wage, and worked you like, well, like Drew working the last piece of ass on this planet."

Luke hit the table with his hand so hard his hat jumped.

"Ha ha ha, fuckin' Drew, man! If there was no ass left on this planet, he'd prolly dive into whatever walked, know what I mean?"

My sides ached from laughing at the way we loved Drew. He always seemed to be the butt of our jokes because he made us feel less serious about life, when all we were was *too* serious about life.

"I remember when I quit that job, I promised myself I'd never go back to doing shit like that again."

Luke laughed and his face relaxed.

"I mean I hated that place, but at least I could grow into a career bartender if I fell in love with it. I respect those people. At least it's actually a craft; you know what I mean?"

His face switched back to the "you're full of shit" look.

"Yeah, but you'd be miserable."

I thought for a moment. "Yeah, I didn't mean what I said—I *was* miserable."

Luke nodded. "Yup."

A man dressed in a black tie and white shirt came in, carrying an apron that had various colored stains on it. I watched him walk up to the bar, order a shot of well whiskey, tip it back, and begin unfolding the apron. He tucked in his shirt, threw on the apron, shook his head like he was shaking off the voices inside, and walked out the door.

"'Member that one time I walked into an interview at some Italian restaurant to be a waiter?"

I nodded.

"I took one look at the wine list I had to mem'rize, then turned round an' walked right out." We both chuckled. "I was like, fuck this! I just looked at myself in the mirror, dressed in a uniform and, well, I couldn't do it, man. I just couldn't do it no more."

I bit my lip. "I get it, man. What's the point of living if all you're doing is working? It's no kind of life. I'd rather be in a box on the street doing what I love."

"Yeah, ya say that, but I'd like to see ya try that."

I leaned back in my chair and stretched my arms out and smiled. "Well, yeah, I'm a big talker, I guess, but seriously, what would you have done if we weren't doing this?"

He frowned, appalled at the very thought of us not succeeding.

"I dunno, prolly some desk job I'd hate. What about you?"

I thought about it for a second, crossing my arms.

"I'd be a chef."

He raised an eyebrow doubting my abilities.

"A chef?"

I nodded. "Yeah, I love food and cooking and drinks and, well, all consumption, I guess."

"I feel ya. At least it'd still be creative."

"Exactly," I said, nodding. "You know what's crazy?"

"What?"

"It's crazy to me how many people don't realize how long we've worked to get where we are. I remember playing so many tiny club shows where five people would show up and we'd get paid with a bar tab."

Luke laughed. "Dude, a bar tab back then was a blessin'."

"Yeah," I said. "It definitely was. I will say, though, I'm glad we had to struggle to get here."

"Me too."

"I think it made us better in all aspects. Playing to no one, then to barely anyone made Ash better at controlling crowds, and it made us better musicians. It made us great at reading the ebb and flow of our environment. Not to mention, it kept us hungry and we hustled harder for a reward."

"Yeah, man, I mean if we hadn't done that, who knows where we'd be?"

"I dunno. Most people think overnight success is a real thing."

"It ain't, though."

"Nope. It's an illusion, like everything else in this fucking world."

The same waitress passed by, slowed, and asked if everything was okay. She looked like she was in tall grass, searching for a way out, being chased by a pride of hungry lions.

"Another two, please," I said.

"Here's to girls."

We drink.

—

"Hmm . . . girls?"

"Hell yeah, man. Can't live with 'em; don't wanna live without 'em."

I laughed, thinking about Em. I missed Em at that moment and wondered where she was in the world and what new things she was falling in love with. A look on a child's face, a speck of brown on a small bird, a fingerprint on a clean window, and all the things she found beautiful that I never appreciated.

I nodded. "They fuel everything, huh?"

"Well, I dunno. I tell ya what, though, they make me wanna be better than every other guy in whatever room I'm in at th' time."

I sighed and shook my head. My hair swung back and forth like octopus tentacles fighting a sailor, and I winced in confusion. "I get that, but I also think that's weird."

Luke scratched his face and leaned in closer. "Well, you've been fuckin' girls ever since you were what?"

I thought about it. "Thirteen."

He leaned back in his chair, making the wood creak in sudden shock. "Yeah, see, I haven't been."

"I guess that's true. So you're saying that right now you're just coming into your sexual maturity?" I smiled at the thought of a twenty-eight-year-old man having the sexual prowess of a teenager.

"Ummm, sure."

I laughed and thought about all the holes and skin my cock has been in and out of. "Yeah, I'm over it."

Luke laughed. *"Over it?"*

"Yeah, man, over it. I don't like the cat-mouse thing anymore. I've slept with . . . I dunno, I lost count somewhere, but now I've learned it's all the same. It's rare that I think back to a random hookup and really cherish it. The best sex I've ever had was always with someone I cared about."

"Yeah, that's what they say," he said.

"You don't think so?"

"Yeah, I do. But I'm not doin' these random hookups to 'member one forever. I'm doin' them to just get off."

"I get that. See, my problem is, I fall in love too easily."

His eyes darted left and right like a Ping-Pong match. "With everyone?"

"Basically. Take our server, for example. She's wild looking. Hair in braids, tan skin, short shorts—shit, she looks like Pocahontas."

He nodded. "Mm-hmm, yeah, she's hot."

"She's been eyeing us ever since we walked in the door. Every time she brings us a shot, she flips her hair and smiles. Then I stare and watch her ass as she walks away. Every time she goes to another table, she doesn't smile. Well, she *does,* but it's not sincere. I see her, and I see a little bit of myself in her."

"I bet ya do," he laughed.

"Not that way—well, that way, yes. But I mean in her spirit. Like, I want to get to know her because at this moment I'm imagining us holding each other, smoking in bed after we just made love for hours. Then I imagine the future with her, where we're seven years out, living in a cabin, chopping wood and raising children with wolves."

"Yer really takin' this Pocahontas thing to heart."

"Well, I'm weird, I guess."

He nodded. "That's for sure."

"Two more and the check."

"Here's to nothing and everything," I said.

"Here's t' you, ya jackass."

We drink.

—

Just as we downed our last shots, Pocahontas walked by another table. She accidentally knocked over a whole tray of glasses, and they tumbled to the floor. Shards of glass flew everywhere, creating the most fantastic sound you've ever heard. Millions of pins randomly dropping on a wood floor, cascading into harmony, shattering like ice on a lake after the season's first warming. She looked at me and started laughing hysterically. She was embarrassed but also seemed like she couldn't have expected anything less. Her hair flipped, she smiled, winked, turned red, and walked off.

I remember thinking she was the most beautiful thing I'd ever seen. When those glasses came down, she walked away as if they shattered and exposed all her secrets. In that split second you could see her vulnerability. You could see the real her, the show she put on, and you could see a warrior protecting herself from the atrocities of the world. She was a wild child. She was everything I wanted to be.

—

We got up and walked out into the night. I looked up and stared at the sky. A shooting star flamed past my eyes and I thought about Jane. We kept walking, smoking, and talking about the world, and I thought about Pocahontas. About halfway to the hotel, a girl was riding by on a bike. She crossed the street, hit a pothole, and went flying through the air, landing on her back. A few people were standing outside and rushed to her aid. I remember thinking that's what was right with the world. Then I looked down at the pothole, thinking that's what's wrong. Fucking potholes.

We got to our hotel. I went to my room, ran a bath, and sat in it. The water was hot and it felt good. I lit a square and reached for my phone. My cousin texted me and asked if I was going to be home for Christmas. I told her I was, but I wasn't going to be attending the family gathering. She told me that Mom missed me and I told her: She has my number.

I threw my phone across the bathroom and just stared at the ceiling. I opened my mind to what the world was giving me. I started to hum and hum louder; I started to sing in a stream of consciousness. Words came out of me like water rushing over a dam.

> I could see Change staring back at me.
> She said, Son, it's time to see
> All the things you're meant to be
> All the things you cannot see
> All the ways and all the means
> Oh, the better man to be.
> I could see Change staring back at me.
> I said, Thank you but listen:
> I've never seen the man,
> I've never met the man,
> I've never been the man
> I'd rather be.

I reached for a bottle of red wine I had opened earlier. I took a pull, gagged, and poured the rest in the water. All around me it billowed through the clear liquid, like a red tide. Everything turned bright red. *This is what it would look like if I slit my wrists,* I thought. But I never had the balls to do anything like that. I never would. For whatever reason, it feels like I'm supposed to be here in this world. I sat back drunk and fell asleep in the tub.

Hours later my phone buzzed. I woke up and the water was cold, and still bloodred. I reached for a towel, got out, and dried off. I remembered throwing my phone, but I didn't remember where. It buzzed again, and I found it next to the wardrobe. It was a text from Francis.

> F: man lil brother, i'm not doing to good these days man, and i'm sorry for all the choices i've made that will soon take me again to prison, away from everyone i hold in the warm part of my heart. know

> that i love you in the deepest and there is no place anyone could ever keep me that can take that from me. i only wish i could have chosen wiser or moved with u from the jump so that i could still be someone for you to be able to look up to or console with about important things. i love you.

The elevator inside me dropped, and I texted him back.

B: i love you too.

I threw my phone on the bed and got dressed. I had to go meet the guys so we could sound check and play for a bunch of drunk Aussies. The monotony of this life was tearing away at me day by day. My one escape had become a chore, and I glided through the show feeling physically there, but not mentally. From what I recall it went well, but I couldn't have cared less.

When we finished, we walked to the dressing room and began to decompress from the show. As I was taking out my in-ear monitors, Asher stared at me.

I looked at him. "What?"

"Brooo, just wondering if you're okay. I mean, you played fine, but I don't even feel like you're here today. Everything cool?"

"I'm fine. Just got a lot on the brain right now."

He bit his lip. "You miss Em? Or?"

I leaned my head back and sighed. "Yeah, but it's more the shit in Texas I gotta deal with."

"Mom stuff?"

I nodded. "Yeah, *and* brother stuff. Well, it's the same thing."

"What do you mean?"

"Well, it's a long story, but I kind of feel like she ruined Francis and my family in general."

Asher wasn't programmed to deal with statements like that. He looked around the room like he was grasping for anyone to help him with his words. "Well, I'm sure you'll get it all figured out. I mean, everything works itself out eventually, right? Brooo, you'll be fine."

I wanted to punch him in his cliché-spouting face, but instead I fake smiled. "Thanks, man. I know." I looked over at Hank, who was cleaning off Luke's hat, which had somehow got Drew's weed trimmings all over it. "What's the plan for tonight?"

He brushed the hat and looked at me. "The usual except the label wants to hang."

I nodded. "What's the name of the bar, then?"

"Shady Pines."

"And when are we leaving?"

He brushed the hat more, getting the last of the crumbs off, then looked at his phone. "In exactly two minutes."

"Great. Have you ever heard of this place?"

"Emily from the label says it's amazing. I think it's some sort of country-western bar."

"Oh."

I wiped my face and lit up a square. "Well, I'm ready."

SHADY PINES

It was a fine bar. The wood was recently stained and smelled like cedar, and the walls were covered in fresh taxidermy: fox, moose, raccoon—you name it. Everywhere you'd walk, they'd stare at you, watching your every move, making you question everything you've ever done, or were planning on doing. It felt like they knew your secrets, the ones that were innocent, the ones that were embarrassing, and especially the ones you hated. Their frozen snarls, sharp teeth, and exposed tongues were a reminder that no one is happy about dying. As if even at their last breath, they were pissed and fighting. I looked up at the light fixtures. They were made out of deer antlers. I couldn't tell if they were real or not, but either way it was ominous. This place was death.

I turned to our label rep and asked if Shady Pines was chosen because she thinks Americans like everything western? Her response was "No, it was chosen 'cause *we* like everything western. It's romantic. It reminds me of the Marlboro man, you know, that manly cowboy." I nodded and pulled out a square, stuck it in my mouth, then looked at the walls again. I began to imagine Mom and Francis up there, mounted on the walls, staring at each other. Mom's face would be angry and tired, with her mouth open, looking like a wolf. Francis's face would be calm and reserved, almost as if he expected this day was coming, like it was a shadow on his back. I took the square out of my mouth and threw it on the ground. Then I walked out of Shady Pines and never looked back.

—

I got to the hotel and packed my bags. Then walked out of my clothes and into bed. I stared at the ceiling, thinking about the image of Mom and France on the wall. It was haunting and stuck to me like honey. I was happy that we were headed back to the States tomorrow. No matter how much I hated it, no matter how much I avoided it, at least I'd be closer to the problem in Texas. My phone buzzed. It was Hank texting me to see where I was. Good ole Hank. I told him I wasn't feeling the bar and went back to my room. His response was: Copy. See you tomorrow at exactly nine a.m.

KANSAS CITY, KANSAS

We all walked into a restaurant that served chicken wings, grilled or fried, in three different flavors: mild, hot, and extra-hot. The servers were all young, with blonde, blue, red, purple, or brown hair, and wore short flannel skirts with white button-up shirts that weren't buttoned too high. If you could ogle their cleavage, they'd make more money.

We were greeted by a dark birdie with a smile. Her lipstick was carefully applied for the third time today, but we focused more on her knee-high white socks and the black ribbon bows on each side, left for us to unwrap. Then our eyes slid down to the shiny black penny shoes that had a strap with a buckle across. I could see a blurred reflection of my face, and I imagined a world of bondage just as she intended.

Her name was Roxy, and her name tag said that she was "employee of the month" exactly two and a half years ago. Her complexion was pale in comparison to her personality. Her smile, though fake, felt genuine. She asked, "How many?" And Hank slowly held up five fingers. Luke and his hat stood there looking awkward, not wanting to bring attention to the fact that he found her attractive. Asher stared at her breasts probably because he felt like he was supposed to, and Drew was miles deep in his phone, looking for the newest piece of ass that had recently posted a picture on Instagram. Roxy showed us to our table and we all followed behind, scouting the restaurant for talent. The place was a sports bar, with HD flat-screen TVs, wooden shelves that were held up by semi-rusted steel rods protruding from the redbrick wall, and vintage sports memorabilia—fakes, of course.

In the men's room, you'd walk to the four-foot-long porcelain pisser, stare at a fading picture of the 1952 New York Yankees, and piss in dead ice, trying not to get any on your pants or shoes. Naturally I failed. "They're just shoes," I said aloud to no one.

The light-colored wooden tables were full of obese half-bearded men with green and black trucker hats and jeans that didn't quite cover their ass cracks. The ones who fit into the booths were also wearing trucker hats, but they looked like meth heads. They all had worn, sad faces that told stories of failed families and dead-end jobs, and they all carried a faint stench of must and chemicals, maybe from cooking blue crystal in their closets. Their hands were like brick masons', with tears and calluses and occasional blood blisters from the skin being pinched in a way it hadn't been before. They all had missing or black teeth rotting from all the sugar they consumed, and their hair was thinning from their hats squashing it down. They came to this godforsaken shithole to stare at birdies and dream, 'cause here the girls wore short flannel skirts and unbuttoned shirts and were paid to flirt and give you heart attacks on a plate, while your pathetic cock hit the underside of the table in hopes of getting some action from a young thing, even though reality always made sure you didn't.

—

We sat down and stared at the wondrous flock around us, licking our lips not because we were hungry, but because we were thirsty. Eventually a young server and her shadow came up to greet us with that same fake, lipsticked smile. She had brittle, dreadlocked hair that looked like pieces of hay wrapped around itself, and it looked like it needed a good dry shampoo. Her round nose was decorated with a golden septum ring and her tongue with a silver ball. They looked less like fashion statements and more like sexual accessories. Her makeup was poorly done, as though she had never properly learned from her mother or she had no friends to teach her. The neon blues and pinks and sparkly glitter told a story of being young and on her own. She was trashy but acceptable; you could roll around in her for a good long minute. The small brown beauty mark above her right eye made me think someone appreciated it as much as I did, and that at least once in her life she was loved because of it.

The shadow girl, however, was more my speed. She was a brunette with an asymmetrical haircut, where one side of her hair covered a few parts of her milky face with sinewy triangles. She was skinny, not the skinny that didn't eat, but the kind that was fortunate enough to have good genetics and wide enough hips to never question whether she had an eating disorder. Her space-like eyes were rosy brown and looked perfect for hiding secrets. Her breasts were perky and a good size, more than a handful, and her makeup was tastefully done. Not too much, not too little, just the way it should always be. Her mouth was semicrooked, and her smile was a nice shade of burgundy. She was holding a white menu and small yellow notepad, and I noticed her nails with chipped black paint and how they looked just long enough to tickle my parts. She would turn around to other tables and her hair would follow behind. She'd smile to the tables of sad men and ask them if they needed anything else. Most of the time, it took several seconds for them to realize she was talking since all they could think about was her smile and the way her shirt sounded when it rubbed against the table. She would bend and her skirt would rise like an eyelid exposing her tight little ass in tight little-boy shorts, and she was well aware of the fact that everyone behind her was looking. It would peek from under her skirt, saying, "Hello," and it made every man in the place hungrier than before.

Asher, with his wide eyes and robot grin, poked me in the ribs with his finger, clueing me in to the fact that our shadow waitress was hot. I slapped his hand and shook my head. "I know, you ass, I know!"

He laughed and hit me on the back out of excitement and whispered, "Dude, I think any one of us could have her."

I looked at him and thought to myself how I'd like to take a shovel and zonk him on the head.

"No shit, we could," I said.

Luke ordered a bunch of wings. "All hot'n buffalo, with a round a light beer ta wash 'em down."

Drew just sat back in his chair, overwhelmed by all the women. "Duuudes, I think I'm in heaven."

Two by two the beers came out. Every time Shadow Girl would bring something, she would eye me and smile. I would in turn look her over head to toe, smile, and take sips of my yellow beer.

"You're not from around here, are y'all?" Her accent was thick and southern.

Hank, buried deep in his phone, without looking up, said, "What makes you say that?"

She looked at Hank and seemed slightly flustered since his gaze didn't meet hers. "I dunno. I mean, y'all sure don't dress like you're from here."

I peeked over her shoulder and sure enough the entire table behind us was staring at her ass. I sunk back into my chair, listening to the chatter in the restaurant and the heavy breathing from one of the obese men.

"Well, I guess that's true," I said.

Her eyes flashed at me and she smiled, biting her crooked lip. "Y'all in a band or something?"

I stared at her, making note of a light patch of freckles on her nose. "Eh, we're more a pack of traveling gypsies."

She laughed. "What's that mean?" Her smile looked like a bow without an arrow, and she leaned in a bit more, letting her breasts take over.

Drew instantly sat up and at the same time let out a small burp, causing the whole table to look at him in disgust. "Whoa, excuse me. Yeeaah, we're in a band."

Hank, Asher, and I all turned back to her. Luke and his hat were laughing.

"Which one? Have I heard y'all before?"

"I dunno, maybe you've heard of us," I said. I named the band.

Her face flushed robin red. "No way! I totally know you guys. Y'all got that one song, that, what's it called?"

Drew predictably named the song, then started humming it.

"Yeah, that one!" she said.

I looked at Drew and thought about choking him with her knee-high sock. "Thanks for that, Drew. Seriously, I thought I almost forgot how it went." I rolled my eyes and took a big sip of my beer.

The rest of the guys all laughed, then ignored her. She was talking to the table, but her eyes were looking at me. I hoped she was wondering if my hands looked the same when I was a child, or if I could be the man who wrote love notes for her to wake up to on Sunday mornings. Part of me hoped she was thinking that I could be the one to look at her and not see the short skirt and pair of tits but rather her beautiful mind.

"What in the hell y'all doing out here in the middle of nowhere?"

My eyes closed and snapped me out of my thoughts. "Well, we're just passing through," I said. "We had a show, but we don't have to be at the next one till tomorrow. We're here for most of the night."

"Most of it?" she asked.

I nodded. "We leave at three."

"Hmm, that's not long at all." She looked over her shoulder. "Hey, I'll be right back. I need to go check on my trainer—I think she's gettin' high in the bathroom or somethin'."

I raised my eyebrow. "What kind of high?"

"Green, I think. Why? Want some?" She fingered her sleeve and smiled, not noticing the table next to her, trying to get her attention.

"Maybe later tonight," I said, leaving it open. She looked me up and down, stood up straight, and said, "I'll see what I can do."

As she walked, the bottom of her ass slipped out, exposing a small birthmark on her right cheek. It was in the shape of a puzzle piece or the state of Louisiana, I don't know. As she disappeared, I couldn't help but imagine her as a little girl, somewhere in the country on some farm, wearing oversized brown cowboy boots and a small white Stetson with a feather poking from the hatband. I imagined her kicking up dry dirt, creating clouds of dust, and dancing around, trying to turn them into tornadoes. She would play in dandelions, smiling, pretending she was a lion, laughing as her pride attacked a defenseless beetle. I imagined her getting lost in the tall grass and finding ladybugs, not just the red ones, but the orange ones too, and naming them after her school friends. How she ended up half-naked, serving gross food to even grosser men, I wasn't sure, but I knew at the very least, it was an interesting story.

I looked down at my white plate. I'd eaten only one wing. I wasn't that hungry. The guys managed to tear through almost all of them, leaving behind a graveyard of bare gray bones sitting in bits of buttery orange hot sauce, and I think they were about to order twelve more. I grabbed my beer and took a sip, only it tasted funny.

Hank sighed. "Sure, go ahead and drink my beer," he said as slowly as molasses.

"Oh, my bad." I reached for mine and sipped—much better. For the first time in over five minutes, although I'm sure he'd know more accurately, Hank put his phone down and looked around. I took it as an opportunity to engage in conversation. "Say, what do you think of our server?"

He looked at her, then turned calmly to me, silently counting in his head. "Well. She smells like a hippie with all that patchouli she's got on, and she has a snag tooth, but hey, I'd like to see her naked. She's got a cute butt."

"No, not that one, though she does have a cute butt—the other one."

He looked at her and blinked his eyes. "Oh yeah, she's a cutie."

I began frantically tapping my fingers on the table. "Why is everything 'cute' to you? Whatever happened to 'I'd totally bang her' or 'I'd bite her on the ass'?"

"I don't know; it's just how I talk, I guess."

Hank had all the same thoughts as the rest of us, but he worded them differently, or kept them to himself. He grew up with sisters and a strong motherly presence, and they taught him how all women should be treated. One time his mother slapped him on the hand with a ruler for noticing his sister's growing breasts, even though he hadn't said anything. His friends all lost their virginity at the age of sixteen, while Hank, on the other hand, was scared to because of his strong desire not to sin against God or, for that matter, his mother. In recent years, his faith became distant and he couldn't decide which one out of over three thousand gods to believe in, but he always trusted numbers. Numbers didn't lie.

"You speak like your favorite flavor of ice cream is vanilla," I said.

Hank stared at me. "It is."

"Oh fuck."

"Alright. I'd totally bang her. But at this point she seems like she's into you."

I laughed. "I think I'm gonna invite her back to the bus."

Drew's ears perked up. "Heeey, if you do, tell her to bring some friends for the rest of us."

I closed one eye. "Okay, done deal." Drew dipped his finger in the orange sauce and licked it. "Hank, is the liquor stocked?" I asked.

"At the beginning of tour we started with seven bottles, the three whiskeys were drunk, the two tequilas haven't been touched, the one vodka fell off the shelf and broke, and the gin was half-gone. We should be all good."

"Cool. I think she's gonna bring some smoke too."

"Waaait, what kind?" asked Drew.

I smiled. "Your favorite. It's green and smells delicious."

"Niiice!" said Drew.

Shadow Girl came out of the bathroom looking like she had unnecessarily fixed herself up. Her makeup was reapplied, and her shirt was unbuttoned slightly more, revealing three little marks on her left breast that when connected made a triangle. She shook her ass walking to the table and, predictably, everyone stared. She leaned over and handed me a torn white piece of paper with green writing.

"Here's my number. I get off at ten and I can come meet you wherever, and I got what you asked for." She smiled and bit her crooked lip again.

I looked at the paper. It was folded, but a looped *L* was sticking out the top. "Sounds good. Say, you got any friends for the rest of these degenerates?"

"Well, I can bring Ashley." She pointed to her dreadlocked trainer, who had just walked out of the bathroom. *She does look like an Ashley,* I thought. "And I have a few other girls I can call up. A few of them got boyfriends, though."

I licked my teeth with a closed mouth, thinking they needed to be brushed. "That's okay, as long as they don't bring them," I said.

She smiled and fidgeted with her skirt, attempting to pull it down so the table behind her could breathe and go back to eating their fried chicken parts. "I'll see what I can do."

I grinned and thought, *Famous last words.*

She walked away, looked back, and waved.

I unfolded the note fully. It had the name "Pearl" written on it in her looped cursive. Below that was her number, only her fours looked like nines. And below that was a lipstick kiss. I smiled and put the note in my pocket. It seemed like the entire restaurant had been listening in on our conversation. When she left, no one turned around and stared at her ass. I did, of course, but no one else. Instead, they all stared at our table with contempt. At that moment, they hated me for achieving what they wanted. When they were done thinking about the ways they could kill this weird group of *skinny-jeaned faggots,* they stared into their beer like the sad barflies they were.

I looked around.

"Let's get the fuck out of this terrible place," I said.

We all stood up, wiped our faces clean of orange sauce and chicken grease, threw more than enough cash on the table, and left.

THE BUS

Later that night Pearl showed up with six other girls. Four of them were just as captivating as she was: skinny, porcelain skinned, smelling like cherries. One of them was pierced, dreadlocked Ashley, and another was round. Not round like a ball, but round like a button. She wasn't fat, she wasn't skinny, and she had a cute and kind face. We drank Don Julio with soda water and lime, and the girls drank Chopin Vodka and soda. Drew and Hank would occasionally go outside with a few of the girls and smoke up. They'd come in high, weightless, narrow eyed, and drunk—all pretending like this was where they wanted to be. A picture, a video, and hell, even just a story was enough to make them stay. Asher and Luke were silently fighting with their eyes over who would get the girl they were both into. I saw them do a rock-paper-scissors game to decide. "Rock, paper, scissors, fuck!" Then they both laughed hysterically, acknowledging that the fate of that girl and a fuck relied on a child's game. She was a notch in the belt, a line on an insignificant piece of paper, a scratch in a record no one noticed.

Asher ended up with the round girl, but he sat there smiling, probably thinking of her pretty, circular face, and how it would look between his legs. Everyone was using someone for a fuck or a good story, or even the false hope of fifteen minutes of fame with their peers. I wanted to think I was more into the thought of holding Pearl's hand for a while, or noticing the way she smelled when she flipped her hair. But all I wanted to do at the moment was bite her. She sat down in a corner bench on the bus, so naturally I sat next to her. Her dress was beautifully colored in reds, blues, and yellows, and made you want to smile and feel happy even if you were a miserable piece of shit like me. When she walked in, everyone complimented her on it, and I imagined taking it off. I'm sure they did too. She was wearing dark-blue heels that exposed a tattoo she had on her right foot, and her walnut hair was down and shimmered in the lights like armor in the sun.

I was staring at her, not saying anything, just thinking, and she began to look uncomfortable. My eyes clicked like a bullet in a chamber. I said, "So what do you do here for fun?"

She looked at me, clearly glad that I broke the silence, but perhaps disappointed by my question.

"Ya mean, like, in this town?"

I looked around, feeling stupid, knowing the shallow question would be answered, but even I wasn't that interested. "Yeah."

She laughed and rolled her eyes. "Truthfully, this is it."

"What? Hang out with guys in rock bands and get drunk?" I asked.

She grinned. "The drunk part," she said.

I forgot about her accent. She sounded like a modern-day Vivien Leigh but not so slow, and not so farm. It was intriguing and sexy. I smiled and took a sip of my tequila. It was cold and fizzy and felt good on my cotton mouth.

"Are you from here?"

She twisted her lip and fingered her drink. "No, I'm from Arkansas. I came here about six months ago."

Seems about right, I thought. "Why'd you choose this place?"

"Well, I have an aunt an' uncle that live here. Thought I'd come stay with them for a while. You know, family trouble at home."

"That's all families seem to be, huh?"

"What, trouble?"

I began to think about my mother.

Her expression turned serious and then she looked into her cup, grinning. "Well, I'm the trouble, to be honest."

"What do you mean?" I asked.

"Well, don't judge me, okay?"

A million reasons why she'd say something like that crept into my mind like bugs through cracks in a wall.

"Okay, I won't." *I might not get laid,* I thought. *Hell, I might not want to.*

"Well, I'm a recoverin' addict."

I made it a point not to change my facial expression even though I was thinking about Francis. "What are you recovering from?"

"I'd rather not say," she said, and began rubbing her elbow.

"Okay. That's crazy."

She turned red. "Don't judge me!"

"Hey, I'm not." I stared into my drink, thinking about whether I was going to tell her about France and my mother. I decided it might benefit me if I did.

"Truthfully, my brother's an addict. He's addicted to heroin and is currently using. To be honest, I don't think he's even trying to stop."

She looked at me, probably wondering if I was telling the truth. "It's hard."

"I can't imagine," I said.

"You know, the hardest part is figurin' out why you do it. You go to counselin' and try to address the root of the issues. My shrink told me I did it as a way to deal with my past," she said.

The only thing my shrink ever told me was that playing music and writing were the only ways I was able to cope with my past. All that money spent just to find out that my real therapy was the thing I was passionate about in life. Everything I was already doing. He did say my misery was self-inflicted, but I chalk that up to enjoying cloudy days. Sunshine isn't for everyone.

"What do you mean?" I asked.

She licked her lips and stared at a speck of dust floating in the air, then nothing. "Well, my dad was an abusive drunk and my mother doesn't do anythin' about it. I guess I didn' wanna be home or face any of it, so I tried it one day, and for the moment it made me forget about all those horrible things. I felt incredible. You coulda hit me over the head with a baseball bat, and I wouldn'a cared."

I looked around and thought about her with a needle in her arm and someone bludgeoning her to death, blood shooting everywhere, skull bits on the concrete; then I thought about Francis sleeping—the only time he seemed to be at peace. Then I thought about what to say and looked at her black-hole eyes.

"Well, I'm glad you're finding peace with it; I'm glad you stopped using. I mean, I don't even know you, but I'm glad you're becoming someone you'd prefer to be."

She lowered her head, and I saw a face I had seen on Francis a thousand times. I knew what she was thinking about.

"You're sweet," she said, sorrowfully smiling.

"I'm just being honest. I hope my brother finds peace like you did."

She took a big gulp of her drink. "Well, I got a ways to go, but for now I think I'm alright."

I looked at her neck and how she swallowed her drink, and how it made the space between her clavicles move and how it accentuated her breasts. "You look more than alright to me."

She laughed and bit her lip again.

"So what happened with everything at home?"

She tilted her head like a confused dog. "What do you mean?"

"Well, is your dad still there?"

"Yeah. He's still there, more'n likely not changed at all. I can't figure out why my mom won't do nothin' 'bout it."

I thought about it for a moment. "Love's weird, I guess."

"I can't fathom why or how she could ever love that drunk idiot bastard." She sighed. "What about you?"

"What about me?"

"Well, you told me about your brother, but you didn't say anythin' about you. Clearly he's running away from somethin', but what're *you* runnin' away from?"

I thought about it for a second. "Nothing that I can think of."

She smiled. "Bullshit, we're all runnin' from somethin'."

I looked around the bus, then at my feet. "I guess everyone's past has shitty moments."

We sat silent for a minute; I sipped my drink, and she just stared, waiting.

"I guess my mom was pretty crazy. Never physically abusive or anything, but she pretty much fucked up the whole family."

I knew my situation was nowhere near as shitty as hers.

"She had postpartum depression with my brother, cheated on my dad, got remarried, then my stepfather died. One day she blamed me for something I didn't do, and I never heard from her after that. I dunno, it doesn't sound so bad, but parts are. She basically abandoned us 'cause she couldn't deal with her own shit."

Her face lit up suddenly. Maybe she didn't feel so small and alone. "I'm sorry you had to go through that."

"Me too, but it is what it is. Not much else can be said."

"Well, I tell you what, there's always two sides to the story. If ya ever hear from her again maybe you should ask her—heck, maybe you should reach out to her."

"I've heard her side, and I *have* reached out. For *years*, I reached out. Something's wrong with her mentally. The other day she stopped recognizing my brother. Also, she blames my padre for everything, but I dunno. What happened to them is none of my business, but after hearing everything for years and years and years, I came to my own conclusions."

She nodded. "What did ya figure out?"

"That she can't face her own problems, that she always runs away, that she's got deep issues. She shouldn't have been married."

"So what happens if she dies?"

Those words hit me like a hammer. "What do you mean?"

"Well, I dunno. Wouldn't you have regrets?"

"Yes, I would. But it wouldn't be anything I couldn't live with."

She narrowed her eyes. "I know what you mean." Her head turned away again. "The only thing I'd regret if I never saw my dad again is not gettin' to tell him that he lost. That he tried so hard to ruin my life, and that he lost."

We sat in silence for a few moments, staring at the broken ice in our cups; the white part was never as attractive as the clear part. I looked up at her face and her smile seemed to wane, but it wasn't fake.

"I didn't expect our conversation to be so heavy!" she softly shouted.

We both laughed.

"Me either. Sometimes strangers are the best listeners, I guess."

She reached for my hand and held it. I squeezed hers, feeling the flesh exciting me. "I need another drink."

She agreed. "Me too—hey, got any cigarettes?"

I winked, closed my eye, and ruffled through my pockets. "Yeah, let's do that too."

We walked over to the bus sink, poured ourselves two more drinks into red Solo cups, and walked outside. She took a square and lit it, and I did the same. I grabbed her arm. "Let's go over here." I took her to the side of the bus where no one could see us.

We stood there looking at each other, smoking and smiling. She started to pull on my arm, and I started to squeeze her back. We threw our squares and immediately pushed into each other's faces. Her lips tasted like strawberry, and her hair smelled like lavender. I started to get a hard-on and she pulled me closer. We kissed, tongues flowing in and out of each other's mouths, and I reached for her right breast. She started panting hard and a little drop of sweat formed. We stopped kissing, and she fixed her dress.

"How long did you say you were here for?" she asked.

I walked to the door of the bus and opened it. I popped my head in.

"Hank! Hank!!" I was yelling over the music.

Annoyed at me for interrupting his conversation with one of the porcelain birds, he turned his head on a slow-five count and asked me, "What?"

My right eye ticked because who the fuck was he to be upset at me for asking him a question?

"When are we leaving?"

He said something I couldn't hear, so I walked in all the way. I looked around and Asher, Luke, and two porcelains were gone. Drew was sitting there with dreadlocked Ashley and another beak, high as a cloud. I turned the music down for a second and repeated my question, this time with a fuck-you attitude.

"When are we leaving?"

Hank looked at his phone. "Thirty minutes, not before and better not be after."

My eyes widened. "Holy shit—thirty minutes!?"

Hank's eyes glazed over as he snuck back into his head, no doubt remembering the exact time he told everyone what time bus call was.

"Yes, I told you earlier today—at two p.m.—that we leave at three tonight."

I shook my head, doubting myself and not Hank. "Okay. Hey, give me a key to that room we have."

I turned the music back up and then ran out of the bus. I looked at Pearl and pointed to the hotel. "Wanna go in there for twenty minutes?"

She laughed and without hesitation said, "Yes."

We walked in holding hands, me in front, her in back, straight to the elevator. She was probably remembering the last time someone led her to bed and how she woke up regretting it. When they finished fucking, did they stick needles in their arms and fade into the floor like spilled water? Did she wake up alone, cold and naked? This time would be different.

We managed to avoid all the eyes looking at us, knowing what was about to go down. In the elevator, I kept grabbing her ass and she would just smile and laugh. We got to the room and I immediately picked her up and threw her on the bed. We started making out and I started tearing off her clothes like a carrot peeler. First her dress. She wasn't wearing a bra, and her breasts were magnificent. Her stomach was flat, and she was wearing a light-blue thong with lace. I kissed her mouth, and then moved to sucking on her breasts and grabbing her back. I worked my way down and kissed on her cunt through her thong, teasing her with my tongue. She moaned and her nipples became hard. I worked my way all the way down her legs and started to lick on her tattooed right foot. I flipped her over, and she grabbed the sheets tight and white knuckled. I kissed her neck and then her back, and then her lower back. I made her put her ass in the air, and I bit her birthmark. Right as I moved to take off her thong, she stopped me.

"Wait, wait. You're gonna hate me."

"What?"

"Well, I'm on my period."

"So what!"

I turned her back around and made her put her ass in the air again, and I slowly pulled her thong off, licking her ass. The string to her tampon was hanging out of her, and I tugged at it a little with my teeth. I licked all around her, and then moved her into the sixty-nine position. She pulled down my pants and started to go down on me. I started to lick her clit, and she was moaning and shaking. She came and all of her pulsated, then she finished me off. She got off from me and started to kiss me. She passed me a little bit of my own cum. We both swallowed and then lay next to each other on the bed, naked and panting.

"That was incredible," I said. The taste of my own cum was salty, but her cherry lip gloss made it taste fine.

"Yes, it was." A drop of sweat rolled down her chest slowly, not fighting gravity, the perfect picture of a good time.

I lay there thinking about how beautiful she was covered in sweat. "What time is it?" I asked.

She reached over and turned around the blinking clock, red numbers flashing on black.

"Twenty minutes!"

"What?! Ha ha, that's amazing. And it means we still have time to smoke a square together!"

"Yes! We did it!" she laughed.

I kissed her, inhaling her lavender hair, walked into the bathroom, and closed the door. I lifted the seat up to piss and began whistling some nonspecific tune. When I was done, I avoided looking in the mirror like always and walked out. She was standing up naked, putting on her dress. At that moment, she looked like my mother.

I was nine, and it was time to go to school. I was at my mother's house, which at that point was my grandmother's house. It had a shag tri-toned brown carpet that covered most of the floor, and the exterior was a light shade of blue. The lawn was huge and had a few giant oak trees that my cousins, France, and I would climb every now and then. In the back was a toolshed, where my grandfather kept all of his tools and where my grandmother did all of her laundry.

I had finished breakfast, which consisted of Cream of Wheat and burnt toast, and walked into my mother's room. She was naked, and I remember staring at her breasts for a minute and thinking that her nipples were dark. I also remember thinking she was beautiful. When she saw me staring, she started to yell at me. She covered herself up, and told me I should be ashamed of myself, and that I was starting to get to an age where it was inappropriate to stare. I don't remember what I said next, but she slapped me and I started crying. I remember the pain, and I remember she was wearing her ring at the time. Then she started to cry. I ran out of the room feeling embarrassed, like I had done something wrong. My grandmother saw me and asked me what happened. I looked at her and told her Mother had slapped me. She stomped over to my mother and started to yell at her in Spanish. Years later, when I think about that moment, I remember hearing my mother yell at Francis the same way my grandmother yelled at her.

Pearl got dressed, and we walked outside hand in hand. I kissed her and said goodbye, and she grabbed my hand hard. She told me to watch myself out there, especially in LA, since that was our next stop. She smiled and said, "It's the land of hussies and fake people, and they're worse than you 'n' me . . . but not that much worse." I laughed and told her I would, then gave her a kiss and wished her good luck. She asked me for a square, so I handed her one, lit it up, and started to walk on the bus.

She stood in front of the window with her back to me, staring at the brightly freckled sky. The moon was nowhere to be seen, but she glowed enough to light the air.

Then she started to speak. "You know, it's incredible."

I stopped in front of the door. "What is?"

She kept staring at the sky. "This night. I mean . . . I feel like all life should be like this. We're endin' this on a high note. I don't wanna see you ever again, and I know you don't wanna see me ever again. We both know that if we did, we'd give each other the chance to ruin whatever this night was for both of us."

She paused, and I was silent. "It's better this way," she said.

She never looked back.

When I walked in, everyone was either saying goodbye to their birds, or they were already in bed. I walked to my bunk, wondering about Pearl and her future and, more interesting to me, her past. What made her father abusive? Maybe Pearl's grandfather was also an abusive drunk asshole.

What about my grandmother and mother's relationship, and Francis? Pearl reminded me of my mother; hell, she even looked like my mother. Where did Mom's issues all come from? I know my grandmother's a bitch, but what made her that way? Roots grow deep, and their soil must be healthy and well tended for them not to be rotten. Grandmother was rotten; she was Mother's poison.

HOLLYWOOD HILLS

We rented a house in the hills of Los Angeles. I say house, but it was more like a mansion. You walked in, and there was a set of wooden stairs that went up, and a set of stairs that went down. Upstairs, large hardwood-floored halls led to bedrooms. Each of them had a Jacuzzi or a claw-foot tub, a balcony, and one even had a swing. I opted for the claw-foot, as I liked to sit with my legs and arms hanging out of the hot water, smoke squares, and just think. Drew, miles deep in Instagram ass, took the swing in hopes of putting it to good use. I set my leather bags down, walked to the balcony, and looked out. A house in the hills was high up there. It overlooked all the other houses and made you feel like you were in a castle. It took twenty fucking minutes to get up the damn hill, so it had better be impressive. All these pathetic people lived here, thinking it was important to have social status in a world that moves too fast to remember anything or anyone. What a time to be barely alive.

We had a label showcase and decided that we should take advantage of it and have a small vacation as well. Three days, no more, no less. I heard Luke and Asher arguing about who would get the big room, so I closed the balcony door and just sat.

The birds were chirping away, talking about the new neighbors who had just moved in for the week. The sun was beating down hard on the lush green hills, reminding everyone how big and strong it was. In the distance a red-tailed hawk was hovering, surveying the area, looking for its next meal. I grunted and thought about it gnawing on a mouse. "Peaceful," I said aloud to no one, and took out a square. I thumbed through my pocket and somehow still had the matchbook from Norway. I pulled out one of the few remaining white-tipped matches and lit up. I inhaled deeply and stared at the book like it was an old family heirloom that held our secrets and passions. Then I threw it over the balcony, imagining jumping off myself. It managed to land in the orange-leaf-covered hot tub down below.

Luke, his hat, and Ash were still arguing about the rooms, so I opened the door and screamed, "Put your dicks away!"

They both yelled simultaneously, "Fuck you!"

I smiled and yelled back, "Yeah, yeah, fuck me!" At least they agreed about something.

I needed a drink. I walked into the kitchen. It was new; it didn't look lived-in at all. The brushed-steel sinks were sterile, and the jet-black oven was still encased in a plastic film, waiting for someone to unwrap it like a present and use it. I opened the distressed white cabinets and found that Hank had stocked us deep: three bottles of 1800—one Silver, two Reposado; two bottles of Eagle Rare whiskey; and one bottle of Grey Goose for the skirts, if any were over. I grabbed a Reposado and poured one over ice with Perrier. I sipped at it, and every time it touched my tongue, I sighed in relief.

I walked into the living room and saw the red-felt-covered pool table. Once again, this house looked so mismatched. I wondered how much smut had been filmed here. I sat down on the couch, carefully looking for cum stains. The yelling from the bedrooms had subsided, and everything was quiet. *Finally*, I thought. Then Hank slowly walked in and loudly made announcements to the whole house.

"Listen up! We need to leave the house in ten minutes so we can make sound check in forty-five! The car will be here in three minutes, so if you're ready now, get in the car when it arrives. The venue is No Vacancy, and it's a cool spot. If you have any guests, let me know by the time we're done with sound check, which will be at six thirty!"

I looked up from my drink. "Goddamn it, Hank, can you stop fucking yelling?"

He calmly looked at me, no doubt counting how many words had just spewed out of my mouth. (Seven, to be exact.) He looked over my head, not in my eyes.

"How is everyone going to hear me?" Then he looked at me like I had just called his mother a cunt or something.

"No one is listening."

"Yes, but if I don't say anything, you guys are going to be mad at me and say I didn't give you any info beforehand."

"Everyone's a fucking hypocrite." I giggled.

He smiled, probably thinking that—while grateful for the job—he would like to slowly peel away our faces one at a time, taking only one minute each so that it was done in a crude fashion and without attention to detail.

Twenty minutes later we all piled into a black Escalade and made our way to the venue.

"So, where we goin' again?" Luke and his hat asked. His accent reminded me of Pearl's, but crazier.

"God-fucking-damn it!" yelled Hank.

"See what I mean?" I smiled.

—

We arrived at No Vacancy and were greeted by the club's owner. He was a tall Asian American man who was wearing a stylish gray fedora made of sleek badger fur. Apparently, he always wore it so you could pick him out of a crowd, and after we complimented him on it, he claimed that, in a way, "The hat seems more important than my face." He was right—without the hat, he was forgettable.

He had us set up upstairs with bottles of liquor and various finger foods that Hank requested. The venue itself was beautiful and looked like a big brown Victorian house. You could drive right past it and never know it existed, but that was the point. Whore hotels were supposed to be inconspicuous. When you walked in the back door, if the doorman felt you were attractive enough to enter, you had to walk up a dark and damp stairway. When you got to the top, there were three wooden doors, with no signs, no nothing. Just three wooden doors anxiously waiting for you to open them. The first door was locked, and had us all saying, "What the fuck?" The second door opened but to a broom closet that had a blue broom with corn bristles in the corner. Luke and his hat said, "Alright, Drew, time to get to work, señor," and had everyone laughing. The third door opened to a bedroom with a lovely brunette bird with big bird eyes in lingerie, sitting on the bed with her bird legs spread. Her panties had a slight rise in the crotch, making her lips look thick.

The whole place was a glorification of prostitution, and I didn't mind it. We walked in, stepped over a few dark leather books. There were vintage hats and sandpapered dressers, and a few old paintings on the wall. But the most important visual was the girl. She asked if we had been there before, then went through a whole rehearsed talk about how there's only one entrance and you have to find your way out and yada, yada, yada. Then she pushed a button and the bed split in half, exposing the springs and cotton guts, revealing a set of stairs underneath it that went down to the club. It was a lot of frills, and made you feel important, like you knew a secret no one else knew. Only, everyone knew about it.

We got to the greenroom and made ourselves a drink. Hank said something calculated and inaudible, but we all knew he was trying to get us to go downstairs to sound check. So we walked down and started to go through our usual routine, only this time, the in-ear monitor system that the company had provided was shit. I swear to God it was from the fucking '90s.

"Every time I move, my ears go in and out," I said. I lit up a square. "Is this happening to anyone else?"

"Yeeeah, same for me," said Drew.

"Yeah," said Luke.

Asher just nodded.

I turned to Hank, who was staring at the sound tech. "This isn't going to work, Hank."

He looked at me, then shifted his eyes slowly to the tech, then back to me.

"Okay, hold on, we're going to move one of the antennas and try to boost the signal."

I watched the skinny piece-of-shit plugged-ear sound-company guy move as slow as a constipated bowel movement and attempt to reposition the antenna paddle. He sauntered back, pulling at a beer with a shit-eating grin, and I remember thinking what an asshole this guy was. Hank looked back at me. "Is that better?"

My eye twitched, and I blew out a puff of smoke. "I dunno." I clicked off, started a song, and the sound kept going in and out. It was like listening to the radio while someone who was a particular asshole periodically turned it off. If this was a show where we didn't rely on ears, and clicks, and we were trying to sound like shit, maybe I wouldn't have cared, but that's never the case.

"Still in and out." I was starting to become frustrated.

The sound prick fiddled with a few knobs to make it look like he was doing something, and after explaining what he was doing to Hank, who looked like he was thinking of dropping this guy down a well after he gutted him like a fish, he asked, "How about now?"

I bit the inside of my lip and started another song.

"Same shit." I watched the sound prick take another pull of his beer, and the sweat on his upper lip started to gross me out. I couldn't help but think this human was a shit stain on the underwear of a forgotten and faceless profession.

"How about now?"

I started another song—same shit. I got up from my throne, took off my ears, and threw the pack into the middle of the floor. It hit the concrete with such force that the metal casing cracked, revealing the D batteries that it used for power. (Normally they use AAs.) I watched the arc of the device, and from the moment it left my hand, the shit-eating grin on the sound-fuck's face disappeared.

"What the fuck is this shit anyway? It's heavier than a fucking VCR. Hank, this is bullshit, and I'm not sound checking until you get a normal set of ears for us. We're supposed to all be professional—I don't fucking know what this guy's trying to be."

I pointed to the sound prick with two fingers in the shape of a gun. "This is bullshit; I'm fucking done."

The sound idiot looked at me like I had just taken away his paycheck. "Hey, man, you can't do that. That's company equipment! I'll get chewed out for this!"

I shook my head. "I'm doing you a fucking favor. This shit deserves to be in a museum. I'm sure you're fine at what you do, but we're not a fucking bar band. If your boss has a problem, tell him to call me so I can tell him to go fuck himself."

Hank walked over, stopped, looked at me, and said, "Are you sure you can't make this work?"

"Goddamn it, Hank, *no*! And you know what? We're not in a position where we should *have* to make this work. If you asked me if it was okay to play a different drum kit—sure. If you asked me if it was okay that I had chicken instead of fish—sure. But not fucking this. Not the stuff that should always be consistent, never the show."

He sighed. "Okay, you're right." Then he grabbed the ear packs. "Let me make a call."

I lit up another square. Everyone other than the band was probably thinking I was an asshole, but I didn't care. They didn't do this every day. And as far as I was concerned, they could all rot in hell. One by one, they started to come up to me and apologize, pretending like they actually cared, or their apology affected me in some shape or form. I know I'm an asshole. I would never claim not to be.

Hank buried his ear in his phone and called another company. After going over the numbers, he said, "New packs will be here in twenty minutes."

I rolled my eyes. "New packs should have been the first thing that was here, before we showed up." Then I smiled.

Hank seemed to be relieved by my smile. He grinned. "It's not what I requested."

"Double-check it next time; we shouldn't be put in this position. The band should never look like the bad guy."

Hank laughed. "I'm pretty sure I'm the one who told you that."

I shrugged my shoulders and pursed my lips for a second, trying to remember when he told me that, but I knew he was right and could probably tell me the exact date and time.

I walked over to a table and poured two shots of Jameson and handed one to Hank.

"Cheers, you prick." We downed them.

Fifteen minutes later the packs showed up. We sound checked smoothly and decided it was time to get some food.

BUTCHERS & BARBERS

Butchers & Barbers was a new American restaurant that had crispy chicken on brussels sprouts, steaks with fingerling potatoes, and all things gastropub. When you walked in, an aroma of citrusy old-fashioneds kicked you in the nose and made you look up. High on the walls were vintage, weathered, even burnt-in-the-corner pictures of mustached boxers promoting a new hair wax, illustrated cuts of meat so you knew the difference between a skirt and a shell steak, and old barber chairs with illustrations of straight razors. The few portraits of naked pinups that were in the corner seemed like a shrine to the "good ole days."

Hank told me that the cocktails were incredible, so I ordered some version of an old-fashioned they concocted that tasted slightly like a root beer. I loved it. The cold Buffalo Trace bourbon hit my throat like a frozen lake, and the bitters on the back end reminded me of tree bark. The sugar and root flavor balanced out the drink, making it a journey instead of an affair.

We were seated at a table in the back, past all the other beautiful people, in a private room located behind a bookcase. After we sat and bickered like brothers about stupid nothings, the chef came out and greeted us. He was skinny-fat, with sleeves of tattoos and gray hair. His ring finger on his right hand had a tan line where you could tell a big, fat gold ring rested when he wasn't cooking. We did the usual introduction, and he pretended to know and care about us, which made us feel good, and said he would take care of the ordering.

Tonight our meal was going to be family-style. Luke and Drew were into the idea, I didn't care much, but I could tell Asher wasn't. He had that only-child thing about him, and he was about to speak up, but Luke quickly shook his head and kicked Ash under the table, telling him to hold his tongue. Asher's eyes widened even more than usual, not out of pain, but because he hated eating food with us. According to him, he never got what he wanted.

The food came out on three big white plates. One had charred carrots, turnips, and beetroots, with a green herb sauce that tasted like heaven. One brandished three bone-in rib eyes that were all perfectly medium-rare. The other had greens consisting of leeks, carrot tops, and chard. Drew was the first to grab, as usual, putting an entire steak on his plate. Luke and his hat said, "What in the hell do you think yer doin'?"

Drew spit back: "Whoooa, man, what do you mean?"

I began to tap my silver fork on the table slowly and looked at Drew. "We should cut the steak so everyone gets some. This isn't your personal steak."

Luke chimed in, "Yeah, ya idiot." His hat nodded.

Drew looked at me, made his eyes big, puffed his cheeks like Dizzy Gillespie, then blew out the hottest air I've ever seen. At the same time, he moved his upper body like a snake, saying, "Welll, myyy baaad, brooos. No need to be a bunch of dicks," then forked the steak and slowly put it back on the plate. The whole table erupted in laughter and the silverware scraping sounds were drowned out.

When we finished our meal, we left the private room and sat at the bar. We preferred not to look at each other all the time. I ordered another one of the root beer drinks, and after a few I felt pretty good.

The bartender was cute. She was a brunette fox with tight black Levis and a halter top from somewhere I didn't know. She had tattoos on her hands in various shapes and lines that reminded me of Aztec symbols. They were surrounded by different ring stacks of gold that really made you look and focus on her hands. I figured she decorated them because she used them a lot. Her eyes reminded me of paint splatters—one was blue and the other hazel. After about five seconds of analyzing her, I decided I better speak up 'cause she was staring and it was getting weird. I took a sip of my drink and smiled at her.

"What brings you guys here?" she asked.

"Playing next door," I said.

Like a pro she smiled and pretended to be more interested than she was. "Cool! What band?"

I told her the name. "Hmm, never heard of you."

Just then Drew predictably started to say, "We have that one song that goes—"

Luke and his hat interrupted. "Shut up, Drew! Damn you to hell!"

I looked at them like they were stupid, then back at the bartender, who didn't have any reaction. "Well, I've never heard of *you* either," I said.

She smiled. "Ha ha, smart-ass. What do you think of that drink?"

I looked down at it. It was half-gone, and the large square ice cube had barely melted. "It's my third one."

"Good. I invented that drink."

I tipped my glass in her direction. "Well, cheers."

"To you." She grabbed for a metal shaker to start on another drink and smiled.

Like a spider building a web, she was magnificent to watch. She would reach left without looking and grab the bitters; she would reach right to rinse a glass as she was reaching down to grab the bourbon or gin. She'd always start with the smallest ingredient in case she spilled something or messed up the recipe so it wasn't a huge loss. And when she stirred, she was all wrist and straight-armed. She was a master. As she was shaking a cocktail, I took note of her posture. She stood straight and gracefully, and her neck extended like a swan. She was perfect.

"The ballerina of bartenders," I said to my ice cube. "Today was a good day."

The black chrysanthemums that decorated her upper arm reminded me of an oil painting. "I like your tattoos," I said.

She smiled at me, stirring the drink. "Thanks, I like yours."

"You kind of look like a ballerina when you bartend."

"I try. What are you doing after the show?"

I blinked. "I dunno yet."

"Go to Beacher's. It's a wild time."

"Will you be there?" I asked.

She smiled again. "Probably."

"Well, okay, then."

We paid our tab and tipped generously. I lit up a square and walked toward No Vacancy. When we got there, the crowd was huge, drunk, and loud. We walked upstairs and put on our new in-ears to play the show. I felt good for the first time in a while. The stage was calling my name. When we were done, I went back upstairs and sat down in an old wooden chair with a velvet cushion. I could feel reality creeping back in, so I tried to be alone. I poured myself another drink as the shitty sound-prick guy walked by and looked at me without saying a word. The owner then came up to us and started to make friends with Luke and Asher. He was nice and invited us to another one of his clubs. We said, "Fuck it," and decided to go. I walked downstairs and the black SUVs were all lined up and ready. One of the owner's friends, known as "the Italian," who was small but jacked like a pit bull, looked at me and asked if I wanted to go in his white Porsche.

"Can you fit two?"

He laughed and said, "Not really."

THE PORSCHE

Luke and I attempted to hop in the car. However, this vehicle was not meant to fit more than two people. The two "seats" in the back were for show. We climbed in and pulled, and tugged, and finally sat down with both of our heads touching the ceiling. Luke and his hat desperately searched for a seat belt and to his horror didn't find one. The Italian turned and looked at us, laughed, then screamed, "Hold on, boys!" and we screeched out of the parking lot like a horde of rats being chased by a fireball. Tires were smoking and the noise was ear piercing. We went from zero to seventy in three seconds. If we happened to come to a red light, we would suddenly stop, then peel out again when it turned green, inviting us to speed into our short futures. When we'd turn, we'd swerve and drift like an ice cube on a metal table, leaving tire marks behind us like a trail of melted water. I looked at Luke, and his eyes were the size of golf balls. All he could do was scream and hold on to his hat. It even looked like he was whispering a prayer at one point. When we got on the highway, we hit one twenty and zoomed in and out of cars like the cops were chasing us.

"Holy shit, this is how I die, this is how I die," I said, my voice drowned out by the engine.

The whole time, the Italian was in the front seat laughing and hitting the ceiling with his fist, his other hand on the wheel. I swear I saw horns start to form out of his bald head. When he turned around to look and laugh at us, it was as though his tongue grew and his eyes turned nuclear yellow. At one point, we sped in between two cars that were both in their respective lanes. We were so close to them you could touch their mirrors with your fingers at the same time. Luke, his hat, and I turned to each other in silence, looked at the Italian, then back at each other, and began screaming our heads off.

BREAK ROOM

We got to Break Room so quickly that we had to wait a good fifteen minutes for the rest of the crew to catch up. It wasn't bad, though, 'cause Luke, his hat, and I stood outside in silence and smoked squares to make our hearts calm down. Our fear left us with the smoke, but only after two squares each. When the rest of the crew got there, they asked about the ride. We just shook our heads, not really knowing what to say.

We walked into a kitchen through the back door. "This must be the reveal," I said to the walls. We kept walking down a gray-bricked hall, and then came to a Snapple machine. Standing there was a beautiful black girl with big kinky hair, asking us if we'd ever been here before. *Same shit,* I thought, shuffling my feet. She pushed the peach tea button and the door slid open to a loud club full of beautiful people. We walked in and it was hot, sweaty, and musty. The girls all dressed like they were there to be seen. They were all in black; couture dresses, black denim, black leathers, all black everything.

We made our way to the bar and each ordered whiskey drinks—a Boulevardier for me. We engaged in the same bullshit conversation that you always have with new people. I didn't talk much 'cause I couldn't hear anything, and I hate not being able to hear anything. I just stood at the bar, sipped at my drink, and looked around the room like all the other nobodies. Periodically I would go outside to the back area. There was a long brown wooden deck and a slab of concrete.

There they had a few tables with video games built into them, but I was more interested in the ashtrays. I would light up a square, and just stand there and think about nonsense. Mom would crawl through my mind, followed by *Why the fuck am I here?* followed by *That girl's hot,* and finally *I should get another drink.* I'd walk back in, and the loud, terrible music would remind me why I went outside in the first place.

At some point after the third time I went out to smoke, I walked around the club to find the guys. They were all in the back in a karaoke room, where everyone was taking turns singing songs, making them worse than they were, and where they also could talk among themselves without having to wear out their vocal cords or eardrums. It was a nice escape, until it wasn't. In the corner of the room was some famous actor—he seemed to be alone, but he was smiling and enjoying himself. It was the best performance I've ever seen from him. The Italian got up and started singing Third Eye Blind's "Jumper." He claimed it was a song he had to sing every time in honor of tradition. None of us complained, even though by this point Third Eye Blind was nothing but a memory to most people, including me.

—

I was lying on my grandmother's shag-carpeted floor when I first listened to that song. I bought the CD and was flipping through the crisp, new-ink-smelling paper, staring at the pictures and reading the lyrics, thinking how perfect it was. I popped the disc into the black boom box and lay there taking it all in. The nuances of the guitar strums, the way the sound of the snare drum changed from verse to chorus, the breaths in between the words, and the colors the sound produced in my head—it was glorious. It got me high. I was so inspired that I started learning how to play piano by ear. I would try to play at my mother's house, but she would tell me to quit as if someone were always sleeping. When I was at my grandpadre's house, I would play along to songs I heard on the radio, and he would just sit and listen. Part of me wondered if he was just happy to hear my padre's old piano being played again, but it didn't matter. It felt special. He'd smile, with his paper-skinned hands folded in his lap, then he would grab his cane, hobble over, and say, "Play that song, 'Love.'" I would play it, and he would ask me to play it again, and again. It reminded him of my grandmother, who'd passed away.

Neither of us knew the name of the song, but to him, and eventually to me, "Love" is what it encompassed.

I walked to the bathroom to take a piss. The line was small, maybe about four or five people ahead of me. It was tiled in black and white, and the short Mexican bathroom attendant was throwing towels at people when they were done, trying to make tips. He was in a vest and tie, and I felt bad for him 'cause looking around made me realize how many cheap, miserable pricks there were. I bought a pack of squares from him, figuring he got them in bulk and makes about a five-dollar profit on each box. That was enough to not have to keep tipping him every time I walked in. He thanked me, not for buying the cigarettes, I think, but probably for acknowledging him at all.

I made my way to the smoking patio, passing the table-service sections full of beautiful people lighting up joints and blowing lines of white powder out in the open. I looked a bit farther and saw Asher with a key up to his nose and white powder on the end of it. He inhaled, arching his back and bending in a way I had never seen a robot bend before. One finger was pushing his other nostril closed so he'd have no problem transferring from key to circuits. His eyes were closed and his mouth was pursed. It looked like he was putting on a show, but he always looked that way. When he finally opened his eyes, his pupils were three times their normal size and flickering in the orange candlelight.

I walked up to him, grabbed him by the arm, and dragged him outside.

"What the fuck are you doing?" I asked.

"Dude, chill! I'm just partying a little bit!"

I looked around and made sure no one was listening.

"Do you know what could happen if this got out? You're in fucking public!"

"Dude, how's that any different than being drunk? It's not, it's the same thing."

"Yeah, the difference is, it's fucking illegal, you *asshole.* The last thing I need is you getting arrested with a drug charge. Then, soon, we're gonna get double-checked every time we go through any sort of security. Then our bus is going to get pulled over and searched all the time, not to mention everyone thinking you have a legit problem.

Then you'll have to go to rehab, and you'll have to stop playing shows, and that means we won't make any fucking money. Not to mention if you actually *do* have a problem; what the fuck happens then? Maybe you're okay with being a burnout, fucking washed-up musician, but goddamn it, I'm not!"

"Okay, okay, okay, geesh, man, I'm freaking sorry!"

Just then he looked up and rolled his eyes—he wasn't sorry at all.

I shook him to get his programmed attention back. "Look, I don't care what you do; it's your fucking body. But do it in the bathroom like every other person who's trying to hide their fucked-up habits."

He closed one orange glowing eye. "You're right, you're right. I'm sorry, dude." Then he opened his eye, exposing his shrunken pupil.

"You fucking robot, you're not sorry. You're just programmed to say that or some shit. Fuck you. Stop saying you're sorry when you're clearly not!"

"Shit, Bell, calm the fuck down!"

I shook my head and calmly said, "I need another drink," then put a square in my mouth and lit up. I looked up at the sky. "What the hell are we doing here?"

He looked up at the sky. "What do you mean?"

"I mean, what the hell are we doing here? Here. Right here, in this terrible place?"

He didn't get it—what was so wrong with having fun?

"C'mon, man, it's not so bad. We're just having a good time, trying to get laid, I guess."

I hated the answer, but couldn't fault him for not knowing how else to respond. "You know, for a bunch of successful, attractive musicians, you wouldn't think it would be so hard."

He laughed. "I know, right? I mean, the chase is kind of fun."

I thought of a fox chasing a rabbit through tall grass. The blades would part with each paw moving forward, and the bugs would fly out, creating a warning sign for all the other rabbits.

"Yeah, ha. I guess I just don't like it anymore."

His face contorted into a confused look. "It?" he asked.

"Well, I guess I don't like people."

"I know what would make you feel better." He was sneering and holding up a little silver vial.

I looked at it, and then I looked at him. He had this frightening smile highlighted by candlelight like the villain in a slasher movie. I looked at him, and then I looked at the vial, swinging back and forth in his hand like a pocket watch. It would shine a sliver of light into my eye every time it hit the candle in just the right way. Then Asher's teeth started to glow and get larger and larger, and his skin changed colors to red. I didn't want to do it, but I grabbed it and went to the bathroom.

The Mexican greeted me again. I just looked at him and fake smiled. When he saw me waiting for the stall, his expression changed from smiling to disappointed. He knew what was going down. No one takes a shit at a club. He looked at me like he knew I didn't want to do it. Then he shrugged, wiped his hands with a white towel, threw it in the trash, sat down on his seat, and opened his phone. I walked into the stall and slammed the black door shut behind me. It made a boom that sounded like the gateway to hell closing. I pulled open the silver vial and felt the little bits of powder crunching on the metal cap. I pulled out a brass key, stuck it in, and pulled out a bump. I put it to my nose and . . .

—

Inhale.

My brain flooded.

—

Francis and I were young, sitting in the den. My padre and mother were arguing over something, and they had just told us they were getting a divorce. I sat there, not knowing what that meant, while Francis cried. Tears were rolling down his face, and he was lying on the floor next to me. I reached over and gave him a hug and asked him why he was crying. He told me 'cause things were going to be different now.

I said, "Don't worry; you're my brother, that'll never change."

He didn't say anything. He just lay there while we listened to the screaming in the kitchen, and cried. When they were done fighting, our padre came over to us and told us to come sit in his lap. He said we had to go live with our mother for a while. I didn't realize it at the time, but they were fighting about

Francis. He didn't want to live with my mother, and my father didn't want him to either. When we pulled away from the driveway, Francis just stared at the house.

—

Exhale.

Blink rapidly.

Inhale.

—

I was ten and I was having my first sleepover birthday party at my padre's house. We had pizza, an ice cream cake with both vanilla and chocolate fudge, root beer, and even a piñata. After all the festivities, there were twenty kids on the floor, all ready for bed. Padre came into the room and sat at the piano. He played a few bars of this fast, ominous chordal tune that made me feel scared. He turned around and made his eyes big, then began telling us the story of The Hound of the Baskervilles. *He told his own version, of course, and the ending wound up not being scary at all. In fact it was funny, and all of us were laughing. But during the story, I was enamored of his natural talent for drama. He would get quiet at all the right times, then loud! His eyebrows would furrow, and his shoulders would creep. He had us in a trance and he knew it. My father was my hero.*

—

Exhale.

Someone was pounding on the door.

THE FIGHT

I sat on the toilet, blank, and finally snapped back when the pounding on the door became a sound that wasn't just in my head. The Mexican bathroom attendant was yelling at me for taking too long. I walked out, licked my lips, adjusted my jacket, said thanks, and threw a twenty into his tip jar. He didn't notice, so I cleared my throat to get his attention. He didn't look, so I tried again but louder. When he still wouldn't look, I shrugged my shoulders and walked out. I passed a beautiful, jet-black-haired raven who had a tattoo of a knife in between her breasts. I didn't see her face, but her legs were perfect. All I could think about was resting her tits on my head from behind me so it looked like a pagan ritual with a dagger about to be plunged into my skull.

I let the fantasy go, then found Hank. He was smiling, not speaking, and had a glass of Cynar in his hand. I walked up to him, and he counted my steps from when he saw me to when I stopped.

"Let's go to Beacher's."

Hank downed his drink, pulled out his phone, typed faster than ever, and said, "Okay, your car will be here in six minutes."

Drew and I walked outside to get in the car ten minutes later.

The driver was annoyed. "Where's your friend?" he asked.

I looked at his fat eyes in the mirror, knowing Asher always took forever to say bye. "He's coming, just hold on."

"Well, I've been waiting for twenty minutes and you guys are costing me money. We gotta go." His hairy knuckles were gripping the steering wheel, making the sound of skin on leather. I reached for my seat belt, thinking that it would at least seem like more of a commitment.

"What are you talking about, man? You're getting paid for this. You're getting paid for sitting here—just relax."

His black eyes grew wide in fury, and drops of sweat started gliding down his balding head.

"Just tell your friend to get out here."

Drew pointed. "Look, maaan, here he comes."

Ash came running and got in the front seat.

"Sorry, guys, I was chatting with a girl I'm meeting at the club later." He closed the door, and it scraped on the curbside.

The driver started yelling. "What the fuck!? You just ruined my door! You're going to pay to get it fixed!"

Asher looked at us, then at the driver. There was an awkward moment of silence. "I didn't do anything, man! I'm not paying for that. Maybe next time don't park so close to the curb when you drive this low of a car."

"Fuck you, man, you're paying for this."

I couldn't take anyone talking to my friends that way. If this overweight, sweaty beast of a man was going to cuss, I was going to cuss right back at him.

"Hey, what the fuck is your problem? My friend didn't do anything wrong; you fucking did! Also, who the fuck do you think you are that you can talk to customers this way? Is this how you talk to your mother?"

There was another awkward silence, and Ash and Drew were both looking at me, wide-eyed. The driver's breathing became heavier and he started to stutter. "What d-d-did you say about my mother?"

I shook my head like I was disappointed in him. "Man, fuck you. Let's get the fuck out of this piece-of-shit car."

We climbed out, and he kept yelling at us, sweat flying off his head. He sped off screaming and punching the steering wheel. Then he looked back and saw us all flick him off.

The three of us were walking down the lamp-lighted street, and I lit up a square. "Fuck that guy!"

Drew sighed. "Yeeeah, that guy was crazy."

Asher pulled out his phone to call another car. "Not my fault he parked so close; what a jerk!"

Just as Asher finished his sentence, we saw the driver speed back around. You could hear him screaming through the windows. He lurched to the curb, then struggled to get out of the car and continued to yell at us.

"Hey, man, you want a piece of me? Let's settle this right now."

This guy was nuts.

"Get back in your car and drive the fuck off," I said. "You're not worth my time."

"Fuck you, man!" His short legs looked like two uncooked hot dogs 'cause you couldn't see his knees from under his long basketball shorts, and his tennis shoes were crushed from the weight. He started to come my way.

I laughed at him, and started to hit my knees, then my chest, and then my head, thinking I had to act crazy to protect these other two idiots.

"I mean, think about it, man. There's three of us; you wouldn't win in a fight!"

Drew and Asher were standing behind me, frozen like ice sculptures. I knew Drew's only thought was *Oooh, shit.* Asher's was *This could be a good story to tell that girl later.* I knew they would back me up, but they weren't fighters. I don't think they've ever been in a fight. It was up to me, if it came down to it.

I could tell the driver was beginning to regret his decision. He began blinking rapidly and rubbing his face. He looked red. "Fuck it," he said, "I'll take my chances, you faggots."

This guy was five six and weighed about two hundred pounds. Getting him in the gut would be pointless. If he got on top of me, it would all be over. I decided that since I had the reach and height, I would let him throw the first punch and then try to crack him on the chin. If I landed, he would go down from his body weight and its own fight with gravity. If I didn't land, there was a good chance I could use his weight against him and get him on the ground, then just give repeated blows to his fat face. I knew it was all a crapshoot, but as long as he didn't have a weapon, I had a chance.

"Well, c'mon, then."

He came at me with a right hook, fast for a fat guy. I saw his hairy knuckles come at me in slow motion. In the background, I could see his blurry pork face squinting with his lips pursed. Luck was on my side. I dodged it, then reached back and put all my weight into my own right hook. I landed it on his left cheek. He wasn't knocked out but he went down. I didn't continue.

"Fuck you, man!" He was out of breath, trying to keep going. I was panting from all the adrenaline and the coke. I yelled, "Look, fuck you too! Why would you come at me and my friends!? Huh? Why would you fight a losing fight? You should have just driven off!"

The driver sat on the ground out of breath, shaking his head, but didn't say anything else.

Drew and Asher grabbed me, and we started running down the empty street.

"Holy shit, maaan, that was an epic puuunch!"

"Shut up, Drew!" yelled Asher. "You should have walked away, Bell."

I nodded, feeling like he was right, but at the same time feeling unstoppable.

"I just don't understand why he came back around," I said.

"Maybe he had a bad day," said Drew.

"Maybe," I said.

BEACHER'S

Our new car eventually came and picked up the three of us. This driver was smiling and had kind eyes. Everyone was silent, and Asher was thumbing his silver vial, ready for more. We got to Beacher's, nodded to the bouncers, and they waved us in. All around me were beautiful birdies, foxes, and owls dressed in expensive clothes with beautiful faces and incredibly well-cared-for skin, drinking cocktails and laughing. They all watched you go in, trying to see who you were and if you could be interested in them. Of course you were interested in them, I mean, c'mon. A few midgets were walking around dressed in costumes: the pope, King Tut, a nurse, not serving any other purpose except shock value. It was hard to shock us after we'd lived in NYC for so long.

Beacher's was another variety-show place like the Box, just not as crazy. The stage was smaller and seemed a little less taken care of. The decor was circus-like, and it felt like you were in a giant tent. We missed most of the show, but after the singing and the lesbian finger part, the last thing was a half-naked dance routine. I watched the troop in cat masks getting on their knees with their tits bouncing every which way. Then I zoned out, feeling numb, gripping my sore knuckles, and the constant ringing in my ears began to grow . . .

Louder.

It was a hot summer day, and the sun was shining through the leaves of the pecan trees in the back. I was fifteen and at my mother's house. She told me that we had to go meet my aunt at the bank for some reason, and she wanted me to come with her. We got in the car, buckled up, and listened to George Strait on the radio. On the way there, we made a wrong turn. Farther into the drive, we made another.

"Mom, are you okay?" I asked.

"What do you mean?"

"You're not going the right way."

She looked at the street signs, then at nothing. "I'm not?"

"No, not even close; you alright?"

"Yeah . . . Oh wow, you're right. We're not going the right way. That's weird. I must be getting old."

I looked at her, then at the leather on the seats, and thought to myself how odd it was. I thought maybe she was *getting old.*

Louder.

My grandfather hid his talents. He was always artistic, and he worked as a car upholsterer. He made the most beautiful custom interior leather seats you'd ever seen. They were all sorts of colors, and the craftsmanship was incredible. One day I walked into his shed and saw all his paintings. They were gorgeous interpretations of circus scenes, carnival rides, hot-air balloons, and the stunning landscapes that surrounded them. He even had a few that looked like people from the 1920s. One of the women he painted looked like my mother. She had on a big hat and a purple dress with a white blouse. She was smiling and playing with a dog. She looked happy. I remember picking up the painting and feeling the canvas with my fingers. It felt rough, and the paint felt thick. I ran inside and asked my grandmother if she had ever seen the paintings my grandfather made, and she said, "Yes."

"Why aren't they hanging?" I asked.

"Because there's no room," she said.

I went to the living room to talk to my grandfather. He was sitting in his chair, watching TV. I asked him about his paintings, and he told me he never followed through with his dreams because his family was more important. When my grandmother went to sleep in her room that night, and my grandfather went to his, I snuck outside and grabbed the painting that looked like my mother. I walked inside and put it on the piano. The next morning when I woke up, it was gone.

"Bell, are you okay?"

Asher was squeezing my arm and looking at me, concerned.

Beacher's was buzzing, but I didn't comprehend where I was right away. "What?"

He asked me again, blinking incredibly fast. "Are you okay?"

I turned my head, popping my neck, and looked at him, nodding. "Yeah, I'm fine."

He smiled. He had his arm on someone's shoulder. "Hey, this is Mr. Brainwash."

I began to speak as if I was programmed to. I didn't even realize what I was saying. "Hi, I'm Bell. It's incredible to meet you; I'm a huge fan."

Mr. Brainwash's paintings and street art made you feel like an activist. He was a social injustice painter who made fun of society and all of its hypocrisies. His existence itself was thought to be performance art.

"It's nice to meet you too." He hugged me and then grabbed both of my arms. "Hey, I can tell there's something really special about you. I can just feel it. I know there's stuff you struggle with, and I know you feel like it holds you back, but it doesn't. It fuels you. You're gonna go far in life; I can tell you that right now."

I looked him in his twinkling eyes and thought to myself how full of shit he was. I knew he was high like me.

"Thanks."

He smiled and said, "No, thank you."

I shook his hand and turned toward the bar. I needed another drink.

The bartender birdie from Butchers & Barbers saw me from across the room and began to walk in my direction. She must have realized how pale, drunk, and high I was 'cause she walked right past me, biting her lip. She smelled like lemon.

"Damn!" I was fucked up, but she wasn't yet. I assume she was hoping to get high for free, but getting drugs from someone who's fading faster than water stains on a black shirt was damn near impossible. She stopped and started talking to a man in a three-piece suit. She must have thought he had drugs or money. Better yet, both.

—

I began to white out again, and my vision started to go.

—

Louder.

—

Francis was a child, sitting on a white floor in a white room with nothing around except the feeling of emptiness. The floor was cold, and the ceiling had no end. His body glowed olive in the opaque white room. A young version of my mother appeared, sitting in front of him with her back turned. They were both naked, hugging their legs, crying, rocking back and forth. Their motion was in sync, back and forth, back and forth, never stopping, like a metronome. Their hair was the same shade of brown, but my mother's looked lighter and was falling to her shoulders, covering her face, while France's was short and looked black in the white room. I saw my grandmother standing in a long black Victorian-looking dress, facing a wall with her back turned to my mother in silence, showing no emotion or reaction. All you could see was the back of her head. There was no sound, just emptiness. I ran up to my grandmother, but every time I put my hand on her shoulder to face her children, her face didn't exist. I'd grab her shoulder, spin her around, and, to my surprise, it was always the back of her head. After I repeated the process a few times, I noticed my mother and France's rocking had become out of sync. I looked back at my grandmother and her dress began to rot and peel off onto the floor like dead black roots. Slowly it fell, leaving behind a pile of dead black tendrils on the floor. The last part to fall brought with it my grandmother's hair. Her face became exposed but looked black and hollowed out. She looked through me, and her two eyeholes became the deep abyss. Her mouth opened and she screamed.

—

Louder.

I passed out.

LAX

"Bell, wake up. Wake up, Bell."

I opened my eyes and everything was blurry. "What? What do you want?"

I couldn't quite make out who was talking to me, but it sounded like Asher. "We gotta go. You passed out and they're kicking us out."

He put my arm over his shoulder.

"How long was I out for?"

"I dunno, twenty seconds or so. Not that long. We managed to catch you and sit you down. Are you okay?"

I was hazy. "No, Ash, I'm not." I began shaking my head. "I need to go home."

Ash didn't say anything. He pulled out his phone and called a car. We made our way to the back of the club and walked out. "I'm sorry, Ash, I'm sorry. I dunno . . . I dunno."

The drive was silent and the roads were listening. Palm trees rose high in the skies and watched our car turn every corner. I was staring out the window, still hearing the ringing in my ears, when Ash finally spoke. "When I lost my dad, I didn't get a chance to tell him how I felt. I didn't get a chance to tell him I loved him one last time. I didn't get a chance to hug him goodbye. Go home, Bell. Go home."

A tear rolled down my cheek, and I grabbed my hair. "I'll tell Hank to book me a flight in the morning."

"I'm already way ahead of you."

When we got to the house, I went straight to my room and flopped on the bed. The crickets outside were singing, along with the birds. I closed my eyes and disappeared into the black nothingness.

AA FLIGHT 27

I woke up the next day at noon to a text from Hank with my flight info.

Flight 27 to San Antonio TX 4:00 p.m. gate 32

"Fuck!"

I stretched out my arms and legs to get my endorphins running, but even they seemed slower today. I lay in bed, staring at the ceiling, not having any daydreams or fantasies. I just lay there and thought about last night and how stupid I felt. My hangover was knocking on my eyeballs like it needed to be let out, so I went to the bathroom and vomited. When I finished, I turned on the shower and got in, letting the water hit my face. It felt soothing, but my mind couldn't focus on it. I didn't want to go to Texas. I didn't want to face my mother. What was I gonna say? I feel like my family crumbled because of her. What was I gonna do? I got out, avoided the mirror, packed my bags, and called a car. I found a blue Gatorade in the fridge with a sparkling water and a note. It read:

Bell,
Good Luck.
I'm proud of you.
-H-

Next to the fridge was a bottle of Advil. I smiled, poured myself a glass of blue and sparkling, popped two pills, and finished it in two sips. Ten minutes later, a young, long-haired, boho-looking driver pulled in and saw me waiting with my bag.

"Hey, man, are you Bell?"

"Yeah."

"Cool. LAX, right?"

"Yeah."

I must've looked like hell 'cause he began to seem concerned. "You alright?"

I nodded. "Hungover."

"Oh damn, long night, huh?"

I winced. "You have no idea."

—

When we landed, I exited the plane and felt like I was on autopilot. I glided through the even slower people here, hailed a cab without even realizing it, and somehow managed to have a conversation with the driver, though I couldn't tell you what it was about. All I remember is the car flying down Loop 410 in the far left lane, speeding and weaving through traffic—mostly trucks 'cause that's what Texas does. We passed the tall palm-tree-like neon signs for Taco Cabana and Chester's Hamburgers, which all brought back great memories from childhood. Chester's always had the best fries with the skin still attached. When we exited onto Interstate 35, we got off on Huebner and made our way to Babcock, past the Chinese restaurant Mom and I always went to. I never remember the name, but it always had the best lemon chicken. We made a left onto Hollyhock, and passed the Maronite Catholic Church, which Padre always revered but never went to, then turned left into my neighborhood. I asked the driver to let me out at the front gate, paid him, and punched in the gate code; it was still the same code from when I was eight. I pulled out a square, lit up, and waited for the gate to open. The neighborhood looked the same, but just a little more lived-in. I made a left on Lost Oak and eyed my home. The tall red-brick house with the crepe myrtle outside and the steep driveway. The oak trees surrounding, standing tall and proud. I'll always remember it that way, even though now the trees have slumped and the brick has faded much like the feeling of our once-perfect family. I still had my keys, so I unlocked the door quietly and went upstairs to my room. I was alone in the house except for the cats, and I was still hungover. I stripped off my clothes and curled up in my bed. I fell asleep to the deafening silence.

SAN ANTONIO, TEXAS

I woke up in my bedroom. It hadn't changed since I was a child. The stiff beige carpet with the red soda stain in the corner; the tall white pull-out doors on the closets that had a brass knob missing; the popcorn ceiling that kept me awake at night, trying to find different faces and shapes and monsters; the flat, circular light fixture that reminded me of a button; and the big window that my bed faced, which looked over the tall oak trees that would shake with the wind and frighten me. This place was my sanctuary. It was where I hid all of my secrets, played with my brother and friends; it was where I once got on my knees and prayed to God for my first crush to love me back; and it was where I cried when Padre went to the hospital because he needed a new kidney. I hadn't been there in just under a year, and it only came back to life and breathed when I was home. It welcomed me with a beating heart, and it comforted me when France was in bad shape. When I wasn't home, it kept my memories safe because that's all it had. I loved my room. I was happiest when I was in it.

—

I opened my eyes and felt the soft sheets between my fingers. I pulled them off and sat on the edge of my bed, noticing the squeak the springs made. I put my feet on the floor, stretched my arms out, yawned, and went downstairs. Walking down the stairs reminded me of Christmas.

The living room had giant ceilings, and every year when the family celebrated, we did so in that room with a twelve-foot tree. That's all behind us now.

I found Padre sitting at the kitchen table, eating crispy bacon and burnt toast, coffee cup steaming, reading the newspaper. It made me smile because that's how I'll always remember him.

"Mornin', Padre."

He spoke without looking up from the paper. "Good morning, rock star. When did you get in?"

I poured myself some coffee. The brand was always a cheap one and reminded me of gas station coffee, but Padre liked it bitter and strong.

"Last night around nine, I guess. Where's Francis?"

He lowered the paper and glanced at me through his clear-framed glasses. "I have no clue."

I could tell he was thinking I looked like shit. It was good to see him anyway. The deep wrinkles on his cheeks had become peppered with gray-and-white hair, the roots of a distinguished beard. All his life he'd been clean-shaven because his father told him that was the only way people would take him seriously. But in his old age, he felt differently. His slacks were neatly pressed, and his white-collared shirt was freshly dry-cleaned. He always looked busy and entrenched in his business.

"Hey, Padre, you got a sec? I kinda need to talk to you."

He put down his newspaper and looked at me, concerned. I could see he was imagining all the bad things I could possibly tell him: I have an STD, or AIDS, or I impregnated a girl, or I was diagnosed with cancer, or I'm using drugs and becoming like Francis. The last thing he needed was for me to become like France. I mean that was the last thing any of us needed. He looked up to the ceiling, then down. I could tell he had started to pray.

"What's up?" he asked.

"Well, okay, I know this is kind of strange, but when you were married to Mom, did you ever notice anything weird about her? Like, I mean, mentally. Did you ever notice her forgetting things?"

He sighed. "No."

When they divorced, Padre said it felt as if someone had "taken his heart, where his family rested, and squeezed it repeatedly until it was broken and left with no one to repair it." After the separation and court custody battles, he decided that loving someone else was not an option. I guess he couldn't trust love unless it was unconditional, and to him, the only place he found it was in his children.

"Francis told me something the other day about her not recognizing him, or something to that effect," he said.

"Yeah." My eyes shifted around a bit. "You know the whole postpartum thing?"

He scrunched his eyes, took another sip of coffee. He had tried to get my mother to counseling, but every time they'd begin to make progress, she'd run away. He always believed he was at fault, and he told me he hoped God understood that.

"Of course, Bell."

"Well, I mean, Mom tried to get help, right?"

He nodded. "She would go talk to a therapist, but she never stuck it out and never got anywhere. When I talked to the therapist, she told me that they would get so close to a breakthrough, but then your mother would just leave."

I took a sip of the hot brown gasoline to distract myself from not being able to understand the situation. "That's weird."

He nodded.

"One morning before we got married, I woke up and she was in tears. I asked what was wrong. She started saying your grandmother wasn't happy for her finding love. She wasn't happy for us—it was terrible. All I could do was let her cry and tell her it was all going to be okay, and she'd come around."

He looked down and massaged his arm where her tears once gathered.

"It's sad, really. She has a lot of issues, Son. There are things she never dealt with the right way, things that have to do with your grandmother and grandfather, and things we might never know about. She was never going to get anywhere with Francis until she dealt with those issues."

I nodded and bit the inside of my lip. "What should I do?"

"What do you mean?"

"I just feel like if she has all these mental issues, and France tells me she's not recognizing him anymore, she's going to forget me. She's wanted nothing to do with me the last seven years. She's going to forget me."

He began to shake his head. They got divorced over twenty years ago, and he couldn't fully understand the situation either.

"She loves you, Bell. And I'm sure she's just as proud of you as I am. She's not going to forget you."

My emotions began to pool at the center of my face, and I started to well up. "What if she doesn't recognize me?"

"If she doesn't recognize you, what can you do? You can't do anything." He stood up out of his chair. "Just know that she loves you. I know that you love her, Bell. You need to go see her and tell her your feelings. If you don't, you'll regret it your whole life."

A tear rolled down my cheek, and I wiped my face. I knew he was right, hell, that's why I came here in the first place.

"I know."

Padre began pacing around the kitchen.

"You know, I've thought about this a lot. I loved your mother, I still do, but something tells me all of this happened the way it was supposed to. You're my two boys. You, Francis, and God are all I've got." He began shaking his head. "Your brother's a mess, but you're not. I'm so proud of you." He sighed and rubbed his temple. "I just hope France doesn't turn out to be like your mother."

I put down the cup and bent over to pick up Misdemeanor, our cat that Francis appropriately named. He was a calico and his colors looked as confusing as this entire family situation. He comforted me.

"What do you mean?"

Padre stopped pacing and turned toward me.

"Ignoring his issues. It's why he does drugs. To hide the pain."

Misdemeanor began purring and wagging his tail. He was staring at a blue jay, which landed outside the window, with childlike wonder. I put him down and he ran off.

"I know. Mom really fucked him up, huh?"

He began shaking his head again, while I was remembering the times I'd walked in on Francis putting needles in various parts of his body. Padre told me he had also seen it a few times. No parent should have to see that.

"No, not just your mother. He made a lot of bad choices, Bell. Listen, it's not important who did what. Go and see your mother."

I shifted my eyes to Misdemeanor, who was still staring at the blue jay. His curiosity reminded me of Francis as a child.

"I'm going to, Padre."

I began to feel better. Not just because I was going to talk to Mom, but because I knew that at the end of the day, I always had Padre. He was my saving grace, and he prayed enough for all of us to get into heaven, if there was one. Even if I didn't believe, he did, and I could respect and appreciate that.

"I am. I'm just a little, well, scared, I guess."

He nodded and gazed at me with his dark-brown eyes, and his still-stalky frame was shrinking, but it was like staring at myself from the future. I looked just like him. I felt numb.

"I just feel like I know the answers already."

"Maybe so, Bell."

I gave Padre a hug. "You know, I think Grandma had the whole postpartum thing too."

He held me a minute.

"You know, I think you're right."

I wondered how often he had thought the same thing.

My grandfather was always overcompensating for my grandmother. He helped my mother with buying cars, painting walls, getting secret loans, and achieving her master's degree. Her brothers and sisters would gang up on her, and he would come to her rescue because my grandmother didn't. He tucked her in at night, read her bedtime stories, and kissed her forehead because my grandmother didn't. He showered her with presents on birthdays because even though he would constantly remind grandmother of the date, she rarely remembered. She was his favorite daughter.

I walked upstairs and knocked on France's door. He didn't answer but it was unlocked, so I walked in. I could hear him breathing, and I saw he was asleep on the bed. His boots were still on, and he was in his jeans and one of the band's shirts. His eyes were half-open but he looked like he was at peace. I glanced around at his trashed room and shook my head. Large and small holes covered the wall where his fists had punched through the drywall. Next to a faded poster of Jesus was a red-and-green dartboard that had a single black dart in the bull's-eye. A white rosary hung from it, motionless. My mother gave that to him for Easter when we were young. A thick blue wool blanket covered the only window in his room to block out the sun. Part of me thought it was so he couldn't see this horror of a room, but he said he was up all night, and it was the only way he could sleep in pitch-black. Next to the dartboard was a framed picture of us in front of my aunt's house. He was eight and had a bad bowl cut; I was four and was missing a few baby teeth. In the background, I could see the faint red from the rosebush. He told me once that he would source numbers and try to counterfeit checks to get money. I could see the papers all over the floor. They looked like tax and bank records. Next to them was a sealed envelope with the words "Mom & Dad" scribbled on it. I grabbed it and put it in my pocket. Dirty socks were everywhere, and a pile of shirts toppled over in the walk-in closet. In one corner of the room there was a black tin full of unused needles next to bent silver spoons with bits of leftover cotton that all had burn marks. The used needles, I imagine, were lost in the pile of socks. Bloodstains from the needles spattered his dresser and various parts of his mattress, and there were cigarette butts and water glasses everywhere. I stood there silent and angry. Not at him, but at my mother's failure to love. Not at him, but at a god I didn't believe in. Not at him, but at myself for being another person in his life who left him. I closed my eyes, took a deep breath, and whispered, "Okay, here we go," to the silence. I looked at Francis one more time, then walked out and closed his door. I walked to my room, my sanctuary, then I got dressed and borrowed Padre's black Nissan. It was time to see her.

4934 ADAMS STREET, TX

I drove around my old neighborhood, passing all the white-and-red-bricked houses. This place hasn't changed a bit, except for the new families and the trees growing taller. When we moved in, it was new. Now I can feel the years of memories settling into the rooftops. I passed the gray mailboxes in the farthest cul-de-sac and remembered driving by them every day with my mother, coming home from school.

I turned out of the oblong neighborhood's black gates and lit up a square. On the way, I stopped at a grocery store to pick up a Dutch apple pie, Mom's favorite. She didn't like the crusty American style because there was too much dough, but she loved the Dutch because of how the crumbles felt grainy and sweet on her teeth.

I drove like a robot, with only my mother's house in mind, and nothing else. Back roads turned into on-ramps, which turned into highways, then to exit ramps, and finally to back roads again. I found myself at her new address, 4934 Adams Street, and got out of the car. I pulled out my pack of squares and lit one up, surveying the house. It was a small brownstone with a thirsty yellow lawn and one large oak tree. The dead leaves from the oak needed to be raked; they made her yard look like a rotting Thanksgiving cornucopia. The driveway had an oil stain, and the garage could have used another coat of blue paint. I would have preferred a darker shade, but Mom always liked brighter colors. One time when France was learning to drive, he managed to plow right through the garage door. I didn't see it happen, but it all played out in my head; he hits the wrong pedal, so the car goes flying forward and crashes into the garage door with a loud boom, scaring Padre. Somehow he figures out which pedal is the brake and hits it hard. Padre then runs out—making the sign of the cross, screaming in his robe, not knowing what had just happened—only to find France behind the wheel, doe-eyed and scared. Just like most other times, Padre forgives him, thanks God, and loves him unconditionally. Mom is nowhere to be found. I giggled, finished the square, and lit up another.

Blood was rushing through my body like an angry current and making me red-hot. I was shaking, upset, and needed to calm down. I took a deep breath, shook my shoulders, and walked up the concrete path through the dying lawn, then to the door, and rang the doorbell. It rang once, and I stood there, still. The blackbirds were chirping; I could hear them gossiping about the bad son who has finally come to confront his mother. I rang again, trying to drown out the birds, and then I saw her peering through a white curtain from the front window. The birds stopped, or at least my hearing did. After a few seconds, she opened the door just enough to peek out and speak.

"Who's there?"

My blood stopped moving. "It's Bell, Mom."

"Bell?"

"Yeah, your son *Bell*."

I stood there frozen, thinking about the last time Francis did this. She almost called the cops on him—was she about to do the same to me? Did she even recognize who I was? I almost yelled "I'm not a thief," but thankfully she opened the door all the way and gave me another once-over, I'm assuming out of confusion. Then she blinked her eyes rapidly and motioned back with her head. "Well, come in."

Through her blue mom jeans and oversized cream sweater, I could see she still had the same thin and soft body. Even though she was older, her skin was still remarkable; I guess all those years of expensive lotions had paid off. Her hair, though thick and full, had started to gray.

I stood there staring at her, thinking about what I had missed the last seven years, and nervously walked into the house. As I shut the door, I looked to my left and saw a sea-foam-green coatrack holding a few bright raincoats and windbreakers with a colorful sign on top:

"Home Sweet Home." To my right was a light-blue living room that looked barely used. In the formal dining room, the large oval chestnut family table had a white lace tablecloth with red flowers stitched in, protecting the wood from dust, and the china cabinet was full of blue-and-white plates with gold trim and crystal champagne glasses that were likely pulled out for celebrations only. I made note of the beautiful painting of a hot-air balloon hanging on the wall. A smiling child was pointing at the balloon that was all colors of the rainbow. He looked like he had never seen one before, and this looked like a real memory. I recognized it from my childhood. It was my grandfather's.

We kept walking in silence through the den, which had a large dark-green leather sofa, a burgundy La-Z-Boy with a mint-green telephone on a walnut side table next to it, and a big gray flat-screen TV in the corner. The place looked weird. So many colors that didn't match but in a strange way did. We walked into the modest kitchen that contained only a currant-red stove, a few white cabinets with brass knobs, a farm-style sink, and an out-of-place tiny black microwave. It was the only black thing in the house as far as I could tell.

I stood there quiet, not really knowing what to say, and she stood there looking at me with her arms folded, wondering what I was going to say.

I cleared my throat. "I brought you an apple pie; I know it's your favorite."

She uncrossed her arms, half smiled, and held out her hand. "Thank you. Do you drink coffee?"

I nodded. "Yeah."

"I'll go put some on."

She grabbed two apricot-colored plates from the cabinet and placed them next to the pie. Then she grabbed a knife and two forks and sliced two perfect triangles.

When she plated the pie, I noticed the tan line from her wedding ring still hadn't worn off. Not the ring from Padre, but the ring from my departed stepfather. Part of me thought that maybe she still wears it every now and then.

She handed me the plate, I said, "Thank you," and we sat down at the table, both not really knowing what to say.

I took a forkful of pie and said, "It's good," to break the silence.

She took a forkful and nodded in agreement. "Mm-hmm."

I looked around the room, then sighed, tapped my finger on my leg, and said, "Well, how are you, Mom?"

She blinked rapidly like she did before at the door. Then she looked at me and mumbled, "What do you need now, Francis?" She sighed while her shoulders deflated.

"No, it's Bell," I said. When I was young, she'd say "Francis" all the time and mean "Bell." Padre did it too. This time it sounded different.

She looked at me. "Bell?" Then she smiled and spoke up, "Well, I'm fine, mostly." Her eyes darted left to right as if she wasn't sure about the words that came out of her mouth. "You know . . ."

I shifted in my chair. "Mostly?"

She began nodding, glad that I repeated what she said.

"Mm-hmm. I went to the doctor the other day, Dr. Patel, and he ran some tests. But it's nothing serious. Just something I need to get taken care of."

As she spoke, her voice sounded as soft as I remembered. It was as though she were speaking to a small child or a small dog that she was meeting for the first time. She was full of love, and you could hear it.

I began to feel nervous again and scratched my head. "Well, like, what kind of tests?"

She moved her head back and forth from right to left, nodding, and grinned. "Well, I have 'woman' issues." She sighed. "A small growth in my right breast, but Dr. Patel says it's nothing."

The blood rushed back, and I became mad at the world in hot fury. My face was red, and I felt a tingle in my toes. "Cancer, Mom!?"

She shook her head. "No, no, no, not that. It's benign. Sometimes we get those things, Bell. It happens more often than you think. No need to get all worked up."

My blood cooled again, and her voice calmed me down. I'd always heard about people getting benign growths, but why did no one tell me about hers? I scratched my cheek, then looked at her face.

"Sorry, just haven't seen you in forever and the first thing I hear about is a growth in your body that's not supposed to be there . . . You're okay? Are you sure?"

She stopped moving and just looked at me and smiled. "I'm fine, Francis."

My soul skipped. "It's Bell, Mom. I'm Bell."

She narrowed her eyes. "What? Oh. I know who you are!"

She was confused. *But she knows who I am. She knows her son's face. She knows every inch of me, from my birthmark on my left inner thigh that looks like the shape of South America to the one tiny mole I have on the top of my right hand. She was in labor with me for twenty hours; she knows who I fucking am!*

"I know who you are." She chuckled and smiled.

I nodded, took another bite of my pie, and felt the crumbs in my teeth. I wasn't a fan of Dutch apple; I liked the doughy American. I put my fork down and took a deep breath.

"Mom, you know it's been seven years since I've seen you?"

She looked at me like I was a psychopath. "What are you talking about, *seven* years?" She took a sip of coffee.

I stared into my crumb pie nervously. "It's been seven years since I've seen you."

She stopped chewing. "I thought I saw you the other day. You always come around and ask for money. Has it been seven years?" She shook her head. "I don't think so. Maybe *you* need to go to the doctor and get *your* head checked." She fiddled with her pie for a second, then put her fork down. "Has it really been that long?"

After hearing it come out of my mouth, it sounded just as crazy to me. I raised my eyebrows. "Yeah, seven years."

"Well, why, France . . . uh, Bell?" She turned her head and looked at the wall. She was flushed red and didn't want me to notice.

I remembered waking her up on a Christmas morning. I ran to her bedroom and she was asleep. The sun had just started to rise and was lighting her face. She looked so peaceful, and I remember thinking how beautiful she was. Padre was still sleeping quietly and lying on his side, turned away from her, lightly breathing and dreaming. I ran into the room, tapped her on the shoulder, and whispered about how Santa had come and left us so many presents. She opened one eye and smiled at me and told me to come lie next to her for thirty more minutes. I lay next to her and just stared as she slept. Those thirty minutes felt like an eternity.

Then I started to remember the feeling of loneliness. I didn't understand what happened to us.

"Well, you left me at Padre's on Christmas. Why did you do that?"

She turned her head and looked at me, angry. "What are you talking about?"

Flustered, I said, "You were supposed to come pick me up, but you never did."

"When?"

"You forgot, didn't you? You didn't come pick me up 'cause you forgot."

"No, I don't know what you mean." Her tone became annoyed. She was still confused.

"Seven years ago, you were supposed to come grab me from home, like we do every year, and you said on the phone you would be there at six thirty, but then you never showed up. I called you, but you didn't answer. I called and called and called, and you never came."

"No, no, no, no. I don't know what you're talking about." She shook her head. "I'm a good mother; I would never leave my children anywhere!" Then she raised her eyebrows. "Are you clean?"

"Mom, it's Bell," I said, confused.

"I know who you are, Bell; why do you keep doing that?"

I stood up angrily. "'Cause I'm not Francis. I don't have problems with drugs; I'm a successful man, damn it!" She got quiet and looked down at her pie, then at me. "I gotta go pee," I said.

I walked to the bathroom, passing old pictures. There were some of her and my stepfather dressed in their Sunday best, posing next to a long staircase, looking happy with their arms around each other; there were a few of her and me from a vacation we took to Port Isabel when I was little; and there was one of France, smiling big and missing a front tooth that was taken when he was in prekindergarten at a school called Bright Ideas.

I touched the wall, needing to feel something to remind me of how real this all was. Then I found the bathroom, walked in, and locked the door behind me. On the sink, amid a well-used toothbrush and a bar of Dial soap, were five different prescription bottles, all with my mother's name on them.

> Marisola Tierra
> Galantamine
> Take one pill daily with food.

Side effects include: Nausea, vomiting, loss of
appetite, headache, confusion, dizziness.

The bright-orange plastic bottles contrasted with the white surface in a way that looked radioactive. The white labels all had her name printed in Courier font, each letter as rigid as her disease. Take with food, until you forget how to swallow.

I sat on the toilet and cried, head in hands, turning red as an ember. After a few minutes, I got up and wiped away my tears. I looked at myself in the mirror and just stared. I hated my reflection because I had her thick, dark hair; I had her straight, triangular nose; and part of me had her creative, free spirit. But right now it was hard to hate any of that. I walked out to the kitchen, passing the memories on the wall and found my grandmother sitting in the room, talking to my mother.

She was a Spanish fly—more wasp than fly—small and mean. Her hair was fully gray and in an appropriate beehive cut. Her skin was like paper; she was frail, but when she got the chance to yell, she found the energy. Not because she hated me but because hard love is the only love she knows. She worked too hard to get far in life to not be treated with respect, and when she was in the room she demanded it. Everything was her way or the door, and she wasn't about to give her ungrateful grandson who'd abandoned his mother a warm welcome.

She looked at me and snarled, "What are you doing here?" She had aged into an old dog.

I snarled back, "What are *you* doing here?"

"I live here with your mother. The one *you* abandoned," she growled.

I nodded, and thought, *Fuck you.* "Well, it's good to see you too."

She stood by my mother like she was protecting a small child, and her dark-brown housedress made her look like a guard.

"You shouldn't be here." She sounded as sharp as I remembered.

"Why not?"

"'Cause *you're* upsetting your mother."

"Well, she is *my* mother, and it's been long enough."

She grinned at me. "That's your fault, isn't it?"

"Mother, shut up," said Mom.

"You're not a good son. How could you just steal from your mother the way you did?"

I looked at her angrily, then at my mother. "First of all, I have no idea what the fuck you're talking about; I didn't steal anything. Second, what do *you* know about anything anyway? This is between me and *my* mother, not you."

She shook her head. "You took thousands of dollars from your mother years ago, and never gave it back. You stole from her when she had nothing. You're an ungrateful child, and you should leave!" she said again, and pointed her bony finger toward the door.

I pulled out a square coolly and smiled. "Once again, I have no idea what you're talking about—I didn't fucking take anything from anybody, and I will leave when I'm good and ready."

She and Mom started arguing in Spanish. I couldn't understand any of it, but my grandmother looked at me and snarled, then walked to her room and slammed the door behind her as I flicked her off in front of my shirt so Mom couldn't see. I turned to my mom in a rush, hot as a fireplace poker.

"Mom, are you happy here? 'Cause I don't know how anyone could be living with that old bitch."

She was on the couch, and her hands were folded in her lap. "Bela, that's your grandmother. Don't talk that way! And I'm fine." It sounded like acceptance and resignation all at the same time. Where else would she go? Who would take care of her? What if she forgot to take her meds? Or what if she forgets what comes after Saturday, or even worse starts to not recognize people? She wouldn't even realize she was doing it half the time.

I looked down at the floor. "I'm sorry. I know better. She's just blaming me for something that never happened, and I feel like it started this whole thing." I felt my heart in my feet. "Mom, I'm sorry I left you."

She looked at me. "What do you mean?"

"I mean, I'm sorry I left you, and moved to Brooklyn. I'm sorry I abandoned you, Mom." I began to cry. "I just had to leave this place, this city, this state . . . I couldn't be here anymore, with you and Padre, and Francis! I felt smothered and terrified. I felt if I stayed here, I would get older with nothing to look forward to, I would never achieve my dreams, I would die alone . . . I felt helpless and I didn't know what to do!" I began to talk with my hands, tears streaming down my face. "I had to go, Mom, I had to go!"

She started to tear up and just stared at me, then she reached for my face and touched it with her palm to comfort me.

"Bela, you did what you had to do. I don't blame you. I love you." I shook my head, and she motioned for me to sit with her. "Calm down, Bell, calm down." I let her hold me.

"I couldn't be here anymore, Mom. There was nothing here for me."

She held my head. "I know, Bell, I know."

The room was heartbeat quiet except for me trying to catch my breath.

"You did what you had to do, Bell."

"Everyone always leaves."

We sat in silence, listening to the ticking of the gold clocks in the room. A faint song from crickets outside hummed, and the sound of oak leaves rubbing in the wind echoed in the house.

I looked up at her. "Mom, France is lost; he needs you. He needs you to be there for him."

"Francis?" Her voice changed back to soft as if she had a sudden warm memory.

"Yes, Francis."

"I sure do miss him. When does he get back from Boston?"

I was confused. "What do you mean?"

She shook her head as if the memory turned cold. "Nothing."

I was still in her arms when her voice changed. "You only come here when you want money. Then you just buy drugs. Are you clean? 'Cause I can't support this anymore; I won't!"

"Mom, calm down, it's Bell."

"Bell? I know it's you, Bell. I know it's you." Her nerves made her hands tremble, and she held back a stutter, but her presence felt the same as it always did.

We both got quiet again. I stared at the table, and she stared at the floor. Then I looked at her. She was beautiful. Her mind was going, but her heart wasn't.

I sat there and became flooded with memories.

When she left my brother and me at Padre's house with the brown teddy bear card, she held us harder and longer that day.

Getting braces on our teeth together. Every time she smiled, it was a badge of love for her son. Helping her move into her first apartment after the divorce, and riding on the back of my uncle's blue pickup truck, laughing together. Johnson City every Christmas; we would drive to see the lights because they were magnificent. We would sing Christmas carols, and look out our windows at the big houses while she dreamt of buying one, one day. And all of us sitting around our kitchen table, laughing and celebrating her birthday. She took a finger of frosting and wiped it on France's nose. Everyone laughed.

I got up from her embrace, touched her face, and kissed her on the forehead. "I gotta go, Mom."

"Where are you going?"

I put my hands on my face. "I just have to go; I can't be here."

"Well, that was fast. Did I say or do something to upset you?"

"No, I just . . . I just gotta go."

She looked frantic. "Okay. I wish you'd stay longer—you just got here."

I nodded but didn't say anything.

She started crying. "I love you, Bell."

"I love you too."

I walked toward the door feeling empty and weightless, like all that was left of me was my skin. Nothing was going to change, except I couldn't be mad at her anymore.

She blinked rapidly through her tears. "I'm sorry life turned out like this."

I looked back at her. "It's not your fault." I reached into my pocket for the keys, and felt the weight of France's letter.

THE LETTER

YOU SAY HANG ON ITS WORTH IT. I SAY INSANITY & SUFFERING THROUGH IT. JUST TO GET TO WHERE I'M NOT WANTED, TO TAKE A SABOTAGED TRIP, TO SPEND A MOMENT WITH YOU WHERE PRETENTIONS INTERSECT WITH BACK ROOM WHISPERS OF PITY. HOPE IS WHAT YOU DO WHEN YOU HAVE NO CONTROL. PRAY IS WHAT YOU DO WHEN YOUR HOPE'S WEARING THIN. LOOK AT THE CROSS; A SYMBOL REMINDING YOU TO ADD UP YOUR SINS. GUILT IS A SECOND-HAND EMOTION THAT FORCES YOU INTO SORROW AND WORSE, PITY. WHICH BLEED THROUGH THE VAIL IN ONE'S EYES AND IN VANE YOU TRY YOUR BEST TO CONTROL YOUR SUBTLE BODY LANGUAGE & TONE OF VOICE WHICH IS A SLAP IN THE FACE TO ME. POOR ME, IF I WERE ONLY WHAT YOU ALL LABEL ME AS. YOU WERE SO QUICK TO SEEK OUT ANSWERS FROM ANYONE WHO WOULD TELL YOU WHAT YOU NEEDED TO HEAR SO YOU COULD CLEAR YOURSELVES OF ANY FAULT OR FEELING OF GUILT OR SHAME, HOT POTATO THE BLAME & SPITEFULLY SO. I COULDN'T COMPREHEND THE SITUATION AT ALL—SHELTERED INNOCENCE FULL OF LOVE

& SECURITY, OVERNIGHT THE VAIL WAS TORN VIOLENTLY & SO SUDDEN. I MISSED SOMETHING. I TOLD MYSELF, I NEVER FATHOMED THAT I WAS IN THE PRESENCE OF HATE, HURT, BETRAYED BY EVERYONE I LOVED ... CONFUSION, FEAR, PANIC, QUESTIONS, OH SO MANY QUESTION ALL THE TIME IN MY HEAD. HOW COULD THIS HAPPEN? CAUGHT IN A GAME OF EVIL, THAT BLAME & THIS & MEAN HURTFUL & THAT & NO WAY BACK TO WHERE I USED TO BE, NO WAY BACK TO WHERE WE USED TO BE, NO WAY BECAUSE IT EXISTED NO MORE. NOW THEY REALIZE HOW FRAGILE THE HEART & MIND IS OF THE CHILD THEY SELFISHLY USED AS A WEAPON AGAINST EACH OTHER, BACK & FORTH STABBING, SLICING, CUTTING DOWN TO SIZE. COLD PREMEDITATED, CALCULATED ... & OVER & OVER, FIRST ONE, THEN THE OTHER, THEN AGAIN, & AGAIN. THE WHOLE TIME USING ME TO CUT DOWN THE WORLD I KNEW, THE SAFE PLACE I COMFORTABLY TRUSTED & CALLED HOME. LOVE WAS AN ILLUSION, TRUST WAS FAKE—USED & DISCARDED IN A WORLD I DIDN'T UNDERSTAND ... REALITY OF WHAT I WAS PIECING TOGETHER WITH MISSING PIECES & NO PICTURE ON THE BOX TO GUIDE ME. I WAS ONCE WHOLE & WARM. NOW I'M HURT AND HUMILIATED, NOW I'M COLD AND EMPTY, IN A STATE OF DISBELIEF. BELL WAS OKAY BECAUSE HE PLAYED NO PART IN YOUR WAR, WHICH MADE ME GERMINATE & GROW MY SEED OF HATE ... YOU DIDN'T LET HIM. AFTER THINGS WERE ALL SAID & DONE, & THE AFTERMATH WAS TAKING IT'S TOLL, THEY WOULD TAKE ME TO APPOINTMENTS WITH THESE JACKASS PHD'S, WHO WOULD TRY IN VAIN TO EARN MY TRUST WITH A COOKIE OR JOLLY RANCHERS SO THEY COULD TRY TO FIGURE OUT JUST WHY I WAS SO ... DIFFERENT FROM WHAT I WAS A YEAR AGO; LIKE THEY REALLY DIDN'T KNOW ... THEY KNEW EXACTLY WHAT THEY HAD DONE, BUT NOW THEY NEEDED ME

TO SIT ON A COUCH & ANSWER ALL THESE QUESTIONS THAT WERE MEANT TO ONCE AGAIN TRICK ME INTO OVERLOOKING THE 1 OR 2 TARGETED QUESTIONS THEY WANTED ME TO ANSWER . . . TO THIS TRUSTWORTHY PRICK WITH A LEGAL PAD IN HIS LAP WHO WOULD MEET WITH THE BETRAYERS BEHIND CLOSED DOORS AFTER HE & I WERE ALL DONE. & AGAIN, THEY BOTH KNEW EXACTLY WHAT WAS WRONG WITH ME. THEY WERE SO PERSISTENT ON GETTING ME TO THE IRRITATING APPOINTMENTS, THIS DR. THAT COUNSELOR THE OTHER REALLY 'SUPER GENIUS' CHINESE DR. WHO LABELED ME AS ADD-ADHD WHICH I FOUND TO BE A GREAT EXCUSE FOR JUST ABOUT EVERYTHING. SO WHY THE FUCK COULDN'T THEY INVEST A LIL' BIT OF TIME TO SOOTHE MY PAIN AND ASK ME THEMSELVES? THEY KNEW ME, I WAS MOLDED FROM THEIR GUIDANCE, FROM THEIR BLOOD. ARE YOU TELLING ME THEY COULDN'T GET ME TO TALK? IF THAT'S WHAT'S IN STOCK, I AINT BUYING IT. SO MY ATTITUDE & POINT OF VIEW DRASTICALLY SHIFTED & I SOMEWHERE AROUND THAT TIME DEVELOPED A MUTE BUTTON FOR MY CONSCIENCE & DOING THE WRONG THING FELT RIGHT. DOING THE WRONG THING FELT GOOD, CAUSE GOOD GOT ME NOWHERE. GOOD GOT ME A MOTHER WHO DIDN'T KNOW HOW TO LOVE ME, A FATHER WHO PITIED ME BECAUSE OF IT, AND YEARS OF THERAPY BECAUSE THEY COULDN'T FACE IT. I DON'T BLAME YOU FOR EVERYTHING. YOU WERE LIKE EVERYONE ELSE IN THIS WORLD, ALONE AND AFRAID. YOU DIDN'T KNOW HOW TO FACE THE THINGS YOU SHOULD HAVE. BUT PLEASE DON'T PITY ME, EITHER OF YOU. I MADE CHOICES THAT GOT ME TO WHERE I AM. NOW I HAVE TO FACE THEM AND HOPEFULLY LEARN FROM YOUR MISTAKES. DON'T PITY ME, I DON'T WANT IT, I DON'T DESERVE IT, I WON'T ACCEPT IT.

-F -

MEXICO CITY, MEXICO

I got home, folded France's letter, and put it back in my pocket. I lit up a square and stared at the sky, knowing that not much would change. The next morning Hank texted me a reminder of my flight and our show in Mexico City. I responded: Copy. You Prick. Then smiled. I walked into France's room to say goodbye. He had just woken up.

"Hey, I gotta run," I said.

He smiled at me. "Where you going?"

"Mexico."

"Mexico? Shit, don't get stuck there. Fucking famous band guy, always on the run, leaving me here with all the old people so they don't die."

He looked down at his shirt, then pointed to the logo and smiled. I laughed and missed him at the same time. "Well, someone's gotta watch out for all of them while I'm gone. I love you."

"I love you too, bro. Oh, hey!"

"What?"

"I know I always say it, but don't forget where you came from."

I shook my head. "I can't."

I hugged him, then went downstairs to say goodbye to Padre. He was sitting in his usual chair, drinking his usual coffee. "Hey, my rock-star! How did it go?" he asked.

"About as well as I thought it would."

He took a sip of his coffee. "So not bad? Or?"

I nodded. "I dunno yet."

—

When I arrived in Mexico City, my driver, who didn't speak any English but wouldn't shut the fuck up, took me to our label. We had a TV promo scheduled that day, so it was a lot more hurry up and wait. Eight hours for five interviews. Fucking hell. The last station had a gorgeous Spanish birdie in tight jeans and high heels. Her skin was the color of milked coffee, her hair looked like the grain on a cherrywood table, and her lips were big and ripe. Asher, Luke, and his hat were playing rock-paper-scissors to see who was going to hit on her first. Asher won like he had been programmed to play the game, and Luke said, "C'mon, besta three!" while his hat nodded. Drew was chatting with a different birdie, laughing and cracking bad jokes and rolling a spliff, and Hank was standing there with his arms folded, phone in one hand, counting, watching us, and making sure everything was in its proper place. I lit up a square and stared at the cherrywood birdie. She caught me, but didn't look away. I took a hard pull and walked to the balcony. The sky was blue, the clouds were sparse, and the wind was softly blowing. I looked back and examined her from far away. She was just as beautiful as she was from up close. I looked up to the sun, exhaled the gray smoke, and said, "Glorious," to no one.

ACKNOWLEDGMENTS

For the unending support in helping this story find its way, I am forever indebted to my manager Alex Brahl. It took us a while, but man, did we arrive! To Neil Shulman for your constant encouragement and wisdom; without you, this would have likely collapsed and found itself buried in the dirt of my mind.

To Brendan Kelly, for having the courage to take on this no-name writer's project. My confidence waned until our whiskey-and-tequila editing sessions. Those hours were inspiring, to say the least.

To Zac Taylor, for your sharp reading and wit. *Thanks* for telling me to "go further."

To Jesse DeFlorio, for your dedication to my vision. There is no better artist in this world that can connect the dots I simply can't.

To my brothers, Dave, James, and Zac. None of this would be possible without the chances we took. It's insane to think that four men from opposite sides of life decided the world needed to hear what we had to say. The battles, the wins, the losses—everything we do, we do together. And in this war of life, I could not ask for better companions.

To Alexander, Christina, Scott, and everyone else at Girl Friday, thank you for your guidance in this world I know nothing about. To Clete Smith, your skills are beyond my comprehension, and I am honored to have you in my corner. I hope that one particular line edit will reign as one of your all-time favorites.

To my brother, Michael, this experience has made me feel closer to you than ever before. With you in my life, I never struggle to find inspiration.

To my Padre, you are my hero. Words cannot express how grateful I am for you and everything you sacrificed for us.

To Aunt Jay, thanks for stepping up when others stepped down. You have become the glue in our family, and that's more than anyone could ask for.

Most importantly, to Katie, my first and last reader. Without your brilliance, I would be lost. I've always walked through this life in the dark, but when you decided to hold my hand, your heart began to light my way. I love you, and always will.

ABOUT THE AUTHOR

© Jesse DeFlorio

Matthew Sanchez is a Brooklyn-based songwriter, drummer, producer, and multi-instrumentalist. He got his start at Berklee College of Music in Boston studying orchestral composition and film scoring. After moving to Brooklyn in 2012, Matthew founded rock band American Authors, best known for their hit single "Best Day of My Life." The band has sold more than six million singles and one million albums worldwide. *No One Is Listening* is his first novel.

Made in the USA
San Bernardino, CA
27 May 2019